MONI

ON MY ROOF

To Fred
Keep up the good work!

MARITA WILD

Love and Light
From Marita Wild

MONKEY ON MY ROOF

Monkey on my Roof is a work of fiction. Any similarity to actual persons or events is purely coincidental.

Marita Wild asserts the moral right to be identified as the author of this work.

ISBN 978-1-907897-08-5

Copyright © Marita Wild 2013

Poem Will I Miss It? *And cover photographs also* © *Marita Wild 2013*
Poem India – Himalaya Sunset © *David Lythgoe*

A *NightWriters Editions* book.

NightWriters Editions have been inaugurated in order to focus attention on individual writers living in or near Brighton whose work merits publication.

NightWriters Editions are published by
NightWriters Press
www.nightwriters.org.uk

All rights reserved. No part of this publication may be reproduced, stored in a retrieval system, or transmitted, in any form or by any means, electronic, mechanical, photocopying, recording or otherwise, without the prior permission of the publishers.

MONKEY ON MY ROOF

In whichever universe they now reside
I would like my friend Anna
And my sister Stella to know
that 50% of the royalties from this novel will be
donated to
Cancer Research.

Acknowledgments

I would like to express my gratitude and appreciation to Tim Shelton-Jones for his appraisal and edit of Monkey on my Roof, and to Anthony Dugdale for his patient revision and valued suggestions; thanks also to Jonathan Cunningham for his expertise in bringing it all together and to the members of Brighton NightWriters for their ideas and inspiration.

MONKEY ON MY ROOF

MONKEY ON MY ROOF

PART ONE

WILL I MISS IT?

When I visit the jewelled splendour of the Taj Mahal
And tour the temples and palaces of Rajasthan,
Will I miss it d'you think?
- My small bungalow and its yellow front door
With the path that bends gently to the right,
Of diamond-paned windows where
Cream Roman blinds hang to filter the light.

When the pilgrims bathe in the holy water of the Ganges
And I see the funeral pyres burn in Varanasi,
Will I miss it d'you think?
- That big money plant in the chipped china pot on the table,
At the side of the couch with the green leather seat
That matches the reclining chair
Where I sit to watch Coronation Street.

When I sit on a honey-coloured rooftop in Jaisalmer
Or watch green parakeets fly in Jaipur,
Will I miss it d'you think?
- My pine bed and ancient memories of passionate delight
With the man I loved so long ago; or was it just last night?
And if in some distant silken bedchamber
I happen to betray the betrayer,
Will I miss him do you think?

MONKEY ON MY ROOF

MONKEY ON MY ROOF

1

INDIA!
THE SCENT OF THE AIR!
That matchless combination of flowers, incense, spices and shit. An assault on every sense, sight, sound, touch, and smell.

I breathe in deeply, sigh, and smile at the same time. How could I have forgotten? It always catches me unawares, always surprises me no matter how often I fly here. The air crackling with electric heat. Voices shouting. Music blaring. The sounds of car and motorcycle horns. The main street in Delhi.

A voice says, 'Taxi Madam?'

I gaze at the small man with the soft voice whose hand is plucking at my sleeve.

'You have taxi?' I say in my fractured Hindi.

His eyes widen, the smile broadens, 'Yes Madam,' he answers.

'Can you take me to a cheap hotel in the Parah Ganj?'

'Yes Madam.'

'How much will you charge me?'

He looks at me, assesses the cost of my clothes and backpack and says, '800 Rupees?'

'Make it 200 and it's a deal,' I tell him.

'I'm a poor man, Madam, 700 Rupees is the smallest I can take, and only because I like you. You are like my mother, isn't it?'

'I also am poor; I don't have a lot of money. I can only give you 200 Rupees.'

We barter around like this for a while and finally settle the fare for 350 Rupees.

Through the dusty window of the taxi I watch the city

MONKEY ON MY ROOF

waking up. Dogs stretch and scratch before trotting off in search of food. Beggars raise themselves from the sides of the road to wrap whatever few possessions they own in dirty rags and shuffle off to do the same, or lift their backsides onto small wheeled platforms and push themselves along with the knuckles of both hands dragging in the dirt. Rag pickers race to rummage through the mounds of rubbish before the street cleaners sweep it all away. Women in saris carrying large earthenware pots yawn and gossip as they queue at the water pumps.

Here and there shutters are being taken down from small roadside shops, and at the side of the road a fruit seller waves a stick to stop a monkey stealing the bananas he's arranged on a table set up in the shade of a tree; behind him other monkeys have snatched a bunch each while his back is turned. Another time I'd have laughed aloud, but right now, jet-lagged after the flight, all I want is to lay my head down and sleep.

I register at the hotel the taxi driver takes me to, leave my suitcase standing beside the bathroom door, and lie down fully dressed on the hard mattress. The flight had been a long one, with a three-hour stopover in Dubai, but I can't go to sleep right away. It feels all wrong to sleep when it's broad daylight outside and my head is buzzing inside, filled with the knowledge of just how false my marriage is, and memories of a tsunami that had killed thousands. Finally fatigue overcomes nervous energy and I sleep.

Its five o'clock in the evening, the sound of explosions wake me up. I mumble to myself about the powerful fireworks — it is Diwali Festival of Light after all — and try to go back to sleep. From the street outside come the sounds of people shouting, the whoop of police and ambulance sirens. It doesn't strike me as unusual, at least not unusual for India, whose inhabitants, whether

MONKEY ON MY ROOF

they are police, ambulance drivers, or ordinary citizens can't resist any method of noise-making.

The hotel manager is knocking on the door, 'Don't be alarmed Madam,' he says; eyes shifting nervously at the sound of yet another police siren, 'you are not in danger. The bombs are in the next street only.'

I *hadn't* been alarmed until he'd knocked on the door to give me that news! The next street is less than a hundred yards away!

'The bombs? What bombs? I thought the noise was just the fireworks for Diwali.'

He gives me a pitying look, 'We don't have fireworks that big Madam, not even at Diwali.'

'No I suppose not,' I say as I come slowly awake.

Bloody 'ell! Bombs! Dead people, and hurt people, broken limbs, blood and crying children, 'Oh My God! How terrible! Is there anything I can do to help?'

His smile quivers. 'The police are there.' He reaches across to pull the door shut. 'Better perhaps you stay away, isn't it?'

So here I am in Delhi, and Delhi is a blast.

Perhaps I should have bought travel insurance after all?

Too late now.

Dear God, what shall I do?

God doesn't answer.

Might it be a good idea to leave the hotel and get right away from the Parah Ganj? But outside in the street there could be other bombs waiting to blow bits of me all over Delhi.

There has been one other occasion when I've been so afraid for my life. Boxing Day 2004; the day of the tsunami. Perhaps it's my Karma to be blown to bits in this room in this rundown hotel in Delhi, if so there isn't anything I can do about it. At least I should

MONKEY ON MY ROOF

be able to get a few hours sleep before being blasted up to play a harp on a damp cloud in the sky. Much less likely to be jet-lagged when I knock at St Peter's pearly gates! I climb back onto the bed. But can I sleep? Can I heck! Visions of my dental plate flying through the sky, falling like a shark's smile into the water of one of the pools at the Bahai Lotus temple, and my specs, arms spinning like a helicopter, landing on a prayer mat at the Jama Masjid Mosque, float before my eyes before they close into fretful slumber.

When I open my eyes again the room is dark, the windowpanes filled with velvety night. My watch informs me its eight thirty and my stomach tell me it needs food. There's nothing for it but to get out of bed and go eat.

MONKEY ON MY ROOF

2

If I were to be perfectly honest, I'd have to admit that it had started as a joke.

'Would you like to live here?' Mark had said waving his hand around the golden beach.

'Who wouldn't?' I'd answered as hundreds of others must have done, lying there in idyllic Palolem in idyllic Goa.

'If we sold the house,' he said, 'we could use the money to buy another one here, and still have enough left over to live like lords for the rest of our lives.'

I put down my glass of papaya juice, 'Hang on a minute, what about the monsoon?'

'That shouldn't be a problem.'

'You can't be serious!'

Mark quirked one eyebrow to show that he was.

'Well then,' I had said, because I'm a practical sort of person, 'let's stay here for a year and see how we'd like to live through the rainy season.'

'We can't do that.'

'Why not?'

'What about Pippa?' he said. 'We can't leave her for a year. How can we expect the neighbours to look after her for that long?'

I love Pippa to bits. Who wouldn't love those appealing eyes, and that gentle manner? But Pippa *is* only a cocker spaniel! To think that all this time I've been living with the mistaken belief that I was the Alpha Bitch in our household!

'All right then,' I said, 'you stay at home with the dog, and I'll come back and travel around India for a year on my own.'

Mark often agrees with me even when we both know that

MONKEY ON MY ROOF

what he really wants is to disagree; 'If that's what you want.'

'You wouldn't mind?' I teased.

'No.'

'Then when I get back home, you can go off for a year by yourself. Do your own thing.'

I'd been pulling his leg, but the next day I hadn't been able to resist telling our friends.

'Guess what? I'm coming back to Goa in October to travel around India for a year. All by myself.'

Sheila had jumped up and down, squealing, 'By yourself! Fuckin 'ell! Wow! Right on! Go for it, Sally!'

Doug had stopped rubbing sun tan lotion into his arms and asked, 'What's Mark got to say about that?'

And I'd pulled the band from my brown ponytail — three sun-streaked shades lighter than when we arrived — shook my hair free and drawled nonchalantly, 'Oh he said it was okay.'

Sheila stopped jumping up and down, Doug put down the sun tan lotion. They both looked at Mark sitting on the sun-bed; glass in one hand, bottle of Kingfisher in the other.

Mark finished pouring his beer and raised his head. He hadn't been listening, but the radar he carries around in his brain told him that we were all looking at him, 'What's up?'

'Did I hear right?' Doug asked. 'Did you tell Sally she could bugger off around India for a year by herself?'

Mark's star sign is Leo. What else could he be with that thick mane of wavy hair, greying now, but once as shiny and black as a lump of polished coal? He wears his hair in a ponytail. It gives people who don't know him the impression that he's an ageing hippy, which amuses us both. Nothing could be further from the truth. Died in the wool Tory Thatcherite that's our Mark.

MONKEY ON MY ROOF

Maybe it's the way he moves silently, cat-like, that makes me think of a lion sleeping with one eye open. Mark is quick-witted but on occasion can be slow to react. This was not one of those occasions.

The slumbering lion roared, 'No I didn't!'

'Yes, you did!'

Wickedly I reminded him about the conversation we'd had the day before, knowing that with those two free sprits Sheila and Doug looking on so expectantly he would have no choice but to grit his teeth, give me his hurt puppy look and say, 'Okay! If that's what you want.'

No doubt, he thought, in an absent-minded sort of way, that if he kept quiet the odds were that I'd forget about it. How was he to know that on the very first time we'd arrived at Dabolim Airport to spend a month in Candolim I'd fallen in love with India?

MONKEY ON MY ROOF

3

The idea kept hovering at the back of my mind as Mark and I swam and sunbathed the long lazy days away at Palolem. It hovered there as we stood side by side with the brown-skinned fishermen and helped to push the boats down to the sea, or lent a hand to haul in the fishing nets.

Watching Indian fathers, uncles, friends walking so naturally, hand in hand, or arms around one another's shoulders along the beach, I thought: how sad that this can't happen in England. In English cities, in my city of Liverpool at least, most men wouldn't dream of showing such natural affection.

The thought stayed with me on the trip to Chowdi to stock up on sun tan lotion, as I shared the back seat of an auto rickshaw with a huge dirty red gas bottle.

Squeezing his rickshaw between the brightly painted trucks and HGVs decorated with tinsel and tiny coloured lights. The rickshaw driver steering with one hand and prodding the horn with the other had said, 'Okay I take gas bottle to home for Sita isn't it, to cook rice, Momma?' He'd taken my silence for consent as I clung, white-knuckled, to the sidebars.

Back home in England, the notion that had started as a joke took root, spreading through my brain like Japanese Knot Weed, growing stronger with every passing day. Now at the ripe age of 54, I mused how nice it might be to take a year off with nobody to worry about but myself. One year to travel India. Students take a gap year to travel the world, why couldn't I take a year for myself? To get away from that whole boring routine of housework, laundry, cooking, and all the other small, banal doings of domestic life.

A kind of middle-aged-geriatric gap year.

MONKEY ON MY ROOF

An impossible dream.

Until Liverpool Council decided to downsize, and — out of the blue — my job in their accounts department was made redundant. Suddenly I had money in my bank account. Not a great deal of money it is true, but enough to clear the mortgage... with a bit left over to get me around India if I was sensible.

What was there to stop me?

What indeed: except a husband, my daughters and the dog!

Though to be fair, nobody tried very hard to stop me when I said what I was planning. Rather disappointing really, I'd have loved a good argument.

As a matter of fact; Mark said he was rather looking forward to being able to slob around the house on his own without me being there nagging him to pick his dirty socks up from under the sitting room cushions, and reminding him to hang his jackets in the wardrobe and not on the floor. Which made me pause for a few seconds to wonder just what state things would be in when I got back. I could see him walking around the house like a happy-go-lucky schoolboy, leaving a trail of crumbs and bits of wrappers from the strong mints he is so fond of all over the carpets.

Left on his own my husband would soon become an eighteen-carat-gold slob of the Olympic Team variety.

Moreover, there was always the prospect he'd revert to his old two-timing ways while I was gone. Always been reliable at putting the round peg into the nearest sympathetic round hole while representing himself as the misunderstood square peg has our Mark; who hasn't yet cottoned on to the fact that I understand him only too well.

I understand the reason for that resentment of his which permeates every room in our home. It's because Mark is a

MONKEY ON MY ROOF

perfectionist and I am no longer his perfect woman. No longer that tall girl/woman he imagined other men lusted after. My thickened figure, greying hair, crow's feet around the eyes, repel him. I have gotten fat and old, which he didn't bargain for when he made his marriage vows.

He looks at me when I get undressed, his gaze lingers on my hips and, 'You've put a lot of weight on,' he says, where not so long ago he'd jump from the bed and grab me by what he'd been happy to call my 'Love handles.' He stares at my stretch marks — leftovers from three pregnancies — 'What're those bumps on your thighs? They're ugly. You should see the doctor.'

Every night there's another remark in a critical tone. Nowadays I turn my back to get undressed and cringe myself into a cotton nightdress. The freedom of nude sleeping, the feel of the air on my skin a thing of the past.

Our two eldest daughters — Lisa and Jayne — have jobs and full lives of their own; Lisa is a social worker, Jayne a nurse, they share a flat in the West Derby district, our youngest Emma is in Student digs in Manchester, she's reading English lit at Manchester university. Doesn't stop them all coming home for a good nosh-up on Sundays though!

The three of them looked sideways at me and murmured disbelievingly, 'Go for it Mum,' on that Sunday when I dropped a casual hint over the roast beef and Yorkshire pudding of my plans.

Giving them a withering look, I said, 'I'm serious!'

'Yeah, yeah, yeah,' my husband mumbled grabbing the last slice of roast beef before anyone else could get at it.

They all seemed to think that that was the end of the matter so I served up the apple pie and custard in silence, but if they thought I had forgotten about my geriatric gap year, they were

MONKEY ON MY ROOF

mistaken!

That's the reason why not one of my family believed I was serious until my backpack was standing by the side of the dog basket in the hall, and I was phoning a taxi to take me to the airport. Then the only thing left for them to do was to wish me Bon Voyage.

So if I'm to be completely honest, it wasn't some kind of spiritual wisdom I was seeking when I left my husband and children to travel alone around India for a year like some wrinkly arthritic teenager. However, the small knowledge I've gleaned of Buddhism, with its focus on compassion and meditation, seems to me to be the perfect creed. Then there'd been that Reiki healing session three years ago while on holiday in Goa that had me wondering if all I'd heard was true.

…And there was the Indian man I'd chatted to while on a Zurich train.

The train may have been steam; were steam trains still around in 1972? Gazing out at the Alps, I gushed: 'How beautiful!' Newly married with Mark's arm warm around me, I leaned my head on his shoulder and sighed with delight.

'If you think these mountains are beautiful you must go see the Himalayas,' the Indian businessman who shared the carriage with us said.

'More beautiful than this?' I asked him.

'Beautiful and mystical,' he said, 'nothing compares to the beauty of the Himalayas.'

For the rest of our journey he told us of India. Never before had I heard a person talk of their home country with such natural love. I could feel Mark moving against me, pressing his thigh against mine in that little signal that I knew meant that he was

MONKEY ON MY ROOF

bored, but, fascinated by the expression on the Indian's face, the tone of his voice, the poetry of the words he used, a desire had begun to form in me.

'If what you say is true then someday I must go to India,' I said.

The man smiled as if he knew something I didn't; 'You will.'

That man had been right. But it would be more than thirty years before I got there.

MONKEY ON MY ROOF

4

'No Madam, we don't have restaurant,' the hotel Manager says, 'you go out to Chat House in main bazaar. Or buy food. Eat in your room.'

The hotel staff — usually so friendly, chatting away about their families and friends, and the best tourist spots to visit — shrink away shifty-eyed, afraid to speak, afraid of the police.

Outside troops of police officers and soldiers patrol the streets. Men in uniform with guns and fidgety fingers: scary! It's surreal to see the Parah Ganj stuffed full of armed men, and, at the same time, wherever I look, window ledges, balconies, stairs, and roofs are glittery with small lamps for Diwali. There is even a couple twinkling on top of the cistern in my hotel bathroom.

One of the policemen stops to question a vegetable-seller who'd set up a pitch on what had been a pavement, though whether the pavement has been damaged by the bomb blast, or is in its usual state of disrepair, is difficult to say.

The vegetable-seller has a bloodstained piece of cloth, which has obviously once been part of a white tee shirt, loosely taped to one side of his face. When the police officer has gone, I pick up a bunch of bananas and ask, 'How much for these?'

'One rupee each.'

There are six on the bunch, I hand him a 10-rupee note, and thinking vaguely that perhaps he had been cut by flying splinters when the bombs went off, point to the bandage, 'Did you get caught in the blast?'

The man ducks his head awkwardly as he hands me my change and mumbles, 'Yes Ji. It blew my ear off.'

'Oh I'm so sorry!'

MONKEY ON MY ROOF

'No need for sorry Ji,' he says, 'It was my ear only. Not my head, isn't it?'

He gives me an enormous smile; the smile suffuses his whole body.

'And already you're back at work!'

The man scratches at his uninjured ear, 'My children must eat, or...' he sweeps his arm around eloquently, indicating the two snotty-nosed beggar boys who have magically appeared out of nowhere to tug at my skirt, and at their bare-bummed little sister. She is fearfully eyeing a policeman swinging his bamboo lathi as she squats to release a stream of yellow urine in the gutter.

I regard the fruit and veg seller, his shining smile and radiant eyes, and wonder at his cheerful acceptance. My thoughts must have been showing in my eyes because he hands me two red apples, 'This is my gift to you, Ji,' he says, 'one for you and one for your husband.'

Bananas and apples. At least I won't starve! Now if only I can find somewhere to buy bread...

'Thank you but my husband isn't with me,' I take one of the apples and give him back the other, 'I'm by myself.'

'Where is husband?'

'He's in England.'

The fruit and veg seller is shocked, 'You shouldn't be here alone isn't it. He should have stopped you from coming here only.'

'It's different for Englishwomen. We are used to being alone,' I say.

He frowns and wiggles his head in that familiar Indian neck sway which can mean, Yes, No, Maybe.

How can I make this man understand?

I don't even try; instead, I hand the beggar children a banana

MONKEY ON MY ROOF

each, and ask him where the nearest Internet Shop is, 'I need to phone my husband, let him know that I'm safe.'

He points to a nearby alley, and I rush away before the neighbourhood bush telegraph alerts every beggar for miles around about the crazy English woman handing out free bananas.

The internet shop has an STD phone. It takes three attempts before I manage to get through.

'Oh hello,' Mark says. 'Guess what? There's trouble in the government. Looks like Jack Straw will have to resign.'

And suddenly I am furiously angry.

Thousands of miles away from home, feeling as if I'm in a war zone, surrounded by men with guns, deafened by the sirens of police cars and ambulances; expecting him to ask if I'm okay, to tell me to keep away from danger. I can see him sitting in his armchair, feet up on the coffee table, schooner of malt whisky in one hand, TV remote in the other. And all I get is bloody politics!

I tell him I don't want to know. Hasn't he heard about the bombs going off all around me in the Parah Ganj? Isn't it strange how he, compulsively watching all those news programmes, isn't aware his wife might be in danger? It's been all over the international news on TV after all.

Yes, he has heard, he says, and he's sorry.

But it's too late, and too little.

Now, instead of hitting my credit card in the shops of New Delhi I've decided to move to somewhere safer. I'm off to book a flight to Goa. To a beautiful crescent beach with an island and river at the north end of the beach where people of all ages stretch suntanned bodies into yoga positions or sit lotus-legged on the sand to meditate.

Next door to the internet shop is a travel agent. The travel

MONKEY ON MY ROOF

agents say everyone is leaving Delhi, there are no seats available on the planes but they can fix me up with a car at three times the price.

The fruit and vegetable seller with the wounded ear tells me to get a rickshaw to the airport and book a seat for myself.

'It's easy,' he says, 'and a lot cheaper.'

He's right: within half a day I've packed my stuff, settled my bill and am stepping out of a taxi outside a guesthouse in Palolem south Goa.

Sun surf and sea yippee.

A week later Ailsa, whose reasons for visiting India are very different from mine, stepped off the plane at Dabolim airport into the bright morning sunshine.

And so it began.

MONKEY ON MY ROOF

5

When she walked from the airport wheeling her luggage in a rickety trolley with wonky wheels, Ailsa must have realised that the first thing she needed was a taxi. She would have carried her backpack across the traffic lane to the taxi booth outside Dabolim airport where the local panchayat — council to you and me — makes sure the prices are strictly controlled.

Now I'm not saying that all the taxi drivers in India are thieves and vagabonds, occasionally you'll meet an honest one; though I wouldn't count on it. You're much less likely to get ripped off if you use one of the taxi booths, which India has set up in some of its cities.

When I arrived last week bright inquisitive eyes at the front of the queue inspected me warily. Dark matted hair flopped above those eyes, with bristly designer stubble doing it's best to look respectable below. A student on a gap year, out in India to do voluntary work in an orphanage or hospital, to learn yoga and meditation, and find enlightenment by smoking Ganga. You see them all over India these students. They come in all nationalities, all shapes and sizes, and are easily recognizable by their scruffy jeans, and tee shirts plastered with crude slogans — until they hit the beaches that is, then it's all change to bare-tanned chests and bright lungis for the boys and tiny bikinis for the girls.

This particular student asked, 'Are you going to Palolem?'
I nodded yes.
'Want to share a taxi?'
Squinting at the price board on the taxi booth I said, '1400 rupees, that's about ten pounds each. We can make it cheaper than that.'

MONKEY ON MY ROOF

Raising my voice I'd called to the others in the queue, 'Anyone else here going to Palolem?'

Two other gap-year students stepped forward, 'We are!'

The bored-looking police officer in the taxi booth wrote us a chitty detailing what we should pay, and the four of us followed the driver to the taxi rank. We loaded three huge backpacks and my small one into the boot and squeezed ourselves into the back seat.

Then we were on our way along the hot, dusty, potholed road. Driving through the little towns where men sat on wooden benches to drink chai in teahouses, and eat Masala dosa or puri bhaji in the booths placed at the side of the road. By-passing the thick groves of bamboo, coconut palms and cashew trees, the rice paddies being worked by women in bright saris. Putting behind us the fields encircling small ponds in which water buffaloes stand waist deep, as white ibis wade around them.

The three students looked at it all with big eyes: The way Ailsa must have done when she arrived the following week.

At Palolem I booked in at my usual guesthouse, then took a rickshaw to Chaudi, the nearest town, to visit the small supermarket and buy sun tan lotion, shampoo, flea powder, bleach for the toilet, a toilet brush, coat hangers, a plastic vegetable rack to be used as a bedside table and two tumblers, and I was all set.

My landlady had told me proudly that there was a new bus station in Chaudi, very modern with little shops and restaurants in the waiting areas, and even western-style toilets, so I walked up the lane to catch the bus back.

However I didn't get the chance to examine the facilities. In fact I didn't even get across the road to the bus station. After dodging a lorry and jumping out of the way of a rickshaw driver steering his vehicle around a sacred cow — I'm not sacred enough

MONKEY ON MY ROOF

to be worth avoiding it seems — my leg twisted and I fell. When I tried to get up, tried to put weight on my foot, it hurt so badly that I moaned in pain.

The rickshaw driver stopped and got out, 'You stupid sod,' I shouted at him from my position seated on my bum in the middle of the road, 'Why can't you look where you're going!'

He smiled with relief; if I could shout at him it meant I wasn't dead. Now he wouldn't have to grease the palms of local police to cover up the accident. He picked up my shopping, helped me into the rickshaw and drove me to the Government Hospital; a dingy brick built building with benches set along a crumbling wall outside the main door. This was the waiting area.

With the aid of the rickshaw driver I hobbled to a bench and sat beside a boy who couldn't have been more than fifteen years old. Brown-green pus issued from a huge gaping wound on the boys arm, which was swollen to twice its normal size. The smell from his wound was appalling. I'd never smelt gas gangrene, but I didn't need a medical dictionary to tell me that this was how it must smell.

The boy was raving in delirium; a man sitting next to him wiped the sweat from the boy's forehead with a dirty rag and tried to sooth him.

'What happened to him?' I said to this man. But he didn't speak English.

The rickshaw driver translated, 'He the boy's father, they work in the jungle. Father says the boy clumsy, have accident with machete.'

'The wound is very bad. Why wasn't he brought here earlier?'

'They try to cure it with turmeric, Momma.'

MONKEY ON MY ROOF

'Turmeric! That's for cooking.'
'Is antiseptic also,' the rickshaw driver said.
'It can't be a very good antiseptic then!'
From my other side came a strong smell of kerosene.

A woman in a green sari had arrived to sit beside me. Though she had drawn the end of her sari over her head, I could see that one side of her face and the arm holding the veil was bubbling with blisters, which were bursting to reveal the vivid red raw flesh beneath. I said to the rickshaw driver, 'And her?'

The local language is Konkanese, the rickshaw driver and the woman talked. After a while he told me, 'She cook rice on stove, husband drunk, angry, kick stove. Stove fall over, rice pot fly in air, fall on her.'

But I knew what he was *not* saying. It isn't the first time I'd heard about kerosene stove accidents. Others have told me that these "accidents" are often deliberate because the husband wants rid of the wife. Perhaps this woman wasn't young enough, or hadn't borne him a son. I'd never believed it until then.

A harassed-looking nurse came along and told me to follow her and I was led into a kind of operating room. I'd been expecting to walk into the film set of M.A.S.H. to see blood and dirt on the tiled floor, the bare plaster walls, the windowpanes, but the hospital was surprisingly clean.

A weary Brahmin Doctor wearing a dirty white coat examined my foot in a perfunctory sort of way.

He said, 'You have Bursitis of the Achilles tendon.'
'What does that mean?'
'You must rest your foot for three days,' he told me, 'and don't wear flip flops, wear shoes with a high heel.'
'High heels!'

MONKEY ON MY ROOF

'To take pressure away from the tendon. If the tendon snaps you'll be lame for the rest of your life.'

'How long before I can travel?'

'Who knows? Two months. Maybe longer.'

He gave me a prescription for tablets.

Being there, in that hospital, made me very much aware of how lucky I was not to have been born as a lower caste Indian.

MONKEY ON MY ROOF

6

There are too many power cuts in India! The blasted things usually happen just as I've come out of the shower, and am hopping around with one leg in my knickers trying to remember where the heck I've put the soddin' torch.

There was a power cut tonight; the reason I'm so late getting to Casa Fiesta my favourite restaurant, a place where I am known and liked by the staff and can be certain I won't end up with Delhi Belly. India can be dangerous. A person can't run away from danger if she's got the squitters.

The street outside is noisy I can't quite make out what Prakash the waiter is murmuring under his breath, something about a young girl.

Then, 'This way, Momma,' he says.

Feeling like an idiot in my high-heeled sandals, I hobble behind him between the neem trees and coconut palms. At one of the tables a young woman is sitting alone.

There used to be a TV advert for pensions, it was called the Scottish Widow. The girl at the table isn't wearing the same black cloak; a red-lined cowl doesn't cover her hair. She doesn't need either of those to give off that same aura of desolation.

That look of hers, the sense of hopelessness, stops me in my tracks. Stops me as if the soles of my feet are cemented to the sandy floor. I can't bring myself to walk past that bent blonde head and those round, long-lashed brown eyes gazing with such concentrated despair at the red tablecloth. She seems much too young — in her early twenties — to look so… desperate.

But I can hardly go up to a complete stranger in a restaurant, and declare, 'Hi, there! You look as if you need someone to talk to?'

MONKEY ON MY ROOF

Can I?

So I do the only thing I can think of; which is to lean across the table, take hold of the flex of the sombrero hat that is used as a lampshade, and set the light swinging. Then, when she looks up to see what is happening, I pin a smile on my face and drawl nonchalantly, 'Hi there! You look bloody bored!'

She says, 'I'm not bored! I was thinking.'

And Prakash asks, 'You sitting here, Momma?'

'I don't know,' I tell him because now I'm beginning to think that I've got it wrong and am in danger of making a complete horse's ass of myself. Maybe the young lady prefers to be alone?

The young person in question gives me a long searching look. The kind of look a person gives to a stranger when they feel lost in unknowable territory. Then her eyes soften, and she smiles, 'No. Please! Won't you sit down?'

Her name is Ailsa she says, and she's from Glasgow — not quite the Scottish Widow but near enough. Mum and Dad divorced. Both of them remarried with new families. She hasn't spoken to her mother for the past two years. Her mother prefers her younger sister, the child of her second marriage, Ailsa says resentfully. She never sees her father, he just can't be bothered.

'Second best,' she says bitterly, 'I'm second best!'

I know what that feels like; *my* mother preferred my younger sister over me and wasn't afraid to show it, and I didn't see much of Dad either once my parents split up. It seems Ailsa and I have something in common.

We order our meals, and she tells me that she's looking for a room nearer the beach.

'I'm not bothered about swimming,' she says. Then adds dreamily, 'Just to lie on a sunbed and feel the hot sun on my skin

MONKEY ON MY ROOF

will be enough.'

'The swimming is safe in Palolem,' I tell her.

She lifts her chin in defiance, 'I've been ill. Had to have an operation, so I can't go in the water.'

So that's why she's so thin, the reason her skin has that translucent almost alabaster cast which only seems to come with illness; 'Oh?'

Her face tightens, 'I don't want to talk about it.'

I smile at her, 'You don't have to do anything you don't want to do.'

Just then Prakash brings the food, 'Enjoy dinner, Momma,' he says.

'He calls you Momma. What's that about?'

'It doesn't mean anything. Every westerner over the age of fifty is Momma or Poppa to Indians.'

After a while I say, 'The guest-house I stay at is near the beach. There could be a room available.'

Ailsa smiles, 'Really?'

'Yes. The rooms are basic though, not much furniture — a bed, a chair, a table, and a few pegs behind the door to hang clothes on. But there's a western toilet, *and* a shower in the bathroom. There's no hot water by the way. But the landlady will heat a bucketful on the cauldron in the garden if she's asked nicely. I can show you if you'd like?'

When we've finished eating she says, 'Where's this guest-house you were telling me about then?'

And we dawdle along the road, past the small shops and booths selling tourist souvenirs, to my room.

MONKEY ON MY ROOF

7

The main house is dark and silent, it seems the landlady is either out or having an early night.

A gravel path runs alongside the main house to the rooms at the back.

'Come and look,' I tell Ailsa, 'you mightn't want to stay here once you've seen what it's like.'

Ailsa takes a look at my room; inspects the bathroom, bounces up and down on the spare bed to test the mattress.

She lifts her head to gaze at the ceiling beam, which runs through all the rooms from one end of the building to the other, and I say, 'I suppose I should tell you about the rat that walks along that beam every night.'

'Rat?'

I grin, 'Don't worry, he never comes in the rooms, he's only interested in his dinner. The restaurant owner empties the slops around midnight. He didn't half give me a fright the first time I saw him. Then the cheeky sod turned his head, looked at me as if to say: "Who the heck are you? How dare you interrupt me?" As if it was none of my business and he had a perfect right to be there. Then he carried on strolling along that beam as is he didn't have a care in the world. It made me laugh.'

Ailsa shudders, 'Ugh, rats! Doesn't it give you the shivers?'

'Not a bit, I used to keep white rats as pets when I was a child. Even a rat is entitled to his life. ...His name is Cuthbert.'

That makes her laugh, 'Cuthbert!'

I laugh back at her.

'Cuthbert,' she says again through the laughter. Then her laughter changes. Now there are tears running down her face, she

MONKEY ON MY ROOF

turns away, 'Sorry, sorry, sorry, I have to go.'

I put my hand on her shoulder, 'What's wrong, Ailsa?'

Through great gulping sobs words burst in torrents from her lips. The operation. A cancer, a hysterectomy. Broken dreams of a white wedding, lost visions of her father walking her down the aisle. Children who will never now be born.

Sitting beside her on the bed, I gather her to me and listen, because that's all I know to do, and she doesn't need me to do anything else.

Finally, the sobs slow to hiccups, and she mutters, 'There was a works do last year. Some of us went on to a disco. Greg was there. I knew right away he was the one. It was the same for him. We've been planning to marry.'

'Go on.'

'Greg is just an ordinary guy,' she says, 'not so tall, and his nose is a little bent where it was broken when he played rugby. He drives me to my hospital appointments. Holds my head when I throw up, rubs my back when it aches. How can I carry on without him? But how can I marry him now? It wouldn't be fair. Why would he want to marry a woman who has cancer? A woman who can't have his children?'

It torments her more than the fear of death: never to give birth; never to know that sweet, earth shattering, mind boggling moment; that moment when you hold your child, your small perfect scrap of humanity for the first time.

What can I say? How can I answer her? I mumble some words about keeping positive, the kind of platitudes she must have heard a hundred times before. Those flawlessly faulty words fall like stones from my lips, angrily I wonder why such things happen to people like Ailsa, why can't God — if there is a God — inflict

MONKEY ON MY ROOF

cancer on the wicked amongst us.

Ailsa is quieter now, though she is still hiccupping, 'I'm sorry, Sally,' she says, 'I shouldn't have laid this on you.'

What if she were one of my daughters?

I reach across for a packet of tissues from my vegetable rack bedside table, and wipe the tears and snot from off her face, 'A girl with your illness shouldn't be alone,' I say, 'the bed we're sitting on is going spare. You can stay with me if you like?'

She gives herself a little shake, lifts her chin resolutely and says, 'No, no, I'll be alright. Don't worry about me.'

'It's getting late. You can't walk back like that. The state you're in, you could get eaten by a tiger!'

She gives me a look, 'Really?'

'No, I was joking! Stay the night at least. There's a spare nightie hanging on that peg behind the door.'

'If you're sure...?'

I nod.

Sleep is hard to come by. Small hiccups mingled with quiet breathing from the bed next to mine tell me Ailsa is sleepless too.

It's the kind of night when no matter how often you turn every bone in your body groans in discomfort, a clammy, sweaty, itchy, airless night. A night for me to lie awake and think about why I'm here alone in India.

MONKEY ON MY ROOF

8

My family and friends tell me that I'm crazy to be travelling around India on my own. They point out the dangers of death from typhoid, malaria, religious riots, man-eating tigers and rampaging elephants, not to mention the odd theft and rape. What would they think now, I wonder, if they knew I've invited a strange young woman to share my room?

This morning Ailsa's face is drawn and pale. There are shadows around her eyes from last night's tears. She sits on the side of the bed and murmurs, 'I thought I could do this on my own.'

'You don't have to do it on your own,' I say, unsure if she is talking to me or just thinking aloud. 'You can stay here, the offer's still open.'

Shadowed or not, her gaze is direct. 'Why Sally? Why would you…?'

Gazing back at her I say, 'Don't get me wrong, Ailsa, I'm no Mother Teresa but I have daughters of my own. If one of them was in your position I hope somebody would do the same.'

Only then does she smile, 'Okay,' she says decisively. 'If you and Cuthbert can bear to have me here, I'll stay with you.'

What have I let myself in for? Oh well, in for a penny, in for a pound.

We have breakfast at Casa Fiesta, then we collect Ailsa's backpack from the room she's booked into. A room among the coconut palms right at the back of the village, as far away from the beach as one can get in this small place.

'What shall we do now?' she asks.

'How about we go dump your bag in the room and take off up the beach. I'll introduce you to my friend Manju,' I say. 'In

MONKEY ON MY ROOF

Palolem I eat lunch at River Valley, and dinner at Casa Fiesta.'

Passing the stalls selling sandals and beach wear, jewellery, souvenirs and sun-tan lotion, we walk along the beach road and turn right through the archway onto the beach. The tide is out this morning, the sand swept clean, fishing boats pulled up high away from the sea. Later when the sea has crept nearer the shore, the boats will be rolled down again to take tourists out to watch the dolphins playing around the back of the island. A few people are sitting in the lotus position facing the sea, one of them a man with greying hair, gets up and waves at me before jumping into the surf.

'Who's that?' Ailsa asks.

'I've no idea,' I say airily, not wanting to explain the easy understanding that seems to pass between this man and myself, the smiles and waves — though we've never even wished each other a Good Morning. How can I explain something so inexplicable when I can't explain it to myself?

'He's always there at this time in the morning, always gives me a wave.' I find myself blushing. Not wanting her to read my face, I turn away.

'Really?' Ailsa, who's no fool, lifts her hand, takes hold of my chin, pulls my head back towards her, gazes at my red face and grins.

'I've never spoken to him,' I protest.

'What about this Manju you're taking me to meet?'

Positioned at the side of the river, Manju's camp — one of those universal beach camps — is easy enough to find. Each wooden hut is thatched with palm leaves, and has its own small balcony where towels and bikinis can be thrown over railings to dry. Every hut has a different sign naming it for an Indian river. Hammocks are strung between palm trees. The harmony of the river and trees, the

MONKEY ON MY ROOF

stillness of the hot air, gave the camp an atmosphere of tranquillity.

'His camp runs alongside the river,' I say, and point to the path leading through the coconut grove. 'This is the reason he named it River Valley. Most lunchtimes I eat lunch with Manju. It's my favourite place. That's where I'd be staying if I was young enough to stumble around dodging palm trees, spiders, snakes, and rats while I'm looking for a lavatory in the middle of the night.'

'Sounds ideal,' she says sardonically.

'You'll see it for yourself soon enough.'

'How long have you known Manju?'

'Not so long. I got to know him last year.'

*

I'd been passing his gate and stopped when I saw him sitting under the awning, head in hands.

'Hangover?'

Manju had groaned, flapped his hand, and winced.

'Would you like some aspirin?'

He'd raised his head hopefully, 'You have some?'

Rummaging in my beach bag I found the bottle, and handed it to him.

He shook two into his hand, and called, 'Cook!'

Like some sort of magic trick a smile materialised in the kitchen doorway. The cook's smile always arrives on the scene first. It's the biggest thing about him.

'Make chai,' Manju ordered the smile. He looked at me for the first time, 'You like stay take chai?'

So I'd stayed to drink chai.

'I'm not Indian,' Manju told me. 'I'm South American.'

MONKEY ON MY ROOF

This was just about plausible given his appearance. His shoulder length dark hair hung around his face making him look like a Mexican in a spaghetti western, while the curved hook of his nose and dark hooded eyes gave him an Aztec look.

'South American?' I said, half believing.

'Only half South American,' Manju smiled.

I could tell he wanted me to ask so I'd said, 'What's the other half?'

'Irish. Mother name Mary O'Toole from Donegal,' he'd answered seriously.

'Really? And I suppose your brother is a leprechaun?'

'A lep re cha un---.' He'd stumbled over the pronunciation, 'What?'

'It's a kind of Irish Hindu priest,' I told him.

Manju had given me a quizzical look, 'Stay have lunch, daal and rice,' he'd said. 'No charge!'

MONKEY ON MY ROOF

9

But that was last year. Today the three of us Ailsa, Manju, and me are sitting around the table under the awning. Ailsa is struggling not to laugh as she listens to Manju's tales of his Inca father from Machu Picchu and his Irish mother from Donegal.

My new roommate has a way of crossing her eyes comically when she's not sure of herself; it's very endearing.

She takes a sip from the mug of Masala chai the cook has made and says, 'The wedding must have been… interesting, I take it your father is Hindu. What about your mother? Was she Roman Catholic?'

'No problem,' Manju assures her, 'they were married by a leprechaun.'

Ailsa does that thing again with her eyes and splutters into her mug of chai, 'A what!'

'A kind of Irish Hindu priest,' Manju states.

He looks at me, 'Isn't that right, Sally?'

'Of course it is! Would I lie to you?' I say deadpan.

Watching how we smile at each other Ailsa says, 'You seem to have known each other forever. Are you sure it's only been a year?'

Instantly Manju sobers, 'I'm sure,' he says, '2004. Camp flooded.'

She says, 'What happened?'

'A tsunami is what happened,' I say.

'You were in India? You never told me!'

I shrug, 'There are more important things for you to listen to than the ramblings of a bored and desperate housewife.'

She laughs, 'I've got nothing against bored housewives, or

MONKEY ON MY ROOF

desperate ones for that matter. You may as well tell me, I've got plenty of time. I have a six month visa.'

'There's nothing much to tell,' I say, 'not compared to what had happened in other places.'

'So how come Manju's camp got flooded?'

Manju puts his mug of chai down on the table, 'Tell her, Sally,' he says.

'Okay, Boxing Day 2004! Just a normal day,' I say. 'But then in the afternoon people were saying — it was all over the TV — how while we'd been swimming and sunbathing, rubbing in suntan lotion, chatting with our friends, drinking the odd cocktail: all those lovely relaxing things that people do on holiday... hundreds of other people... people just like us; were drowning.'

I shivered remembering, 'It was the way everyone freaked out that frightened me the most.'

'Freaked out?' Ailsa said.

'Yeah, after dinner Mark had gone back to our room while I went to the Internet shop to phone our daughters and let them know we were safe.'

I lean back in the chair and close my eyes, behind my eyelids I picture that day as if it is a DVD replay on my television.

I'd been in the internet shop about ten minutes when Prakash pulled me out into the street, 'You have to come Momma. The big wave comes! You have to come. Now Momma!'

All hell had broken loose, hundreds of people running on the road, men ran with bundles on their heads, women with babies in their arms dragged howling toddlers, Indians and Europeans all mixed up with rushing dogs, little black pigs, and stampeding cows.

And I'd fought against the crowd, worried for Mark — was he safe? Did he get back to our room? I'd fought until I could fight no

MONKEY ON MY ROOF

more. Until I was forced to run. Running, because there was nothing else I could do. Running faster than I'd ever known possible. More afraid of being trampled underfoot than of the tsunami. When the owner of the internet shop passed me dawdling his motor bike through the crowd I'd pulled at his arm, 'I can't find Mark. Have you seen him? Have you seen my husband?'

'No Momma. No Momma,' panic-stricken face matching mine. 'My wife I must find my wife.'

Later I saw them; his wife sitting astride the pillion of the motor bike, his eyes alive with relief at having found her.

The next few hours were spent standing at the side of the road on a mountain with some other people until the police arrived to tell us it was safe to go back. I got back to the guesthouse to find that the water hadn't reached our lodgings.

Dreading what I would find; had Mark been caught up in the panic, had he gone looking for me and got caught in the tsunami? Was he even now lying by the side of the road trampled and bleeding, or being dashed against the rocks by giant waves? I rushed up the stairs to our room.

Mark was lying in bed: watching TV.

'Oh Thank God!' My sense of relief had been enormous, 'You're okay,' I cried.

Mark didn't move. His mouth didn't flicker in a smile; his eyes didn't come alight with relief. Why didn't he jump out of bed? Why wasn't he glad to see me? To see I was alive, unhurt?

'Weren't you worried about me?' I'd asked standing there bruised and exhausted.

He'd seen nothing of the panic, he said. Didn't know there was any danger.

Why then a few days later did my friend Sheila inform me

MONKEY ON MY ROOF

that Mark had told her I'd deserted him that night. Told her that I had abandoned him?

Mark who is so secretive, who never talks about personal things, whose conversation consists mostly of politics, football, and cooking, had confided in Sheila!

Shocked, I'd exclaimed in surprise, 'I did try to get back to him, I suppose I could have tried harder, but I just didn't have any strength left to fight against that crowd.'

Back in England I'd asked him why he'd felt I'd deserted him, didn't he know me well enough by now to realise that I'd never do that?

His face carefully blank. Mark had denied saying any such thing. Who to believe? My husband or my friend? My friend had never lied to me, my husband had; many times. I changed the subject.

Later Mark told me that a Police Inspector had knocked on the door to warn him that Palolem was being evacuated.

'That contradicts what you said when I got back that night,' I told him.

'What did I say?'

'You said you'd seen nothing of the panic, and didn't know there was any danger.'

'No I didn't.'

I looked him in the face, 'I'd never have got those words wrong.'

Mark shrugged his shoulders and left the room.

I watched him walk away, and that's when I got the idea that perhaps a year away from one another would be good for us. Maybe when I got back home our marriage could be reborn? If we still had a marriage that is.

MONKEY ON MY ROOF

It was after the tsunami that he began to address me as "Mother", by way of a dirty word coming from his mouth.

Before the tsunami; after the tsunami. This is how my life divides.

*

'There wasn't much damage in Palolem,' I tell Ailsa now, 'nothing compared to what happened elsewhere. A few fishing boats lying in splinters against the sea wall, a couple of dead puppies on the beach, two or three beach cafés swept away.'

'My camp was flooded,' says Manju, 'some people take passports, run away. Didn't come back to pay.'

'A lot of people drowned,' I say more sharply than I intended. 'Thousands of them.'

'Not from my camp!' But he looks ashamed. 'What you do now?'

The hands of my watch point to half past two. Turning to Ailsa I exclaim, 'It's time to cross the river for Reiki. Do you want to come, or would you rather stay here and listen to Manju whinge?'

She laughs, 'I'll come with you. See you tomorrow, Manju.'

We finish our chai and wade across the river.

MONKEY ON MY ROOF

10

Today the only things on Yoga beach are a couple of derelict bamboo fruit stalls, and a man and woman sunning themselves on the sand. No noisy holidaymakers playing cricket or throwing Frisbees. Only the whisper of the surf and the swish from the wings of fish eagles, as they circle the rocks that bridge the small cove to the island when the tide is out.

The Reiki master has seen us crossing the river; he appears from an opening in the rocks and walks barefoot towards us.

'Gosh!' Ailsa exclaims.

Everyone says, 'Gosh!' when they first meet him.

Perhaps it's his air of serenity. On the other hand it could be his lithe body, which wouldn't be out of place on a super-fit thirty year old. Possibly, it's his copper brown skin; for most of the year he lives in the jungle with only a canopy for shade against the sun. There again it could be his laser-like brown eyes, which seem to probe right into ones soul. Nobody tells lies to the Reiki Master.

Personally though, I think the surprise comes from his interesting line in bathing attire, which just happens to be the same colour as his skin. And what with the curly grey hairs escaping from the sides — not to mention other dangly bits when he's been a bit careless dressing — it looks at first sight as if he is stark naked!

'Yes. That's my name,' Gosh states.

'Of course!' Ailsa says dryly. 'What else could it be?'

Gosh walks over to give me a hug, while beside me Ailsa shifts from one foot to the other, and stares firmly at the top of the nearest palm tree. I know just how she feels, I didn't know where to look the first time I saw him either.

Aware of the sunbathing couple watching with amusement, I

MONKEY ON MY ROOF

try not to giggle as I say, 'This is Ailsa. She urgently needs some healing.'

'Yes,' Gosh replies, and takes her hand. 'Come and tell me about it.'

They go to sit cross-legged on the beach mats, Ailsa talking and Gosh listening intently.

Other healers, two women and a man, arrive and join them at the healing circle. Ailsa has lost her shyness, she lies down on the straw beach mat and Gosh sits at her head to take up the healing position, so I walk across the hot sand to say 'Hi' to the woman with the big laugh, and the man with the drolly-expressive face.

They seem like my kind of people.

They've moved into the shade of a rock, and are sitting silently, leaning towards one another with that air of easy, well-worn affection that couples get when they've been together a long time. The woman smiles when she notices me standing there, and says, 'Hi. I'm Irene;' she strokes the man's shoulder, 'he is Udo.'

Udo clasps the hand that is resting on his shoulder, with his other hand he pats the sand, 'Come and sit down.'

I lower myself to the floor.

Turning to Irene I ask, 'What part of Germany are you from?'

'How do you know we are German?' Udo asks, 'are you a witch or something?'

His accent couldn't be anything else but German, but I smile mysteriously and say, 'I'm psychic. Be careful! I can read your minds.'

'Can you read mine?' Udo asks.

Glancing at the way his hand is now stroking Irene's arm with unashamed sensuality, I tell him, 'Better not!'

MONKEY ON MY ROOF

Udo grins, and Irene gives out that big laugh again.

Then Ailsa arrives carrying her shoes. Her air of quiet desperation has vanished. In her beach dress and bare feet, with that bright look on her face she seems lit from within, as if in some way a burnt-out light bulb has been replaced by one of a 100 watts.

She lowers herself gently down beside me.

Irene says, 'How was the Reiki?'

People who've had Reiki for the first time frequently can't find the words to describe what happens, are often too overawed to explain the warmth, the colours, the energy. 'Oh er... You know...' struggling for words, Ailsa crosses her eyes and blurts, 'Gosh is going to teach me the First Degree.'

Then she is off, talking nineteen to the dozen about Gosh, and how he is teaching her, and how she is planning to practise to heal herself when she gets back home.

Silently I recall my first Reiki session; a hotel, a swimming pool, and Margaret, one of the guests — noticing how stiffly I'd lowered myself onto the sunbed — offering me healing for my arthritis.

At that time I knew absolutely nothing about Reiki, had never even heard the word spoken. Of course I'd seen it written in big letters, advertised on the tatty faded posters stuck on lamp posts along the road, but I'd never been interested enough to read one of those posters.

Not knowing if she was going to massage me, stick pins in me or pull my toes I'd lain back on the sun bed and closed my eyes obediently. Then Margaret's hands touched my shoulders and the lovely normal sounds of a holiday hotel, the splashes from the swimming pool, people laughing, dogs barking far away, crows squabbling in the palm trees, faded into the distance.

MONKEY ON MY ROOF

Margaret's hands moved from my shoulders to the back of my neck, stayed there for a few minutes, then moved to cover my eyes.
And Wham!

There are no words to describe what happened to me next. I don't think even Shakespeare could describe it; there isn't a dictionary in any language in the world that could even come close. All I can say is that I took hold of that which was offered to me. From that moment, I wanted to give anyone who needed it that same feeling.

MONKEY ON MY ROOF

11

Another power cut. Tonight there are two of us hopping around bumping into one another.

Ailsa thinks it's hilarious, and then she trips over a chair and bangs her head on the bathroom door.

It's difficult to get dressed in the dark, but we manage, and before long are stumbling our way through the pot-holed road to Casa Fiesta, where the two of us stand helplessly just inside the gate, squinting our eyes for a table that isn't crammed to capacity with cheerful, big-eyed, pink-tinged tourists.

'Bloody 'ell,' I say, 'where did this mob come from? Looks like a charabanc outing to Blackpool illuminations. Want to go somewhere else?'

'We can't just leave,' Ailsa says, 'what would Irene and Udo think?'

As we talk, Prakash comes towards us carrying candles to put in the glass shades on the tables, and nods his head towards the back of the restaurant, 'Doug and Sheila round the backside, Momma.'

Ailsa smothers a laugh, and I can't help smiling. Whenever an Indian tells me something is "around the backside" I imagine the first English schoolteacher to come to India with a wicked sense of humour. I picture him capped and gowned, standing in front of a class of small boys.

He's saying, 'All together now class. Repeat after me.'

The children are solemnly chanting, 'Left side, right side, back side.'

Through the gloom at the back of the restaurant, a candle-flame is waving backward and forwards.

MONKEY ON MY ROOF

Sheila's voice skips across the restaurant, 'Over here Sally!'

It is good to see them again, to have Doug bend down and engulf me in an awkward hug. He's tall; six feet two at least, and plump with the kind of thickset body you sometimes see on people from the Netherlands. Which, being as he is half-Dutch, isn't surprising. Small dark-haired Sheila, with her delicate features and big eyes, looks like a tiny pixie next to him. She has to stand on tiptoes while I bend down to embrace her.

Then the power comes on again, the sombrero hat lampshades glow with light, and Irene and Udo arrive to join us.

If anyone should ask me tomorrow what I ate at dinner this evening I won't be able to remember. My memory cells can hold only the moonlight and music, the talk, the laughter.

Like a digital camera my brain takes snapshots; Irene's shoulder sighing with delight when Udo — coming back from the toilet — bends to place a kiss on the back of her neck. Ailsa's face as she tastes her dessert — 'Hello to the Queen' — for the first time. Prakash gazing at Ailsa with an expression that could be mistaken for love, but is really compassion.

Another snapshot: Doug with one arm around Sheila's shoulder as she holds the lighter to his cigarette, the huge painting of Buddha over the bar, and gentle dignified Shiva Prasad the restaurant manager stirring a cocktail with one hand while he slices a lime with the other.

Shiva mixes some wonderful cocktails. How I wish I was as clever at mixing people who haven't met before. I never know how well the ingredients will blend. Tonight I got it right. The conversation and laughter flows as if the six of us are old friends catching up with one another after many years.

'What are you doing Saturday?' Sheila asks.

MONKEY ON MY ROOF

'Saturday,' I tell her, 'Ailsa and me are going to the market.'

*

The market in Chaudi, is not a patch on the one in Anjuna, but Chaudi is only five miles away, ten minutes in a rickshaw at the most. Anjuna is in the north of Goa, a couple of hours at the least, the bus or taxi ride over bumpy unmade roads would certainly be tiring, and might be painful for her, Ailsa says. Anyway, she's never been to an Indian market before. It will be a new experience.

The Saturday market in Chaudi is not so different from any other day of the week, but Ailsa doesn't know that, and stares big-eyed at the few vendors sitting cross-legged at the side of the road, their wares displayed on plastic sheets. They sell bangles, bindis and posters of Hindu Gods. Ailsa buys an armful of Indian bangles for her sister, a couple of cards of bindis for herself, and a poster of Saraswati for me.

'Why Saraswati?' I ask.

'Saraswati is goddess of the arts,' Ailsa tells me, 'I think she is right for you.'

'I'll put her on the wall in the room when we get back,' I declare, 'she'll brighten the place up. Should look good on that bare wall.'

I buy some pink gauze netting, and a poster of Ganesha, and tell Ailsa the story of how the God Shiva came home from battle to find a stranger in bed with his wife.

'Not realising who it is,' I tell her, 'Shiva takes out his sword and cuts the boy's head off. Overcome with remorse when he discovers that he has killed his own son, he then swears an oath to take the head of the next living thing he sees and replace his son's head with it.

MONKEY ON MY ROOF

Unfortunately, Shiva hasn't considered that the next living thing he sees might not be human. But an oath is an oath, especially when you are a god. This is why Ganesha has the head of an elephant, and the body of a human being.'

Ailsa laughs, 'I've met a few people who'd benefit the human race if their heads were cut off,' she says. 'What's the pink netting for?'

'It's to string across the beams, it'll stop the spiders from dropping in my open mouth when I snore in the night,' I tell her. 'And now I have this problem with my foot, I'm stuck here for the next couple of months and I want to make my room more pleasant to come home to.'

'Good idea,' she says.

She's never tasted sugar cane syrup. We go to the wheelbarrow where an Indian woman in a yellow and green sari is running the long canes through a machine and catching the syrup in plastic cups. 'It tastes like nectar,' Ailsa says, 'if Shiva had drunk more of this he'd have been too happy to cut his son's head off!'

We decide to lunch at The Udupi Restaurant, though to call it a restaurant is a bit of an exaggeration; with its plastic-topped tables and benches the place is more like an old-fashioned works canteen, but the food is good and cheap.

My mobile phone beeps, a text from Emma my youngest to say that she's been bragging to her friends at university about her Mum, who like some recycled teenage hippie was sodding off to India for a year. And wasn't it great that Mum wasn't sitting knitting on the couch while she watched Corrie on the telly and waited to die.

'Humm,' I show Ailsa the text, 'considering that I can't knit, seldom watch Coronation Street, and have no intention of dying just

MONKEY ON MY ROOF

yet thank you very much, it's a bit tactless of daughter number three don't you think?'

Ailsa laughs, 'Bet she wishes she was here with you.'

Then she sighs, 'I wish Greg could be sitting next to me on this wooden bench drinking chai, practising Indian head nods and laughing at your jokes while we wait for the waiter to bring our puri bahjis! Isn't it funny, only last week I couldn't get away fast enough! Now I want him here.' She smiles. Then she frowns, 'He was upset when I told him I wanted to come away on my own.'

'If Greg's the paragon you describe, he'll understand,' I tell her.

Ailsa gives a wicked grin, 'Aren't you worried your husband will get into mischief while you're gone?'

'Oh, there's always the chance he'll two-time me while I'm away, but after the last two episodes ...'

'Two episodes!' Ailsa is startled. 'I had no idea! I wouldn't have made that joke if...'

'Yes,' my voice quivers; even now the shockwave has the power to disturb me. 'It's not only the betrayals,' I tell her, 'though they're bad enough. It's what comes after. Mark has a way of transferring his guilt onto my shoulders.'

It's the soul-destroying rounds of accusations, revelations and recriminations. The being made to feel as if I'm the guilty one. His wilful misunderstanding, those heavy sighs every time I make an innocent joke, the cast up eyebrows and hurt puppy looks. It's the having to walk on eggshells around him. Having to watch every word I utter. It's the not being able to make the smallest innocuous remark without it being taken out of context. As if I'm the kind of person who'd throw that up in his face!

As if it's something I'd joke about.

MONKEY ON MY ROOF

'So that's the reason you're here alone!' Ailsa exclaims, 'I've been wondering why your husband wasn't here with you. Once is bad enough, but twice must have been traumatic...'

'Oh it's been more than twice,' I say.

'Why do you stay with him?'

The trouble is,' I bite my lip, 'despite everything I still care about him. Believe it or not he's a nice man, the sort of man who carries old ladies' shopping bags and helps blind people to cross the road.'

I stop talking because the waiter has arrived with our food. He plonks the plates down on the table and gives it a token wipe with a filthy cloth.

After he leaves Ailsa says, 'Go on.'

'We've had some good times together, my husband and me,' I say. 'Mark's no monster. It wouldn't say much for me if I'd married a monster would it? He's just a human being with faults and failings like the rest of us. You'd like him if ever you got to meet him. People do like him. I loved him once and he loved me... I can't help thinking that maybe...'

'He must have hurt you very much,' she says, and I look down suddenly aware that Ailsa is holding my hand...when did that happen?

'That first time...when I found out,' I turn my head to hide the pain on my face, 'it made me sick... sick to my stomach...I couldn't stop vomiting.

MONKEY ON MY ROOF

12

Now it's dinner time. Tonight we eat at Cool Breeze. Emanuel, the Frenchman who runs safaris into the jungle, arrives to sit with us. He is not in a good mood, he tells us: Casa Fiesta doesn't have fish or pineapples.

It seems that Emanuel had asked for fish as usual at Casa Fiesta.

But: 'No fish,' Prakash told him.

'Why not?'

'No fish, it full moon. Can't have fish on full moon.'

'What you say me? Full moon?'

'Fish see nets when it full moon, they dive to bottom of ocean.'

So the Frenchman asked for his cocktail, which has pineapples in it.

'No pineapples,' Prakash told him.

'What you say me? No pineapples!'

'Full moon.'

'Why no pineapples.'

'Pineapples see us climb tree in full moon and jump top of tree, we can't reach them.'

Our waiter at Cool Breeze has been listening to this tale of woe; he says, 'No problem in this restaurant. Full moon not disturbs fish or pineapple here. We give them sun-glasses.'

The Frenchman laughs and becomes his cheerful schoolboy self again.

Was it our lunch of bhajis and chai at the Udupi? The plate of hunter's chicken we shared at Cool Breeze, or the fried ice cream for dessert? Whatever; it's at two o'clock in the morning, and we

MONKEY ON MY ROOF

both have the squitters.— a word that describes wonderfully the physical complaint we are suffering from.

Ailsa loses the race to use the toilet and balances on the pink plastic bucket in the bathroom, trying to make her arm long enough to grab the toilet paper.

'It's not fair!' she groans, 'Your bed is closer to the bathroom than mine. And you've got longer legs!'

From where I sit straining on the white enamel throne I grin at her through gritted teeth, 'Ah, but you're younger than me.'

'What's that got to do with anything?'

'So; you should be able to run faster!'

The pink plastic bucket wobbles.

'Don't make me laugh, it hurts!'

*

This morning my landlady stops us as we leave for the beach, she says the son of Gowri (who is the Rajasthani woman selling bedspreads, cushion covers and rugs to tourists in a stall across the road) will be able to string some rope across the ceiling and drape the pink gauze netting across the beams in my room.

'Where can we find him?' Ailsa asks.

We are both thinking of a strapping teenager whose muscles have become accustomed to putting up the heavy wood frame and tin roof of his mother's stall.

'He's here,' the landlady points to a small thin boy about eight years old who is playing in the courtyard.

'No, I don't think so,' I say.

Too late; he's already rushing towards us like an eager puppy, 'I can do it. Show me! I can do job.'

MONKEY ON MY ROOF

And before we know it he is in my room, perched precariously on top of a rickety bamboo ladder which Ailsa and me are holding; hearts in mouth, convinced that the damn thing will drop to pieces and the little lad fall and break his neck as he reaches and stretches across the ceiling. What with the weight of the boy — who is a lot heavier than he looks — and the ladder pulling on her operation wound Ailsa has gone very pale, and my arms are aching.

There's a knock at the door, the lad's mother is worried too! She's left her stall and crossed the road to my room to take charge of holding the ladder.

What a relief!

After the job is done Gowri speaks to us softly in pidgin English inviting us to drink chai with her.

Ailsa and I look at one another. I ask, 'Shall we? Would you like to?'

'Okay,' she says, and we walk across the road to Gowri's stall.

But hey this is India, there's no such thing as a free lunch, or a free cup of chai for that matter; Gowri has sussed that we are gullible tourists, and the time is ripe for her to rip us off... er sorry I mean sell us her stuff. As we sip our hot milky chai she throws one colourful bedspread after the other down across the floor until it looks like the backdrop of a lunatic landscape painter, 'You like buy preety bedspread?'

'That one would look nice now that you've decorated the place with pink netting,' Ailsa says mischievously.

'I'll buy one if you buy one,' I tell her.

'Okay' she says, 'I can use mine back home when I snuggle down in bed with Greg.' She turns to Gowri, 'How much?'

In India — perhaps more in India than anywhere else in the

MONKEY ON MY ROOF

world — there's always someone, somewhere, trying to rip-off someone else; in the street, in restaurants, in rickshaws and taxis, even over the phone. Interrupted by the constant ringing of Gowri's mobile phone we barter the price in sign language and broken English.

When her mobile interrupts Gowri's sales pitch for the fifth time, her lovely face twists into a snarl. Then this beautiful graceful woman with a face and figure as delicate as a piece of Dresden china shouts down the phone in perfect English, 'Fuck off, I'm trying to do business here!'

It cracks Ailsa and me up so much that we can't stop laughing.

Which is perhaps the reason that Gowri presents us with two cushion covers, free of charge, to go with the bedspreads she's talked us both into buying.

We take the bedspreads back to our room, drape them across the beds, pin the posters of Saraswati and Ganesha on the wall, take what's left of the pink netting and swathe it across the window. Only then do we stand back to admire our handiwork.

I look around doubtfully. 'The room needs something else,' I say.

'A couple of rugs on the floor would finish it off,' Ailsa tells me.

'The supermarket in Chaudi has straw mats, just seventy rupees each.'

So it's a rickshaw back to Chaudi again to practise our Indian head-nodding in Udipi Restaurant where we get a round of applause from the staff. Then we cross the road to the supermarket to buy two red and green straw mats. We take the mats back to Palolem and place them on the floor each side of the beds. The whole lot,

MONKEY ON MY ROOF

bedspread, pink netting, string, poster, and straw mats cost less than five pounds.

The landlady pops her head around the door, 'Momma, your room it look like a Maharaja's palace.'

MONKEY ON MY ROOF

13

Over the next few days Ailsa sunbathes, walks to River Valley to joke with Manju, visits Sheila and Doug at the house they rent in the coconut grove, goes to Gosh for instruction in Reiki. The drawn look disappears from her eyes and mouth, and she laughs more easily.

When she smiles that deep dimple in her left cheek becomes more defined. Her skin and eyes glow, everything about her seems to bounce with health. The change is extraordinary; no longer can she be mistaken for the Scottish Widow in that TV commercial.

We book a day trip with Emanuel the Frenchman who runs trips into the jungle.

Sheila decides that she'd like a day trip too and comes with us. The Frenchman drives us in a battered old jeep to a spice plantation. The owner shows us around the plantation, and then takes us to his house where a lunch of daal and rice is served on banana leaves by his wife.

Their house is decorated with pink, yellow and blue garlands, fresh and paper flowers mingled together. They are everywhere, draped around the doors and windows, hanging from the ceiling, festooned around the walls, you can't tell where one starts and the other ends.

'They got married a couple of weeks ago,' Emanuel tells us.

We smile at the new wife who is exceptionally pretty.

'They look very happy,' Sheila says.

'So perhaps arranged marriages do work after all,' Ailsa comments.

'That remains to be seen,' I say.

At dinner last night the waiter told me that Emanuel once

MONKEY ON MY ROOF

represented France in an Olympic Team. Whether this is true or not I wouldn't know, and I'm not about to ask. Both Emanuel and the waiter are rather relaxed about how they pronounce English. But it isn't difficult for me to imagine this French Tarzan breaking records for skiing and tobogganing.

On the way back to the jeep he picks Ailsa up and carries her through a rice paddy. She's afraid of falling and getting the dirty water on her operation scar, which is still tender. Emanuel: This man, who lives for the outdoors, this scruffy, fearless, rough and tumble Tarzan, carries Ailsa so caringly that my eyes fill with tears.

We drive to a clearing in the jungle which reveals a small temple sited above a pool that fizzes and bubbles.

In his charming French accent Emanuel gives us to understand that the Indians consider the pool to be sacred. He invites us to walk down stone steps and sit at the pool's rim. Three of us dangle our feet in the water. The fourth, Sheila, steps out of her skirt, pulls her tee shirt off and jumps in the sacred pool for a swim among the snakes and frogs. Climbing out again she sits in her black bra and bikini bottoms on the path at the side of the pool. 'Ze snakes, zey are frog snakes,' Emanuel tells us. He casts nervous glances between Sheila and the temple, 'Zey only eat frogs, not feet.'

'You'd better keep your toes out of the water then,' I say.

Emanuel says nothing. Hopefully he doesn't know the English nickname for French people.

Ailsa grins at me, then gives me a nudge to notice the sadhu — Hindu priest — a chunky man wearing a saffron sarong frowning at us from the doorway of his temple. I prod Ailsa and we pull our feet out quickly.

But we soon come to realise that it isn't our feet dangling in

MONKEY ON MY ROOF

the water that is offending him. It's obvious that the murderous expression on his face — enhanced by the red religious stripes on his forehead — is directed at Sheila sunning herself in her black undies. He starts down the steps of the temple. Any minute now he'll come charging at her with a machete.

I tap Sheila on the shoulder and point at the sadhu, 'Hadn't you better put your clothes back on?'

Sheila is one of those energetic people who have been everywhere and done everything; she says imperiously, 'Oh, don't worry about him, he'll have seen it all before.'

The sadhu is glowering at her — if looks could kill.

'Hmm, I can't help thinking you're wrong this time!'

Emanuel walks over to talk to the sadhu. Their conversation is noisy, consisting of raised voices and a lot of arm waving.

Ailsa twitches a lock of her blonde curly hair over one shoulder, and hunches the other nervously. She looks from Sheila to me, then back at Sheila again. Having made a promise to herself to stay positive, Ailsa is stuck for words.

'Ve should go now,' Emanuel says when he comes back, and waits while Sheila puts her clothes back on.

Glaring all the while at Sheila, the sadhu walks down the steps that lead to the pool and lowers himself into the water. He swims around amongst the snakes before intoning his prayers to a statue set on a tiny island in the middle.

*

Back at Casa Fiesta, Prakash tells Ailsa and me that the accident with my foot was sent by Shiva to keep me here so that Ailsa and I could meet.

Who knows, maybe he's right? But I don't want to go down

that path. If it hadn't been for the bombing in Delhi, I'd have been travelling around Rajasthan, and Ailsa and I would never have got to meet.

People died that day in the Pahar Ganj, I'd hate to think it was on my account, or on Ailsa's — dear as she is to me.

MONKEY ON MY ROOF

14

Sand clogs the silver two-inch-heeled evening sandals I brought with me from England, I slip them off to paddle with Ailsa along the edge of the sea to the Cosy Nook Café. What a mistake! Splat, all over my clean white blouse.

'Have you ever noticed how a seagull's cries often sound like laughter?' I say and shake my fist at the sky, but the bird has flown away.

Luckily I'm wearing my bathing suit under my clothes, so I take my blouse off to dunk it in the sea, and manage to get most of the yellowy green muck off; but it still pongs. From the café an aroma of freshly brewed coffee mingled with the smells of papaya juice, eggs and fried onions drifts across the beach, contrasting with the scent of seagull shit. A Buddhist chant trickles peacefully from a CD player, drawing us in.

Putting our shoes back on we walk into the café and sit at the only vacant table facing the sea. Halfway through our breakfast Gosh arrives with Joseph the Ethiopian Shaman. They join us at our table.

Gosh's lean brown body, naked except for a saffron sarong and straw hat, and Joseph in his white robes and red head dress, collect curious stares from the two-week tourists sitting in the café eating and smoking.

This morning Gosh is hard pushed to know whose swimming costume to look down first. His gaze swivels between Ailsa and me. Gosh is a boob man, any shape, any size, any age, any woman. His eyes are loitering on the front of my swimming costume when he asks, 'How is you're foot?'

I smile internally — you won't find it down there — and

MONKEY ON MY ROOF

answer, 'Still painful, it's been nearly two months. I thought it would be better by now. Sheila's told me of a good orthopaedic doctor at the Nusi hospital near Margao. So I'm going there tomorrow.'

'Hmm,' Gosh says, he's still talking to my chest.

Joseph is staring at Gosh staring at my chest, his deep brown voice croons matter-of-factly, 'Sally has very large breasts.'

'Hmm,' Gosh says again.

Joseph looks at me, 'How many children have you?'

'Er, three,' I say.

'And did you breast-feed them all?'

Joseph's voice, usually so soft, explodes into one of those moments of perfect stillness when even the seagulls have stopped calling. Every head in the café swivels around, every pair of eyes fastens on the front of my swimming costume.

Embarrassed I turn my head away. Ailsa nudges me, pointing towards the beach, and — wouldn't you know it today of all days — who should be passing by but the man who waves to me each day. Obviously having overheard what Joseph has said he's laughing too hard to raise his hand and wave.

Was it the silver high heels which brought this on I wonder? Did they make me stand up so straight that my boobs were thrown out of proportion when I got up to greet Gosh and Joseph?

Red-faced I get up to go to a sun bed, and a middle-aged man at the next table asks if he can join me for dinner tonight. No way! I smile sweetly and turn him down.

The new Nepalese waiter has heard Joseph's remarks and smiles at me sympathetically. He interrupts to point out an Indian woman, 'Momma,' he says, 'lady there wants to meet you.'

She is sitting at a table at the back of The Cosy Nook café,

MONKEY ON MY ROOF

long slender hands tipped with perfectly manicured nails delicately holding the cup as she drinks her chai. I've seen her many times before but we've never spoken. An elegant woman with shining black hair coifed in the latest style. Only a wealthy Indian would have the time and money to dress so classily, and use cosmetics so tastefully, I'd thought, supposing her to be some kind of local dignitary, or a Maharani perhaps who wished to remain incognito.

Nothing of the sort.

Her name is Eliza and she's a beautician.

We get on like a house on fire, so I leave Ailsa to her sunbathing and go with Eliza to her salon which is fitted out with a bed — presumably used for massage — and a rickety chair which may or may not be a cast off from a dentist's surgery, plus a water tap but no wash basin.

Eliza cuts my hair and gives me a manicure. Then from somewhere in the bowels of the room she fetches a wooden stool. She fills a plastic bowl with water from the tap, sits on the stool, balances the bowl of water on her lap and proceeds to give me a pedicure.

I remind her of her mother she says, as she scrubs my feet and reminisces about her childhood.

The bowl of water teeters dangerously as she cuts my toenails. Then she gets all choked up and tells me that her mother has never loved her. The stool teeters even more dangerously.

Like flying missiles her arms are flung around my neck and hot wet tears dampen my shoulder. I murmur soothing noises, pat her back with one hand while desperately holding onto the bowl of water with the other, and silently recite to myself 'This Be The Verse' by Phillip Larkin, "They fuck you up your Mum and Dad. They don't mean to but they do..."

MONKEY ON MY ROOF

'I want you to come home with me,' she says, 'come to my house and eat lunch.'

'No, no really,' I protest.

'Why not? Please you come,' she implores.

I look in her eyes, there's no mistaking the appeal waiting there. Why not indeed?

'Where do you live?'

'Ponsulem. Is not far. Behind Chaudi. I take you.'

'Alright,' I agree.

Which I wouldn't have done if I'd known that instead of sitting sedately in a rickshaw I'd be holding on to her ample waist while riding side saddle on a motor scooter.

We wobble all over the road missing by a cat's whisker buses, HGVs, and rickshaws which seem determined on murder and mayhem. I am equally determined not to be their victim, 'Slow down Eliza,' I yell, 'you're going too fast!'

The motor scooter swerves violently as she turns her head to tell me indignantly, 'Momma I'm only doing twelve miles an hour!'

'No way! There must be something wrong with your speedometer,' I say.

But Eliza is turning into the side road which leads to her village and doesn't hear me.

Her home is large, set back from the road down a steep path, a single-storied Portuguese style villa, though at some time in the past somebody has started to build a second storey before running out of money.

There are iron grilles at the windows and a heavy, carved wood door leading from the veranda into the sitting room where her husband is sitting in a wooden armchair watching TV. His English isn't as good as Eliza's, but he does his best to make me welcome;

MONKEY ON MY ROOF

insisting that I drink a glass of the port he pours from what is obviously a much prized bottle.

The décor seems unusual to my westernized eyes, it's strange to see the TV sitting on a plank of wood set on two tree trunks. There is a similar arrangement for the music centre. A cuckoo clock, pendulum swinging, hangs above the door leading to the rest of the house. On the wall — presumably because the family are Roman Catholics — is a picture of Jesus crowned with thorns and surrounded by flashing lights. But décor isn't important when you are being treated with such hospitality.

I am taken into the dining room and seated at the table; Eliza serves me with a special lunch of ladyfinger curry, rice, daal, fried prawns, Bombay duck, and four different kinds of pickle. To follow she has made a dessert of fruit salad.

Eliza's husband and their younger son, who has just arrived home from school, look on. The family doesn't eat with me; I sit there alone feeling out of place and awkward, being waited on as if I'm the Queen of England! Are they checking my table manners I ask myself, or is it that their religion doesn't allow them to eat with foreigners, though I've never heard of Roman Catholics being under that kind of restriction?

The journey back to Palolem is even more electrifying. Eliza's husband insists that he gives me a lift back on his much more powerful motorbike. I'm not allowed to sit side saddle on the pillion he says, but must sit astride it like a normal person. He takes off down the road like a bat out of hell, vroom-vrooming and sounding the horn at everything that crosses his path, and I clutch at his waist, pleading with him to slow down as I wonder what the criteria might be for a Hindu funeral.

Eventually I get it through to Eliza's husband that my hips

MONKEY ON MY ROOF

are unused to high-powered motor bikes and are complaining at being locked around his backside. He is forced to pull over to the side of the road while I get off.

'Sit side-saddle,' he says.

But I can see the local bus lumbering along the road, and hold my arm out for it to stop.

'No fear, I'm getting the bus,' I tell him, 'thank Eliza for lunch, it was lovely.'

MONKEY ON MY ROOF

15

Ailsa and I say goodnight to our friends at Casa Fiesta and make our way along the road. As we walk, wild dogs come squirming, wagging tails, asking have you any food? No? Well at least give us a pat and a tickle behind the ears. Then we are on the path alongside the main house to the guest rooms. The path leads to the small garden where coconut husks are stored to be used as fuel to heat the water in an iron cauldron, and laundry is beaten against a stone before being hung out to dry.

In the garden a huge black apparition is moving towards us. Ailsa gives a squeak and runs, but fear freezes me to the spot. Then I realise that it's a black cow. A very pregnant black cow. I bolt through the gate, unlock the door and go straight into the bathroom. I'm sitting there on the throne when I hear a noise in the passage outside. The deaf woman from the room opposite is knocking on my door, 'Sally are you there?'

Bloody 'ell, can't I even go to the loo in peace!

She goes on calling. There's no point in me answering, she only wears her hearing aid when she talks to anyone interesting; and has made it plain that I don't come into that category. Ailsa is already in bed so I'm forced to jump off the toilet before I'm half done.

The cow has wandered up the passage and is now in the little garden at the back which my landlady only last week planted with bushes and flowers. She lifts her head and stares at me in that arrogant way cows in India have, knowing how secure they are in their sacredness, and dares me to interfere while she makes a meal of a pink hibiscus bush; looking as if she's enjoying every mouthful. I leave the cow to make the most of her meal and knock

MONKEY ON MY ROOF

on the deaf woman's door.

The door opens and she peers around it bleary eyed, half asleep.

I say, 'What's wrong?'

'Nothing is wrong! Why are you knocking on my door?'

'I'm knocking on your door,' I say, 'to see why you were knocking on mine.'

'Well I was knocking on your door,' she answers, 'to see why you were knocking on mine.'

Then the penny drops.

'That wasn't me! The cow must have brushed against it when it came through the passage.'

'The what?'

'The sacred cow,' I say.

'The crow?'

'No! A sacred cow, in the back garden,' I say, trying not to laugh.

'What's it scared of?' she asks.

Then the Irishman, who lodges in the next room to mine appears, all bronzed chest and hairy legs in his tartan shorts. He is carrying a stick and begins to shoo the cow away into the front garden.

'Oh a cow,' the deaf woman says, 'I thought you said there was a scared crow in the garden!'

The cow keeps Ailsa and me awake all night with her mooing, which sets the dogs to howling.

This morning when we leave for Casa Fiesta she is still here, still as black, but quite a bit slimmer with an adorable brown and white calf by her side.

Between mouthfuls of fruit salad and curd — we're eating

breakfast — Ailsa asks, 'How long are you staying in Palolem, Sally?'

'Only until my foot heals. Why? Are you getting fed up with me already?'

She laughs, 'No way! It's just… I was thinking… If you're travelling… I've a six month Indian Visa. Maybe we could travel together?'

'Hum,' I take a slurp at my coffee, 'what's this? Only the other day you were saying how you are longing for Greg to be here with you.'

'Well he's not here is he? And I am,' she turns her head away and says softly, 'Who knows if I'll ever have an opportunity like this again.'

'Still, there's Christmas coming up. I think you should talk to him about it before you decide.'

'I already did. Last night, at the internet café, on Skype.'

Hmmm — wish I'd been a fly on the wall when that conversation took place!

'How did he take it?'

'He was shocked,' she smiles, lowers her head to gaze at a stain on the red tablecloth, 'I was only meant to be away for three weeks and suddenly here I am talking about months.'

'Yes?'

She lifts her head and looks at me defiantly, 'Okay! He's worried and trying not to show it. Said he wanted us to spend Christmas together…'

'And?'

'Then he told me to go for it!'

Despite the heat of the day she gives a little shiver, 'But he made me promise to go straight home if…'

MONKEY ON MY ROOF

Unspoken between us is the fact of her cancer, the question of her survival.

'Please Sally!'

How can I refuse?

'If that's how you feel; but only until the end of March. I have to be in Nepal by April, my visa ends in March,' I explain.

She does that thing with her eyes, 'But there's rioting in Nepal! It's been on TV. Something about the king and his family all being killed.'

I pull a face, 'Rioting or not I still have to be in Nepal in April. Mark will be there, he's decided he wants to climb Mount Everest.'

'Until March then?' she says.

'If you're sure?'

She nods, 'Yay!' she says and jumps out of her chair to give me a hug.

'You have to promise me that you'll let me know if you have any kind of symptoms.' I look at her seriously, 'Even if you only *suspect* that there's something wrong!'

'Oh okay,' she says in a muffled voice, 'you have my promise.'

'Alright then. Tomorrow we'll go to Rainbow Travel and change your air ticket.'

What have I let myself in for?

'When can we start travelling?'

'Can't tell you now. It depends on my foot.'

'What's wrong with it? You've never told me.'

'An accident on the day I got here,' I shudder. 'Indian hospitals are a lot different to ours. The Doctor gave me a prescription for tablets. They don't seem to be working.'

MONKEY ON MY ROOF

'Never mind,' she says, 'I'll buy you a walking stick next time we go to Chaudi.'

Irene and Udo walk back with us after dinner to see our room. Proudly we show off the pink awning, our Rajasthani bedspreads with their embroidered elephants and tiny glittery mirrors. Ailsa points out the posters on the wall, the red and green straw mats. I open the door to show off the balcony with its small plastic table and chairs...

Then I open the door to the bathroom and reach through to switch the light on. I'm telling them how brave Ailsa was this morning to flush a cockroach away down the plughole, when Irene, who has walked into the bathroom in front of me, screeches, 'EEUCH! THERE'S ONE!'

'WHERE? WHERE?' I screech back.

Irene points to the drain, 'There's another!'

'Two more by the toilet,' says Udo.

'Cockroaches! Oh no!' Ailsa says and shudders.

There are roaches are all over the place. We count seven of them in all, and those are only what we can see, heaven knows what might be lurking in the drains!

'What am I going to do?' I moan. Everything about the creatures repels me, 'How can I get to the loo in the middle of the night with these things here?'

'Leave the bathroom light on all night. They don't like the light,' Udo tells us.

'In the morning buy a can of Hit and spray everything in sight,' Irene says, 'You'll never see another cockroach.'

'Are you sure it works?'

'It works,' Udo assures us, 'and when the can is empty you can throw it at them!'

MONKEY ON MY ROOF

But after Irene and Udo go back to their hut Ailsa and I stay awake all night and keep the light on.

MONKEY ON MY ROOF

16

The shop across the road from our guesthouse sells us a can of Hit, just one spray once a month keeps cockroaches away it says on the label. We shall see! We carry it back to the room and spray everything in sight.

In the bathroom baby frogs watch us from the drain in the floor, blinking their beady little eyes as if saying, 'What about us?'

'Does this stuff kill frogs as well as cockroaches?' I ask Ailsa.

She doesn't know. And the frogs are still looking at us with those pleading eyes. So we spend the next half hour chasing them around the bathroom with the plastic jug which is found in every Indian bathroom — the jug one is meant to use in the washing of ones buttocks after going to the loo. Finally the frogs are all safely out in the garden enjoying their freedom.

Only then can we spray the bathroom before going to breakfast at Casa Fiesta.

Over our second cup of coffee Ailsa says, 'I'm planning a day on the beach. What about you Sally?'

'My plan is to get the bus to the NUSI hospital,' I say, 'the bus stop is right outside the restaurant.'

Ailsa and I arrange to meet later at the Cosy Nook café, and go our separate ways.

Bus conductors are still employed on Indian buses. The bus I'm on doesn't go to Margao so I get off at the stop before Chaudi.

It's standing room only on the next bus to come along, and I sway and stumble all over people's feet. An Indian man gets up and gives me his seat. Throughout the journey he stands in the gangway beside me and plays with my hair which I'm wearing loose around

MONKEY ON MY ROOF

my shoulders this morning. He takes one strand of hair at a time, winds it round his fingers to make ringlets, then takes another to make a small plait, he does this without saying a word. The Indian ladies turn around in their seats to watch, they hold the edges of their saris up to their faces and go 'AH'.

Should I stop him or not? I don't know what to do. It seems like a strange way for a man to behave; perhaps he's been a ladies hairdresser in a previous life? Perhaps he's an escaped maniac with a hair fetish? Then again he did get up to give me his seat. So I say nothing, figuring it's the least I can do in return. But I'm bloody glad when we get to the hospital and I can escape. At least he doesn't pinch my behind like they do on the train.

Unlike the Government hospital in Palolem, the NUSI is bright and modern. I have an x-ray, and am shunted in to see the orthopaedic specialist. He gives me exactly the same advice as the Brahmin Doctor in the Government hospital: which is to wear high heeled shoes. Then he presents me with a prescription for tablets to reduce the cyst that has formed on my Achilles tendon and charges me 1000 rupees — about twelve pounds.

When I get back to my room there are half a dozen dead cockroaches lying on the floor. Looks like that can of Hit does exactly what it says on the label.

*

There is a party tonight at the restaurant on the beach road. The party should be fun. At least that's what Doug says when he invites us.

Doug has one of those faces that look as if they are forever smiling. A merry sparkling face, set off by silver hair and a deep

MONKEY ON MY ROOF

tan, his nickname is The Laughing Buddha: it suits him.

'So who gave him that nickname?' Ailsa asks when Doug gets up to go to the loo.

I grin, 'Believe it or not, after we'd eaten Christmas dinner last year, the four of us, Mark, Doug, Sheila and me, stopped to wish Merry Christmas to the restaurant owner. The restaurant we're sitting in now. "Come and sit at my table," Sanjay said. "Have a Christmas drink."'

Mark and me had eaten in his restaurant lots of times. Sanjay had always been very correct, making sure the food was to our liking and that the waiters served with right hands only, left hand, which is only used for toiletry purposes, tucked firmly behind their back. Heaven forbid that one of Sanjay's waiters should carry a plate with his dirty left hand.

I was sitting next to Sanjay at the table, 'You're British aren't you?' he asked me.

'Born and bred,' I told him.

'I love the fucking British! It's the pity the fucking British ever left fucking India, then fucking India wouldn't be in the fucking state it's fucking in now.'

Never before have I heard so many fuckings in one sentence.

Doug and Sheila were both giggling at the expression on my face, which was torn between amusement and outrage. Amusement won, leaving me wondering why it is that a foreign accent twists profanity into comedy.

Then Sanjay stared at Mark, who as usual had slumped in his chair and fallen asleep, 'The Sleeping fucking Buddha,' he said.

Then he'd looked at the laughter on Doug's face, glanced down at his bulging belly still stuffed with all he'd eaten at Christmas dinner and said, 'The Laughing Buddha fucking

MONKEY ON MY ROOF

reincarnated!'
    'You're kidding me!' Ailsa splutters.
    'No,' I say 'that's how Doug got his nickname!'

MONKEY ON MY ROOF

17

Did Doug say this party would be fun? I've had more enjoyment at a crematorium! Everyone — except pure little me on a detox for my Reiki attunement — drunk as skunks. Serves me right for believing anything Doug says... not that I'm calling him a liar. Let's just say that Doug is a bit careless with his veracity, if you get my meaning.

The party tonight is for a social worker; a nutritionist; a woman who runs a charity for homeless Tsunami kids; a gay home designer (whatever a home designer is); and his partner, a male model.

Plus the man who waves to me on the beach.

All six are going back to England tomorrow morning.

All that is except the man from the beach who just sits quietly observing.

Ailsa nudges me, 'Isn't he the man who...?'

I nod, 'Could be,' I say offhandedly, hopeful she hasn't seen that he's the only man at the party I'm interested in.

But Ailsa is nobody's fool, and says, 'Who are you trying to kid?' She's noticed how each time he looks my way my eyes are drawn to him. And it seems to be the same for him.

'This is Stephan,' Doug says as he introduces us, 'I thought it was about time you two got to meet before he leaves.'

Aware that Ailsa is watching us and grinning to herself I try to keep my voice cool, 'You're leaving?'

'Working my way around India, and checking out Vipassana meditation,' he tells me.

As for the others...

The woman who runs the tsunami charity continuously invites us to pat her on the back for her selflessness. The gay

MONKEY ON MY ROOF

couples are such drama queens they could make even Elton John jealous. The nutritionist finds fault with everything; the food is too cold, or too hot, too spicy, or not spicy enough, overcooked or undercooked.

The social worker is forever calling the waiter over (Sanjay the owner is waiting on tonight) and telling him to hurry up, chop chop, look lively man, in the sort of lordly condescending English voice that assumes any person other than those in his immediate circle is his inferior. When he does deign to speak to me he calls me "My Dear" in a manner which makes it plain he considers me to be in my dotage.

To cap it all each time I open my mouth most of the others ignore me. I'm beginning to feel invisible. It's making me angry.

'Hey you,' the social worker calls to Sanjay, 'fetch me a Kingfisher.'

Kingfisher is the Indian beer, which the ex-pats who live here won't drink. They say it's full of glycerine and gives them the runs!

Couldn't happen to a nicer person; hope he spends all night on the loo.

Behind his mask of politeness Sanjay is seething, 'Right away muy zonia,' he says quietly.

The social worker asks, 'What does muy zonia mean?'

Doug and I look at each other, 'It's difficult to translate,' Doug says.

'Doesn't it mean something like your Honour or your Eminence?' I ask innocently.

The man from the beach, who is sitting opposite me and has been in Goa long enough to have got to know some of the Konkanese looks at me and drops one of his eyelids in a surreptitious wink.

MONKEY ON MY ROOF

The social worker preens, and says condescendingly, 'Does it really, my dear?'

Ailsa smothers a laugh. She's heard Emanuel using those words often enough while joking with the waiters and is aware that the social worker wouldn't be preening himself if he knew that Sanjay has accused him of having sex with his own mother.

'Please use my name,' I say, 'I'm not your dear. My name is Sally, not Bambi.'

The nutritionist pokes at her fish curry, 'Much too salty,' she moans, 'why can't they get anything right?'

Sanjay has arrived with the bottle of Kingfisher. He gives her a dirty look.

'The food isn't as bad,' the home designer tells her, 'as the Indian condoms.'

Doug, sitting on my left, says, 'So what's wrong with Indian condoms then?'

'Always past their sell by date, and leak like a sieve,' is the answer.

'You should have bought Cobra condoms, they're the best,' Sheila informs the home designer.

Then the male model puts his oar in, 'That's only because Indian sperms are so fat they can't get through the holes!'

'Stupid little prick!' I whisper to Ailsa, 'Can't he see that murderous look on Sanjay's face? Maybe it's time I confounded these ill-mannered people with my comprehensive knowledge regarding Asian sperm!'

'Go for it Sally,' she whispers back.

'As a matter of fact,' I raise my voice to inform them, 'it is well documented that Asian men have smaller scrotums than any other race of people. This means that they produce lesser and

MONKEY ON MY ROOF

slimmer sperm, because a male may only produce sperm in accordance with the size of his gonads.'

It gets their attention, there is a straightening of backs in seats, a leaning forward of heads, a fastening of eyes on my face.

'It is a scientifically proven fact that the quality of sperm depends, in all nationalities — on the individual.'

With enormous effort, I overcome the urge to laugh and continue with unfaltering sang-froid, 'Asians definitely do not produce thick sperm, which is why the birth rate in India never drops.'

I glance around the table. Except for the social worker — who is being nudged by Stephan to stop him interrupting — my audience is looking at me open-mouthed. There is silence now as they listen to the beautiful lies falling from my lips.

'Any person studying the Karma Sutra will be well aware that the small size of the scrotum in the Asian male bears no relation to the size of the Asian penis, which tends to be twenty-three point six per cent longer, and approximately thirty-two per cent thicker than that of a European male. Indian condoms have to be correspondingly longer and thicker in size, to accommodate the difference. This is why Europeans such as yourselves, who may have what is considered to be a miniscule phallus, have problems with Cobra Condoms!'

Unsure if he has just been insulted the male model asks, 'What are you then; some kind of specialist?'

'No, but I have done my research,' I tell him.

'Research,' Doug murmurs, 'bit of a cock-up there.'

Stephan leans towards me and whispers, 'How much of what you said is true?'

'All of it,' Ailsa says drily, 'Sally never lies. Do you Sally?'

MONKEY ON MY ROOF

Before I can answer, Doug, this person who told me he'd helped the Dalai Lama to escape over the Himalayas from the Chinese, and had given Reiki to the dying Pope, leans across me to whisper, 'Don't believe a word she says, Sally's a bigger bullshitter than me.'

Suddenly the five of us are laughing. The party hasn't turned out to be so bad after all!

Stephan asks, 'How long are you staying in Palolem?'

'Only until my foot is better,' I answer, 'Then I'm away on my travels. Who knows, maybe I'll see you in Dharamsala.'

'I'd be pleased to see you there,' Stephan says quietly.

We look into each other's eyes. Stephan's eyes are an unusual colour, light brown with flecks of green and grey. Something is happening. A faint flicker of sexual attraction between us. The kind of spark I haven't felt for a long time. Had forgotten even existed.

'I seem to be spending all my time with Buddhists, so I may as well check out the Dalai Lama,' I say, unhappily aware that I'm babbling, trying without success to sound nonchalant.

'Is it my shining aura do you think? Or is it the sunburn I got when I fell asleep on the beach? Perhaps I should wear red robes?'

We are still looking into one another's eyes.

'You're fine as you are,' Stephan informs me.

*

'You've definitely pulled there,' Ailsa says when we finally tear ourselves away from the restaurant.

'Maybe,' I say, 'but it isn't going anywhere. Apart from anything else he's leaving in the morning.'

MONKEY ON MY ROOF

'It's cold here at night,' Ailsa says.

Cha Cha's shop is still open. He sells her a red and blue checked blanket for only 100 rupees!

MONKEY ON MY ROOF

18

On those few evenings when Ailsa and I go our separate ways, the German hippy — who lives in the next room — takes it into his head that he is somehow responsible for my safety. What he'd say if he'd seen me trying out a Hookah pipe at Café Del Mar a couple of nights ago I dread to think! Though somehow I don't think he'd be as shocked as the young gap year student who cracked up laughing and dug out his digital camera when he saw me puffing away wreathed in smoke.

By two o'clock in the morning though, I'd had enough of Café Del Mar, and started back along the beach, escorted, despite my protests, by the waiter from the Cosy Nook.

Suddenly my German neighbour was walking towards us.

'Hi,' I exclaimed, 'are you going back to the guesthouse?'

'Ja!'

'Mind if I walk with you?'

He nodded.

'There you are,' I said to the waiter, 'you can stop worrying, this gentleman will see me home.'

The German started lecturing me the moment the waiter walked off.

Why was I walking the beach alone at this time of night? Didn't I know how dangerous it was to walk the beach with strange Indian men? On, and on, and on, until we reached the guest house and said goodnight.

Most nights I'm back at the guest house and in my bed by half past eleven. But since that night, if I'm even ten minutes late my neighbour is sitting on a stool in the passage outside his room, tapping his watch, 'What time is this to come home,' he says, 'I

MONKEY ON MY ROOF

was worried about you.'

It's like having my Dad there keeping an eye on me, I wouldn't mind but he has to be at least twenty years younger than me!

Ailsa and I were late again the other night; not that it made any difference, sleep is impossible because of the noise coming from the restaurant at the back of our balcony. For the last three weeks, an Indian man — we don't know who — has been shouting for hours at the top of his voice. It goes on until two or three o'clock in the morning.

The first time we heard him Ailsa called out, 'For God's sake shut up and let's get some sleep!'

He yelled back hysterically, 'What you say? You want to fucking offend me? I fucking come over there and break your fucking head!'

'Oo er!' shivering with fright the two of us simultaneously buried our heads under our blankets.

The shouting goes on, and on, and on, night after night. When the Irishman in the room on the left calls to him to shut up, and the gentle German hippie in the room on the right complains, they both get the same reaction. Being as we're all cowards we all spend the night cowering under our respective bedclothes!

Yesterday our left side neighbour moved out. He's going home to Ireland he says. Back to Dublin where he can get some sleep.

*

It's three o'clock in the morning. From the restaurant behind the guesthouse the usual pandemonium of shouts and screams keeps us awake.

83

MONKEY ON MY ROOF

A jet-lagged Italian guy has moved into the Irishman's old room; he roars, 'Shut a da up! I want to sleep!'

'You speaking to me? You try to fucking offend me? I come there I break your fuckin' head!'

For a moment there is silence from the Italian guy's room, and I'm thinking that like the rest of us he's buried his head under the blanket.

Then I hear the sound of his balcony door opening...

Whoa! What's happening? Whatever it is, this is going to be too good to miss! In unison Ailsa and I jump out of bed and open the door onto our balcony.

From our right Nick the German hippy has done the same.

Naked except for a pair of black and white checked boxer shorts, the Italian is standing on top of the wall between his balcony and the restaurant, 'Yes! Yes! Yes! I want to a fuckin' offenda you!' he yells at the top of his voice. 'Come outta of there. I break *your* fucking head forra you! I fucking offenda you proper!'

Everything goes quiet. I glance at Ailsa who looks back at me. We are both holding our breath.

Then: 'Sorry, Sorry,' a voice whimpers, 'I have many problems.'

'Youa keepa quiet or you have lotsa morra problems,' the Italian barks.

'Okay, Sorry, Sorry,' the voice says again.

The rest of us give the Italian a round of applause, he turns and bows before he gets down from the wall.

'God is good,' I tell Ailsa, 'he must have been an Italian!'

MONKEY ON MY ROOF

19

Ailsa is yawning and rubbing her eyes as we leave our room this morning.

'Still tired?' I ask.

'Who wouldn't be with that guy shouting and that damn dog howling all night?' she complains.

'The dog is howling for food,' I say. 'If she doesn't eat, she can't make milk for her puppies.'

'Puppies?'

I nod. 'Yes. Four of them hidden under our balcony.'

Ailsa says, 'I'll bring her something back from the restaurant when we've had breakfast.'

We walk up the road to Cuba Bar, where we eat breakfast and persuade the waiter to give us some scraps for the dog. But when we get back we find Momma Ji — our landlady's Mother in Law from Hell — digging the litter of puppies out from under our balcony and putting them one by one into a sack. The mother dog is going frantic but each time it comes near, Mother in Law chases it off with a bamboo stick.

Our German neighbour is watching her; I know he speaks the local language so I ask him to find out what she is doing. She's taking the puppies to the beach to drown them in the ocean he translates.

Ailsa and me recoil in horror.

'No! No!' I exclaim, 'tell her to give them to me.'

Ailsa tries to snatch the sack away from Mother in Law.

She holds on to it and laughs.

'She won't have the dogs on her property,' the German says.

'Tell her she doesn't have to,' I say, 'we can take them to the

85

MONKEY ON MY ROOF

Animal Rescue Centre.'

Sonia Gandhi has set up animal rescue centres in some parts of India. Volunteers run a centre in Chaudi beside the new bus station. The idea is to medicate and delouse any diseased dogs, humanely destroy the ones that are too far gone for treatment, and sterilise the others to keep down the growing population.

Eventually Ma in Law surrenders the sack of puppies to us.

'What a horrible woman!' Ailsa says vehemently. 'How can she bring herself to drown little puppies, when she could take them to the Animal Rescue centre.'

'This is India, you ain't seen nothing yet,' I tell her, 'life is cheap out here.'

With a tender look on her face, Ailsa has taken one of the puppies out of the sack, 'No wonder she's rich,' she says. She is stroking the little dog so gently that I can't bring myself to tell her that the life of these puppies is not just cheap. It's cut price bargain basement! There's not much call for mongrel pups as pets in India, these will probably be put down at the animal rescue centre. My only consolation is that when they are put down it will hopefully be in a more humane manner than putting them in a sack and throwing them into the sea to drown.

The rickshaw driver doesn't want us in his vehicle, 'No Momma,' he says, 'dogs have too many fleas.'

But he relents when Ailsa fetches the flea powder from our room, and we promise to delouse his rickshaw.

We hand the dogs over at the centre. Only one of the staff is on duty, and he doesn't speak much English. It takes some persuasion to get him to take the mother dog as well as the puppies. A hundred rupees, plus the food the waiter gave us and the box of flea powder, sways the balance for the mother dog to be reconciled

MONKEY ON MY ROOF

with her puppies.

All this palaver has taken time, now it's getting on for one o'clock and my tummy is rumbling. A cup of chai and a puri bhaji at the Udipi Restaurant seems to be in order.

Sheila and Doug are sitting at the back of the restaurant with a male friend of theirs just arrived from England.

'Hi girls, come and join us,' Sheila says as we walk in, 'Our friend here is telling us about the man he met yesterday who teaches Transcendental Meditation.'

'I thought TM was illegal,' I declare.

Doug laughs, '*Nothing* is illegal in India.'

'My wife has Parkinson's Disease,' their friend says, 'I thought TM might take the edge off, but she'll have none of it.'

Ailsa does that thing with her eyes, 'What a shame! Now she'll never know if it'd help her or not.'

'No,' he says downcast.

'Tell you what,' I say, 'I'll go and see him if you like.'

'I'll come with you,' Ailsa says. She turns to the man, 'When your wife knows that someone like us has been to him she might change her mind.'

He gives us the address, and tells us to ask for Singh.

The four of us eat our lunch. Then we walk outside to brave the buses, cars, mad motorcyclists, sacred cows and sacred cow pats, until it is safe to cross the road and hire a rickshaw.

On the way back to Palolem we are dropped off at the Seashell Hotel in order to suss out the Mystical Meditation Master.

As the rickshaw drives away Sheila calls out, 'Dinner tonight girls? Schätzchen Bakery eight o'clock.'

'See you there,' I call back, holding my nose as we dodge through wicker baskets full of the fish the women sitting at the side

MONKEY ON MY ROOF

of the road are selling. We step over an open ditch, walk up the path and go through the murky hallway to knock on the end door. A tall blonde woman opens it. She takes us through to the back of the house to a kind of lean-to covered by a bamboo awning.

Under the awning is a single bed. The man on the bed is dressed in a white khurta and matching trousers, and is about sixty years old. He's sitting straight-backed in the lotus position. His face is deeply wrinkled, maybe because of the blue smoke from the ciggie he is smoking. Judging by the fag ends scattered around on the bare earth, he smokes a lot of cigarettes.

He surveys at us with an intense stare through the cigarette smoke, and keeping eye-contact pats the bed, 'Come, sit,' he says, 'what's your names?'

We sit down and tell him our names.

I say, 'I believe you teach Transcendental Meditation.'

'I was trained in TM by Osho at his ashram in Pune,' Singh answers.

'Oh! I thought Osho died a long time ago,' Ailsa declares.

'I knew him before he left his body.'

'Huh?'

'Osho. Never born, never died. Only visited this planet earth,' Singh intones.

Beside me Ailsa gives a smothered gasp, I can feel her shoulders quivering as she tries to conceal her laughter.

But with those piercing brown eyes of Singh's seeming to bore right through me, I don't think it diplomatic to enquire if he knows which planet Osho is on right now.

The blonde woman is his partner, she teaches Yoga, gives Reiki and does Shiatsu massage

which she learned in Japan. She spent five years sitting at the

MONKEY ON MY ROOF

feet of a master in a Japanese Dojo she tells us. I've no idea what a Dojo is but don't bother to ask. Ignorance is often bliss.

Ailsa decides to stick with Gosh and the Reiki he's teaching and give TM a miss, so I'll be doing TM alone. I make an arrangement for tomorrow morning and, dodging little black pigs, little black pig droppings and falling coconuts, we walk back to our room through the coconut grove.

MONKEY ON MY ROOF

20

The Schätzchen Bakery isn't what I would call a bakery, it's more a clothes stall with a few tables set to the side and a kitchen at the back.

When we arrive Sheila and Doug are already there sitting at a round table. They introduce us to the absobloody lovely Indian Doctor who is sitting with them. He really is beautiful this Doctor, tall and slim, black curly hair, sculptured features, and long elegant hands, but he takes himself so seriously, no humour at all. The gorgeous Doctor makes his living by research into mysterious sciences, he says, plus the small and very lucrative matter of Tantric Massage.

'Tantric Massage,' Sheila says innocently as she kicks me under the table, 'what exactly is that?'

'It's a form of very ancient Eastern Medicine,' Doctor tells her looking deeply into her eyes, 'very advantageous to the health.'

'I suppose it's expensive,' Ailsa remarks.

'Of course, but it does take five hours.'

Doug joins the conversation, 'What? All in one go?'

'Yes.'

'You won't be able to do many of those in a day then,' I say.

'I did one today,' the gorgeous creature informs us, 'she come and ask me for a half hour massage, and I tell her No. But she say she only have 250 rupees so I say she could pay me tomorrow.'

'That was very trusting of you,' Doug declares.

'I know she come back. She was very thrilling. Every time I touch her she went...' — here he closes his eyes and gives an incredibly good imitation of the fake orgasm scene in "When Harry met Sally" — 'Even her hands. When I pull her knuckles she say it

MONKEY ON MY ROOF

give her more thrilling than when she have the full love with her husband. With me she was thrilling all over.'

'I'd be thrilling all over too, if he touched me like that,' I murmur to Ailsa.

Sheila grins at me, 'Thrilling all over!' She turns to her husband, 'Did you hear that, Doug?'

The Doctor blinks his soulful black eyes, 'She come again I think.'

'And again and again and again,' Ailsa says wickedly.

'Full power, every hour on the hour, no toilet, no shower,' says Doug.

Sheila kicks me under the table once more.

'Absolutely,' intones the absobloodylovely Doctor and smiles into my eyes.

Whew! I can't afford 5000 rupees so there'll be no five hour tantric massage for me, but I can't resist smiling back at him.

A smile costs nothing.

*

Leaving Ailsa still snoring I creep out the door. Last night I slept like a baby, so this morning I'm full of beans and raring to go. My plan is to eat a breakfast of hot chocolate and croissant at the German bakery — which unlike the Schätzchen really is a bakery with lots of delicious home-made cakes — before I keep my appointment with the Mystical Meditation Master.

At the Seashell Hotel Singh gives me my mantras and instructs me how to use them. Then I am taken inside into the calm room which is used for yoga. Yesterday I'd told Singh that there'd be no lotus position for me; my knees and hips won't allow it.

MONKEY ON MY ROOF

They've arranged a bed where I can sit comfortably. Singh performs a kind of ceremony, and I sit on the bed for twenty minutes to repeat my mantras and meditate.

After the meditation, we sit outside drinking chai, smoking and talking.

'Singh and me met one another in Rishikesh,' his partner tells me, 'I walked into a café, and saw this shining man sitting at a table philosophizing to a group of young people. They were hanging on every word. I've never seen anyone else shine that way, shine like Singh. We've been together ever since.'

Looking at Singh sitting there cross-legged on the bed nodding his head, I can see what she means. The combination of his brown skin against those white robes, his broad face with that aquiline nose above the long upper lip with its black moustache, but most of all those dark eyes with their intense hypnotic stare.

Of course he shines.

'I have ambition to start my own ashram,' Singh says, directing his hypnotic stare deep into my eyes.

I can't look away.

'I will teach the philosophy; Nicole here will do the massage and teach yoga.'

Still keeping eye-contact, Singh asserts, 'and you, Sally, will do the healing Reiki and be the mother of my ashram. An Amma to all the young people who will come.' He tears his eyes away from mine for a moment to glance at the multi-coloured skirt and pink tee shirt I'm wearing, 'You will wear only white robes,' he tells me, 'and every day fresh flowers in your hair.'

An ashram is a place of humble cubicles and even more humble food, where fervent devotees sit in serene meditation, chanting mantras, while saffron clothed sadhus teach philosophy

MONKEY ON MY ROOF

before twisting themselves into yoga positions. I picture myself there, sitting on a throne in my white robes. I'm wearing an ethereal smile and am surrounded by eager, reverent young people who are hanging on my every word.

'Yes, yes, yes!' I exclaim eagerly.

Half way back through the coconut grove I come to my senses. Hang on a minute; I didn't come to India to be the mother of anybody's ashram. Sod that for a lark.

I take my mobile out of my beach bag.

Nicole answers the phone and I ask her when Singh is likely to open his ashram.

'Oh that! It won't be for a couple of years at least,' she says.

Phew, lucky escape!

The coconut grove runs alongside the beach, I take one of the paths down and walk along the water's edge to cool my feet in the surf.

My mobile plays its little tune, Ailsa calling, 'Where are you? How did the TM go?'

'I'm paddling in the surf at the moment,' I tell her, 'on my way to the Cosy Nook. Tell you all about the TM when I get there.'

A young man walking from the sea wearing a very fetching pair of tiny swimming trunks waves and calls my name. It's that beautiful young man who does Tantric massage for five hours, the absobloodylovely Indian Doctor that Sheila and Doug introduced me to last night.

'Come for a swim, Sally,' he says.

Gazing at his tiny swimming trunks I think: No fear! I wouldn't be able to trust myself.

'Erm, no thanks, I haven't had my lunch yet,' I say.

He gives me a puzzled look.

MONKEY ON MY ROOF

But before he can say anything, a woman gets up from the sand and asks can she have her photograph taken with him.

Taking her digital camera I reel off a couple of shots before saying goodbye, and walking up the beach to the Cosy Nook Café to meet Ailsa.

MONKEY ON MY ROOF

21

A relaxing time on a sunbed brings us up to five o'clock, it's time to go back, shower and get ready for dinner. Instead of the beach road we take the short cut through the coconut grove.

At the end of the path onto the road is the Hindu Guest house. From his balcony on the first floor the Doctor calls down to us. Calls us to climb the iron stairs and come visit.

Would I have walked with Ailsa along that path if I'd known he had an apartment there? Who knows? Maybe I would!

Ailsa nudges me, 'What have we got to lose?'

I smile, 'Not our virginity that's for sure!'

We walk up the stairs to his room.

He is still wearing his swimming trunks, 'I've only just come back from the beach,' he says.

There are two beds pushed against the walls on each side of the room, which is his consulting room, treatment room, and living space.

He pats the bed on the left, 'Come and sit down.'

We sit on the very edge.

'You can lie down and rest if you like.'

'No thanks!' I exclaim.

He gives me a hurt look, 'Why not?'

'Oh, er, we've got sand on our feet, we don't want to make your sheets dirty.'

'No problem! Everyone's feet get dirty.'

With that he grabs a pair of pillows from one bed, puts them against the wall of the other. Then he lifts up my feet and swings them round onto the mattress, he does the same to Ailsa. Ailsa and I look at one another and burst out laughing. His actions are so charming, performed with such obvious innocence, that we can't take offence.

There's a knock on the door, and the Israeli woman who had her photo taken with him on the beach walks into the room. She has thick, long, black curly hair. It stretches down her back to her hips.

'You rest there,' the Doctor says, 'I go give her bath, wash her hair.'

He takes the Israeli woman's hand and they disappear into the bathroom to emerge a short time later wrapped in big fluffy white towels. The woman's hair is dripping wet; modestly she dresses herself under the towel, and then uses it to dry her hair.

The Doctor however is doing a sort of dance with the towel, making a meal of drying himself. He says, 'If I drop towel you will be very shocked, no?'

We pretend not to hear.

'What you say if I drop towel?' he persists.

'Why should I say anything?' I tell him, 'I'm a married woman.'

'And I'm from Scotland; I've seen it all before,' says Ailsa.

Just the same she turns her head away.

He drops the towel.

Quickly I look up at the ceiling, the door, the window, anywhere but that brown organ which seems to grow bigger every time my disobedient eye slithers towards it. My memory flashes back to when I was fifteen years old.

I am walking along a country path with Dawn my best friend. It's her birthday and her brothers have clubbed together to buy her an umbrella. Not any old umbrella mind you. Oh no, this is a top of the range, to die for, frilly, saucy umbrella, with a carved handle at one end and a wicked spike at the other. The fashion statement

MONKEY ON MY ROOF

every teenage girl craved for in 1965.

The man walking towards us drops the bike he is wheeling and flaps open the front of his grubby fawn mac.

I stop dead in my tracks.

There are three of us at home, my Mother, my sister, and me. A man's sexual organ hasn't been allowed near our house for as long as I can remember. I've certainly never seen one.

Dawn, being the only girl in a family of five boys, isn't fazed, 'What the bloody hell do you think you're doing you dirty bastid,' she exclaims in her Liverpool accent and raises the umbrella.

To this day I can still hear the sound that brolly made as it swished through the air and whacked down with full force on his family jewels. The man let out a scream, clutched his nether regions and fell to ground moaning and writhing...

Unfortunately Dawn isn't with me, I don't happen to have an umbrella, and the gorgeous Doctor has turned full on flaunting his John Thomas and is saying, 'Do you think I'm a little boy?'

I lower my eyes and gaze pointedly at his groin.

'Do you think I'm a little boy?' he repeats.

Despite what I said at that leaving party last week I'm no expert on the size of Indian male organs: this is the first I've seen.

'I wouldn't know,' I tell him, 'I've never seen an Indian man naked before. But compared to an Englishman, yes, you are a little boy!'

Beside me on the bed Ailsa's shoulders are shaking as she tries to conceal her laughter. The Israeli woman has stopped drying her hair and is making smothered noises into her towel, and the Doctor picks *his* towel up from the floor and wraps it quickly around his waist.

MONKEY ON MY ROOF

Then the owner of the Schätzchen Bakery arrives bringing food. The Doctor goes in the bathroom to dress. More people arrive; Joseph the Ethiopian Shaman, the French girl with her Nepalese boyfriend. We all sit on straw mats on the floor, to eat green salad, chapattis, vegetable curry, fresh fruit salad, and drink coconut milk.

According to the owner of the Schätzchen Bakery, the Doctor is a very high Yogi.

This proclamation inspires the high Yogi to tell a story about a patient who came to him worried because his new-born son had red hair.

'It's possible that one of your ancestors had red hair, and it's carried on to your son,' the Doctor told him.

'But my wife and I both have black hair,' said the man, 'and so have all our families.'

The Doctor asked him, 'How often do you make love with your wife?'

'Once every five months,' the man said.

'There you are then,' the Doctor told him, 'your son's red hair is caused by rust!'

I was wrong about him having no sense of humour, some of the things he tells us have us all crying with laughter. Not just the stories he tells, but the way he mimes the actions as he tells them.

There is a lot of laughing, joking, and discussing of Shiva, Buddha, and the Gita. The party doesn't break up until one thirty in the morning.

Back at the guest house our German neighbour is sitting on a chair in the passage outside his room, he taps his watch, 'What time is this to come back?' he says, 'I was worried about you.'

Ailsa looks at her watch, 'It's half past December. Nearly Christmas!'

MONKEY ON MY ROOF

22

My days are spent sunbathing with Ailsa, discussing Buddhism with the travellers at River Valley, learning about Transcendental Meditation with Singh, and studying for my Reiki Master attunement with Gosh. Cold distant Britain with its mad culture of TV, booze, fags, and debauchery is only a faint memory of my other life... until the Christmas charter planes arrive and disgorge the two-week tourists.

Fat, beer-bellied men wearing gaudy shorts lumber through the surf to sample the booze in the beach shacks. Their women, coifed and made up like Stepford Wives, totter along the sand in stiletto heels to lie bare breasted on sunbeds. Young Indian men arrive from Bombay to leer with wide eyes at the European women. Few of them have ever seen further than the skin on their mother's bare arm, let alone a naked breast. They take photos that they will show to their friends back home to prove how sophisticated they are. Arms around one another, drunks stumble singing and shouting along the sand.

An Indian man lurches towards me, 'Namaste Momma,' he says. Then he throws up, narrowly missing my feet. At least the worst of the lagers louts seem to be on the south side of the beach.

I watch them with distaste, then I remember how Irene had said, "Paradise is for everyone, not just for a few."

Who, after all, am I too judge?

*

This morning Ailsa and I watch as eager boys play football on the beach in the blazing heat, gaggles of girls giggle as they collect sea shells, toddlers toddle in the surf, their eyes full of wonder.

MONKEY ON MY ROOF

Volunteers from the El Shaddai Children's Shelter in Margao have hired a bus to give parentless Indian children a Christmas Eve treat. The children come from Hindu, Muslim, Sikh, Jain, Christian families. What does it matter? Christmas is for everyone.

'Most of these kids are the sons and daughters of beggars who come here from neighbouring states during the tourist season,' I tell Ailsa. 'They're the children abandoned by their parents, left crying on the beach when their parents go back home.'

'Oh isn't it good to see them enjoying themselves,' she exclaims.

One of the volunteers plays football with the boys, helps the girls collect shells, and rescues toddlers from the surf. Then he buys them all ice cream.

He has a sunbed next to mine and tells us he owns a restaurant in Margao. 'Having been abandoned by my parents when I was six years old, I understand these children,' he says.

At thirty years of age he still feels a sense of betrayal, and although his genetic family has been traced he wants nothing to do with them. He was lucky; he was taken in and fostered by a family who treated him well. Though he can never look upon his foster parents as his real family he concedes that without their help he couldn't have made the good successful life he enjoys now.

'Sometimes,' I say, 'I can't help feeling that the children the beggars leave behind have a better life in the children's shelters. At least they get food, clothes, lodgings, and a chance at an education.'

'What will become of them,' Ailsa asks 'when they are too old for the children's shelter?'

'Some will stay and work in the shelter,' the volunteer says, 'some will disappear... who knows where?' Then his face softens into a smile, 'and a lucky few — the bright, pretty ones — will be

MONKEY ON MY ROOF

fostered or adopted by childless couples.'

I smile back at him, 'And become restaurant owners like you?'

At five o clock they all leave the beach to go back to the shelter.

Ailsa and I leave at the same time to get ready for our appointment with Singh and his partner who have invited us to have dinner with them at a restaurant on the beach.

Nightfall in India descends dramatically like a theatre curtain. This Christmas Eve, as usual, firework displays light up the sky to fill the place of the vivid sunset. But Ailsa and I don't enjoy the fireworks because Nicole has PMT — paranoid manic tantrums — and Singh has a new kettle.

According to Nicole when Singh plugged his new kettle in earlier this evening he managed to short circuit the entire electricity supply in their apartment block. It's really pissed her off! People must be feeling the vibes as far as Delhi.

'Not only that,' she glowers at him, 'he's caused a power cut to all the houses on our side of the road.'

Singh disputes that the power cut is his responsibility, and contends that it's the electric wiring that is at fault. Ignoring their bickering, Ailsa and I eat our vegetable curry and drink our chai.

Finally Nicole says to Singh, 'It's Christmas and I want a cocktail. Are you going to buy me one or not?'

He nods, and looks from Ailsa to me enquiringly.

A Reiki Master Attunement requires twenty-one days detox, I've nearly done it. No meat, no fish, no booze, and definitely no cigarettes.

I put a hand to my mouth, and — without knowing where it came from — discover a cigarette, half smoked, between my lips. I

MONKEY ON MY ROOF

look at it in astonishment, 'How did that get there?'

Ailsa nudges me, 'Didn't you say your Christmas Eve was supposed to be quiet and spiritual?'

'Spiritual? You must be joking! My detox is broken!'

'You can buy nicotine patches at the pharmacy in Chaudi,' Nicole informs me.

'Really?'

'Yes! Now how about that cocktail?'

'Oh, all right then,' I say, 'might as well be hung for a sheep as a lamb. It is Christmas Eve after all.'

*

Christmas morning! Champagne breakfast at the Banyan tree.

The cocktails last night weren't wasted, Singh and Nicole are here looking all lovey dovey.

Love is in the air. The French girl has fallen *oh la la!* crazily for the Nepalese chef at Moonlite Eatery, can't keep her eyes off him, looks at him as if she'd like to eat him up in the moonlight.

Everyone seems to have converged on Cosy Nook this morning. We drink lots of Bucks Fizz and dance to Slade's Christmas song.

Doug is talking and laughing on his mobile.

He holds it out to me, 'Someone wants to speak to you, Sally.'

I take the phone, 'Hello?'

'Merry Christmas, Sally. You're still in Palolem, then?'

Oh My God! It's Stephan! Stephan the man who waved at me every day from the beach. Stephan who sat beside me the night I made that dreadful speech at the leaving party. Stephan whose

MONKEY ON MY ROOF

eyes tempt me down paths I'm not permitted to walk.

'Yes,' I squeak.

'Where are you off to next?'

'I'm not sure… erm… erm… ,' damn, I'm babbling again! Now he'll be certain to think I'm an idiot, 'Pune… maybe…'

From the corner of my eye I can see Ailsa grinning, she murmurs smugly from the corner of her mouth, 'Told you you'd pulled.'

Beep. Beep. Beep.

Silence!

Not sure whether to be glad or sorry, I look at Doug in disbelief, 'Your battery's packed up!'

'Never mind,' Doug says, 'next time he phones I'll give him your number.'

'No!' I'm appalled: who knows where that might lead? 'Please don't do that.'

I might be here alone but I'm not free!

Singh has never drunk champers before today, he stumbles past us wishing all and sundry a Meeerrry Chrrristmaaass; over and over again. Alcohol inhibits his magnetic stare. Cross-eyed, off balance, he's finding it difficult to hypnotise while tripping over his feet, now no-one can understand a word he's saying. Finally he passes out on a hammock in River Valley. Nicole stands beside him tenderly lifting his head to place a pillow beneath it.

MONKEY ON MY ROOF

<u>23</u>

It's Boxing Day and Ailsa and I have been invited to spend the night at Eliza the beautician's house, because it's Eliza's birthday. It means us sleeping top and tail in a double bed. But what the heck.

At her house, Eliza has gathered a herb called the Queen of Queens, which, she informs me, is a cure for all ills.

'You have to bathe in it twice a day,' she tells me, 'It will cure your fever.'

So I get undressed and go into the bathroom to pour the concoction over my head. It smells weird, like overcooked cabbage mixed with the perfume from marihuana smoke.

'Don't know how good it will be for your feverish cold,' Ailsa says, 'but you'll know what to blame when the beach dogs follow you.'

A football match tonight has been arranged by the village committee to give the young people a bit of fun. Walking down the hill is no trouble now that my joints have stopped aching. Maybe Eliza's herb has done the trick.

At the side of a field that has been left to lie fallow for just this purpose, goal posts have been erected, and plastic garden chairs lined up in rows with a centre aisle, men on the right, women on the left. Fairy lights and electric starry lanterns are hung all around in the trees, and there are stalls selling an Indian version of hot dogs and hamburgers.

I'm sitting between Eliza and Ailsa. A van with a stereo system is belting out the Chicken song, and every person in this Indian audience starts flapping their elbows, arms at shoulder height.

The match starts with the Tsunami Boys and the Hurricane

MONKEY ON MY ROOF

Katrina team fighting it out on the floodlit pitch. A goal has just been scored, a song blares out over the loudspeaker, 'If you're going to do it, do it with a condom.'

Aware of Ailsa's shoulders shaking silently next to me I try not to look at her, but a vision of the goal-scorer pulling a condom on in the middle of the pitch has me falling about with laughter.

Eliza looks at me disapprovingly. 'Enjoying?' she says, then again 'Enjoying?' as if she's never before seen a person laugh, which makes me laugh more than ever.

'Manchester United was never like this,' I gasp, 'eat your heart out, David Beckham!'

Hurricane Katrina beats the Tsunami Boys two to one. And not a condom in sight.

*

Led by Gosh on Yoga beach, New Year's Eve is World Peace meditation. Nearly one hundred of us sit holding hands around a healing circle made from flowers and lit candles.

I'm one of the older people here; the others are much younger; young enough to be idealistic. I watch the bright faces, so eager and optimistic as they pray for peace in the world, pray for the fighting and killing to stop and very nearly believe that perhaps… just perhaps… they can make a difference.

When the meditation is over, I leave Ailsa on Yoga beach putting the world to rights with the other young people, and wander off by myself.

Across the river it's all going on at Graceful Glen, which is very up market with landscaped gardens, a Reiki room, Meditation space, and a Yoga space. During high season the huts cost 4000

MONKEY ON MY ROOF

rupees a night, and are inhabited mostly by upper class twits with more money than sense.

The owner's wife reads Tarot when she isn't drunk or stoned or shagging some young bit of stuff while her fella is away on business; or so Singh says. Some of my friends are sitting around a long table there. Flowers and candles, plates of samosas, Kashmiri naan bread, empty glasses and bottles, full ashtrays litter the table.

'Hi Sally,' someone shouts, 'come and join us.'

A joint is being passed around, I take my turn to puff on it.

'What a lovely night,' I say to the woman sitting next to me. 'Just look at those stars.'

'Yeess,' she drawls, so stoned she can hardly speak, 'lloookkk aattt ttthhaatt oonnee oovvveerr tthheerree.'

What am I doing here?

Having lived to fifty-one years — plus VAT — my time is precious, who knows how much of it I have left?

I get up to leave. But I've had three or four drags on the joint and am a little stoned myself. My left foot moves to the right, and my right foot to the left, I can't find my way out to the beach and stumble around in the jungle upsetting the pigs and chickens, and waking up the crows. Eventually I arrive at the beach and reel onto the sand.

A young Indian man walks beside me as I bumble my way along. He is very drunk. We walk in silence for a while watching the rockets shoot up, the myriad colours flaring into light in the velvet night. The New Year's Eve fireworks are spectacular this year.

He says, 'Please forgive me.'

'Forgive you?' That wacky baccy was good stuff, I'm still a bit stoned. 'What for?'

MONKEY ON MY ROOF

'Please forgive me!' he slurs again.

And I think: maybe he needs to urinate. 'Of course I'll forgive you,' I say wondering if he wants to hide himself behind that handy fishing boat. 'Go on then.'

At which he takes hold of my arm with one hand, and with his other grabs at a place on my anatomy where neither of his hands should have strayed; only then do I realise that he is actually saying, 'Please fuck with me!'

I swing my beach bag around and hit him as hard as I can, 'Get off, you cheeky sod, I'm old enough to be your Auntie.'

At my age I don't expect that kind of behaviour from young men; or old ones if it comes to that. Though if I wasn't married I might make an exception for Stephan, the guy I met at the party.

The drunken Indian reels off along the beach to disappear behind a beach hut, and I stumble my way back to the guest house.

My gentle German neighbour is sitting outside his room. He taps his watch, 'It's a quarter past two, thousand and six. Happy New Year Sally!'

Happy New Year indeed.

24

Eight o'clock in the morning, breakfast time, and the beach café has been invaded by monkeys who pelt Nicole, Singh, Ailsa and me with overripe red berries from the tree. The berries burst and cover us with something that looks and smells like dog poo.

Singh is thrilled. He collects some of the berries and tells Nicole that Indian men in the Punjab wait for the berries to ripen. Then they boil them up with sugar before drinking the liquid. After that, according to Singh, the men can go on having sex all night and all day without stopping.

'It's better than Viagra,' Singh informs her.

Nicole and I look at one another.

'You'll be lucky tonight,' I tell her.

She shrugs, looks at Singh, pulls a face and says, 'So that's why you have left it so long... Indian men look on the banyan tree as sacred. No wonder, when they have to wait for the berries to ripen!'

'How does it work?' I ask Singh.

Ailsa glances at me po-faced; the little madam loses no opportunity to remind me of my speech at that leaving party, and asks Singh, 'Do the berries fatten sperm? Is it worshipped because sex gets to last a long time?'

Singh gazes deep into her eyes and nods mysteriously.

I nudge Ailsa, 'If I boil some of these berries up with sugar and drink it, will it work for me?'

Nicole laughs, but Singh is shocked, 'It only works for men,' he says.

'That figures!' says Ailsa. 'What's your opinion Sally?'

'Not having had the opportunity to weigh anyone's sperm

MONKEY ON MY ROOF

count yet, or measure their gonads, I can't say,' I tell her.

Singh has been watching my mouth as I talk, he expresses his opinion that I have a serene smile, 'You mustn't lose it,' he says.

According to Nicole, serene smiles tend to be sexually attractive to those Indian men who use banyan tree berries.

To stop the conversation from turning into a slanging match I say, 'The man in the room across from us moved out this afternoon. He makes so much noise late at night that if he'd stayed much longer my serene smile would've turned into a murderous scowl.'

Singh gets up and walks away. Nicole watches him go then turns to me, 'I'm glad he's gone,' she says, 'We've been having a few problems lately.'

*

Dinner tonight with Ailsa, Sheila and Doug at Blue Planet. After we've eaten, Gosh gives a lecture in the Yoga Hall. His lecture is about happiness.

After he's finished speaking I light a cigarette.

Ailsa laughs, 'You smoke too much.'

'I'm going to stop!'

She gives me a quizzical look, 'I've heard that one before!'

'This time I mean it. Gosh's lecture has done what it's supposed to do. It's made me question myself.'

She grins sardonically, 'Oh Yeah!'

'How many times have I quit smoking? How many times have I started again? Year after year, time after time since age seventeen, always quitting, and always restarting: like a self-fulfilling prophecy. Quitting cigarettes might not be the path to perfect happiness but it will give me something to aim for.'

MONKEY ON MY ROOF

'So what are you going to do?'

'I'm going to go cold turkey.'

She laughs, 'I'll believe it when I see it.'

After Sheila has wandered off to bed, and Doug has dragged Ailsa away to the other side of the room to listen to him bullshit some tourists, I tell Gosh how much I've enjoyed his lecture.

'You'll be pleased to know that, thanks to you,' I say, 'I've decided to turn my mobile off and lock myself away in my room for three days so that I can quit smoking.'

'You will really do that?' he asks.

'If I'm away from everyone who smokes it'll be easier to quit,' I tell him. 'It's time I took control of my life, I'm not seventeen anymore.'

*

Carrying the bottles of filtered water I've bought for my three-day cigarette stoppage, I cross the road to say hello to the Kashmiri man who is standing in the gateway of his shop. Two very fat and frowsy Russian women wearing nothing but red and white striped bikinis wobble past.

The Kashmiri eyeballs me, I gaze back at him, 'The things you see when you haven't got a camera,' I say. 'Now I know why the burka was invented.'

The Kashmiri smiles. 'Sally,' he purrs in his sound-alike James Mason voice, 'in my country, in Srinagar, there is a lake.'

'Oh?'

'The lake it is full of very big fish.'

'Yes?'

'No-one in my country catches them to eat them.'

His smile widens, 'We keep them as pets!'

MONKEY ON MY ROOF

Being as I'm more than a touch on the large side myself this makes me laugh. Then I begin to wonder: Am I being kept as a pet in Palolem? Casa Fiesta, Palolem Beach Resort, and River Valley, none of them charge me for drinks, I could get drunk every night if I wanted. What a shame that I'm on the wagon!

*

It worked!

I haven't had a cigarette for over three weeks. In the end my nicotine detox was no problem. Yesterday I had my Attunement. Now at last I can call myself a Reiki Master.

Ailsa says, 'So will I have to curtsey to you now that you're a Reiki master?'

'Yes! And while you're about it you can get out the Brasso and polish my halo.'

'How was it? Was it powerful? Have you given anybody Reiki yet?'

'Yes, it was powerful,' I tell her, 'and no, I haven't Reiki'd anyone yet; only my pillow.'

'Your pillow! Oh yeah!'

'That's right. My pillow is doing very well on the chair in our room. Tomorrow I'm going to teach it the symbols and attune it to second degree.'

MONKEY ON MY ROOF

25

Rats are playing tag around our feet on the platform at Margao Railway Station. Its four o'clock on one of those sleepy humid afternoons when everyone around finds themselves yawning. Two wild dogs lying in the shadow of an abandoned wheelbarrow are fast asleep, but the rats are wide awake.

We've been booked a second-class sleeper coach, air-conditioned. This usually means a bunk in an eight-berth carriage with a broken ceiling fan. The journey will take twelve hours; we aren't looking forward to arriving in Pune at four o'clock in the morning!

The train arrives, we're to share a carriage with a German woman — whose name we discover is Anke. A tall woman about my age whose aura of artless simplicity is contradicted by her strong boned sexy face. She's on her way to an Ayurveda hospital she tells us, a sort of ashram at Lonavala.

'I thought we'd take a look at the Osho Ashram,' I say.

'You'll be in Pune for the Holi Festival?'

'Yes.'

Today is the last full moon day of the winter months, the beginning of Holi, the Festival of Colours. A perfect justification — for anyone that way inclined — to get off their head on ganja. And a good excuse for young men to stroke paints or dyes slowly onto their girlfriends' clothes.

'It took me until October to wash the colours from my hair,' Anke says gazing at my hair which has been bleached nearly as blonde as Ailsa's by the sun.

'You'll enjoy Holi,' she says, 'don't forget to wear your oldest clothes.'

MONKEY ON MY ROOF

She smiles at Ailsa, 'Those Indian boys will have such fun painting you.'

At the end of the month, Anke will be leaving India to go home to Germany, Ailsa will be flying back to Scotland and I have to get to Nepal to renew my Indian visa. We exchange e-mail addresses and agree to meet again in Mumbai.

At Pune railway station homeless people are sleeping on the platform, we have to step over them on our way to the ladies waiting room. The platform stinks of rat urine and garlic, the homeless people stink of curried human piss. The stink from the ladies waiting room beggars belief, you don't want to know what the ladies waiting room stinks of. We pull plastic chairs out onto the platform to spend the next couple of hours holding our noses until we can get a taxi to the guesthouse we've booked in Koregaon Park.

*

Serendipity.

Stephan is here in Pune. He was here when we arrived this morning, seated on a trestle bench at one of the rough wood tables in the German Bakery, his backpack beside of him. He went to the Buddhist ashram at Igatpuri after he left Palolem, he tells us, then decided to stop off in Pune for a couple of days. This evening he leaves to help at a children's home in Bombay, a long-standing arrangement that can't be broken.

Stephan is a widower. Two years ago, a drunk driver jumped a red light and rammed his wife's car.

'Ten o'clock in the morning,' he says bitterly, 'imagine it! Drunk at that time in the morning! Jan was only going to Tesco for

MONKEY ON MY ROOF

the weekly shop.'

He turns his head away, lowers his voice, 'Just my luck to be on duty that day,' he mutters bitterly, 'to be the one called out... it was just a run-of-the-mill traffic accident.'

'On duty?'

'With the police. I used to be a police sergeant.' He shudders, 'Jan died in my arms.'

I mouth the usual platitudes and ask him what she was like as a person.

'She was like you,' he says, 'that first time I saw you on the beach, I thought... That's why I waved.'

'And I thought you must be someone I knew,' I answer, 'that's why I waved back.'

'I'm glad you did.'

We smile at one another and he goes on to tell me that the way I look, my personality, everything about me, reminds him of his dead wife.

'Jan was full of fun,' he reminisces, 'worse than any child she was. Loved the theatre she did.' He smiles, 'I can see her now; jumping up and down in her seat booing the villain and cheering the hero at the Panto.'

'You like the theatre then?' I ask.

'We went a couple of times a month, would have gone more often if I'd been sure of having time off. The Grand in the centre of town, or the Dylan Thomas Theatre on the waterside.' He sighs again, 'Before she died. Before I left the Force. Left Swansea.'

'Where do you live now?' Ailsa asks him.

'Nowhere, everywhere,' he says, 'travelling the world. I sold the house, gave up my job— after what happened. After the accident I couldn't bear to stay in that house. So empty without Jan. But at

MONKEY ON MY ROOF

the same time so full of her... the wallpaper she'd chosen, the curtains she'd hung, the pictures on the wall we'd picked out together...' his voice trails off.

Ailsa has been watching his mouth, watching the words that fall from his lips, she gives a little nod and squeezes my hand, 'Sally,' she says, 'there's an internet café around the corner. I'm off to e-mail Greg, don't know how long I'll be.'

'Okay,' I say, 'where shall we meet?'

'I'll see you back at the guest house,' she says, 'I feel like exploring on my own.'

She stands up smiles at Stephan, 'Nice to meet you again,' and she's gone.

'Have I scared her away?' says Stephan.

'No,' I tell him, 'that's just Ailsa being tactful.'

We talk about the books we've read, movies we've seen, concerts we've been to. Our tastes in music, books, movies, and the theatre are the same. Stephan is the same physical type as my husband, tall and heavily built with lots of thick curly hair, though Stephan is a lot slimmer. I've noticed this many times before, how often we are attracted to the same sort of people. He has a dry sense of humour, but his jokes; unlike my husband's, don't always involve sex.

The more we talk the more my liking for him deepens. What's more, each time I look into Stephan's green-grey eyes, there's that attraction again. That flicker of sexual desire that I thought had died for me a long time ago.

MONKEY ON MY ROOF

26

Ailsa has gone shopping this morning, so I've joined Stephan at his table in the German Bakery. Two large men wearing maroon robes walk past our table and stare at me. I'm the only western woman there wearing a Punjabi suit.

'Those two men come here every day,' Stephan tells me, 'they call themselves Sanyasins. Seekers after truth.'

'Aren't we all? It can be hard to find,' I say.

'There have always been seekers,' he states, and then he grins, 'it's written in stone in the Osho Ashram.'

He takes hold of my hand. His hand is square, with long fingers and round, cared-for finger nails; tiny tufts of hair grow on the pads between his knuckles.

'Hmm,' I say, 'some of these Seekers after truth look quite scary. Hope they don't go in for granny banging.'

Giving my hand a squeeze Stephan says, 'If there's any granny banging to be done I'll be the one to do it.'

Whoa! Too close for comfort! Blushing I slap his hand playfully, 'Behave yourself!'

Stephan seems to be in earnest, which has me feeling both disturbed and reassured; it's a long time since I've had this kind of male attention.

'So tell me Sally. Why are you travelling alone?'

'My husband is the manager of a DIY store,' I say, 'he can't get away.'

'If you were my wife I wouldn't let you out of my sight.'

'Oh,' I say uncomfortably, 'Mark's worked in that same store since he left school.'

Nothing if not consistent is our Mark.

MONKEY ON MY ROOF

Of course he was only a lowly shop assistant when we first bopped together at the Cavern Club, hadn't yet attained the distinction of a manager's high position.

'...?' Stephan looks at me inquiringly.

'His job is very important to him.'

Stephan laughs, 'And just what is important to you, Sally?'

His laugh puts me in mind of the way my friend Dawn had laughed when I told her I suspected Mark was having an affair.

'Don't be daft, Sally,' my oldest friend said, 'when would he ever have the chance? It's a Do It Yourself store for goodness sake! Hello! Men not women.'

'You'd be surprised how many women are interested in DIY,' I'd countered, 'plus his job gives him a good excuse to be out at night "doing the books"'.

And I'd been right. Though it wasn't "the books" he was shagging after hours in the storeroom. No, it was one of his staff. That blonde woman on the enquiries counter. The one who always had a trace of shadow showing in the roots of her hair. Made me wonder what kind of enquiries Mark had been making to discover if all that blonde hair was natural. If so he needn't have bothered; the matching shadow under her nose was a dead giveaway.

Do I sound bitter? I have good reason to feel bitter. After all, I *was* seven months pregnant that first time. He said it wasn't important. It was only sex he said, because I was pregnant and it mightn't be good for the baby, he didn't want to hurt me he said. Don't you know that there's more than one way of hurting a person, I asked him. Yes, he said and swore that it would never happen again, begged me to forgive him. What alternative did I have? Two young children and another on the way? Besides, I still loved him.

Then it happened again. And again.

MONKEY ON MY ROOF

How can I reply to Stephan's question, when I hardly know the answer myself?

'Perhaps I'm a seeker after truth too,' I say.

Which, to be honest, isn't that far from reality!

'I've told you all about myself, but I know nothing about you,' Stephan says.

I force a laugh, 'Think of me as a woman of mystery.'

He wants us to spend the rest of the day together.

Silently I reflect that, given the closeness ripening between us, this may not be such a good idea. Nowadays it is permissible to jump in the sack with all and sundry whenever it takes ones fancy. But I'm an old-fashioned girl; I take my marriage vows seriously.

Then the sane practical side of my brain pooh-poohs the romantic in me and asks: But what can possibly happen? You may never see him again. Just enjoy the day.

I throw caution to the winds.

We put his backpack in a locker at the Railway Station before making our way to the Osho Ashram. Huge bamboo trees grow around The Gateless Gate, initials and dates are carved into the trunks. We stand in the queue, go inside to watch the videos, and take the day tour. Stephan points out the stone with the carving about seekers. The Ashram is fantastically beautiful, and enormously expensive. A Cashram, rather than an Ashram.

When we come out, it's raining. Lightning zips in streaks across ugly, black-rimmed clouds. Holding hands we run through the downpour to the nearest rickshaw. Stephan tells the driver to take us to Pune Camp. The rickshaw man says that the monsoon has started early. Holi always brings a strong moon power, he says, running the two words together. Moonpower. A lovelier word than monsoon.

MONKEY ON MY ROOF

We lunch at The Ram Krishna Restaurant: pav bhaji, sweet and spicy channa chaat masala, and papad rolls.

All too soon, it's time to take a rickshaw to the station for Stephan to catch his train to Mumbai. On the platform, unsure about the usual friendly kiss on cheek, too nervous to kiss mouth to mouth, we shake hands awkwardly as we say farewell.

Back at the guest house Ailsa is waiting, 'How was your day?'

'Perfect,' I say.

MONKEY ON MY ROOF

27

This morning the sun is shining again. At the German Bakery we sit beside Faezeh, an Iranian girl. She is at college here she tells us, and wants to improve her English.

'What are you doing today?' she asks.

'We're looking for a room. The one we have is too expensive.'

'Come and stay with me in my flat.'

'Wha...?'

'It won't cost you anything, and will help me with my English.'

'But we're not English teachers!' Ailsa says.

The very idea has us both smiling. An image — that is if you can call the imaginary echo of a sound an image — of this young woman's English vowels inflected with a mixture of my Scouse accent and Ailsa's Glaswegian burr, comes into my head.

'Conversational English. All you have to do is talk to me.'

'You don't need English lessons,' I say.

And Ailsa hastens to assure her, 'Your English is okay,'

'I want to teach,' the Iranian girl pleads.

Doubtfully we both regard her.

A nice-looking girl with a lively honest face, candid bright brown eyes, dimpled chin, full lips parted in a smile, a way about her that one can't help liking. She shifts uncomfortably under our scrutiny, her hand goes up to tidy her unruly black hair tied at the back with a green ribbon.

'Don't decide right away,' she says, 'come and see my flat.'

The flat is okay; it's out in Lane 7 in Meera Nagar Park, a third floor flat. There is a large living space, balcony, bath and

MONKEY ON MY ROOF

kitchen. We stand in the doorway of the only bedroom, window opposite door, a chest of drawers beneath it, a double bed, a small wardrobe...Faezeh points to the bed, 'You can sleep there, it is most comfortable.'

'What about you?' I ask. 'Where will you sleep?'

She takes us to the living room, 'I will sleep here,' and points to the side of the room where, against the wall, a divan heaped with cushions is being used as a sofa. 'Is bed also.'

I am still doubtful and say to Ailsa, 'Staying here will cost us money in rickshaws to get back and forth.'

'But we can suss out the buses and will be saving on paying rent,' Ailsa answers. She has taken a liking to Faezeh.

These two young girls, roughly the same age, turn bright eager faces towards me willing me to say yes. Harder hearts than mine could only defrost under that double stare.

Reflecting that it might be good for Ailsa to spend time with someone her own age instead of an old fogey like me, what else can I do but smile and say, 'Hmm, we'd be off the tourist trail, get to see Pune in all its glory, warts and all! Okay then; let's go and fetch our backpacks.'

The night is humid, thunder growls in the distant hills. It isn't the thunder that stops me from sleeping; or the humidity. The thoughts buzzing around in my brain are the reason I'm still awake: my God, she's Iranian, is this a trick to rob us, kidnap us, blow us up? Stupid I know, but the newspapers back home are full of bulletins about ayatollahs and terrorists, I try to take everything I read with a pinch of salt and throw the salt away but it's difficult not to be affected.

Then Ailsa, sleeping top to toe with me in the double bed, moves in her sleep and I think of the first night she spent in my

MONKEY ON MY ROOF

room. I was a stranger to her. She must have been just as scared, but she was wise enough, her mind open enough to trust me, to accept my offer in the spirit it was given. Why should I think any the less of Faezeh? I smile, turn over, go to sleep and dream that I'm flying without wings into Holi; into a rainbow of colours.

*

The three of us breakfast at the German Bakery. Fruit salad, curd and honey, coffee and cake.

We sit with two Dutch boys, gap year students, young lads filled with high ideals and good intentions who are spending a few weeks holidaying before working in an orphanage in Bombay.

Though only twenty years old, Rueben is a giant, built like the proverbial brick outhouse, his pleasantly ugly face lights up as he tells us his plans to teach PE.

'That's if I have any spare time after taking care of all those homeless children,' he says.

His friend AJ in contrast to Rueben is slight, narrow boned, still in that unfinished stage between adolescence and adulthood. He is just eighteen, and hopes to work in the kitchen of the children's home, learn to cook curries Indian style.

'I know you from Palolem,' Rueben tells me.

'Really? I don't remember.'

He smiles, pulls out a digital camera, says, 'Be sure your sins will find you out,' and shows me a shot of myself smoking a hookah in Café Del Mar.

'Oh, so it was you with the camera that night,' I laugh. 'But I wasn't stoned; it was only apple flavoured tobacco in the hookah.'

'What are you doing today?' AJ asks Faezeh.

MONKEY ON MY ROOF

'I have lecture this morning. After lecture I am free,' she says.

'What about you Ailsa?' Rueben says.

'I must check my e-mail. There's a cyber café in the lane behind the German Bakery. It's cheap, ten rupees an hour,' she tells him.

Faezeh turns to Rueben and AJ, 'There's a movie at Sam city later. We could all go.'

'What's on?' Rueben asks.

'An Indian comedy,' she says. 'Don't have to know the language to enjoy.'

MONKEY ON MY ROOF

28

Last night all over Pune bonfires burnt in memory of Prahlad's escape from Holika the fire demon. Today is the last full moon day of the winter months, the beginning of Holi.

Hindus call the day before the Holi festival Choti Holi, or Little Holi.

Everybody feels it's their right to enjoy the Spring Festival. Holi knows no impediments. Songs, dance, drinks, food, fun. Life is multi-coloured when it's Holi time.

'Those Indian boys won't get another chance to cop a feel until Holi next year,' says a Sanyasin in a maroon robe.

The German Bakery is heaving; Indians mingle with Europeans of all designs and dimensions. Then there is Faezeh, Ailsa, Rueben, AJ and me. We are wearing our scruffiest clothes. Faezeh and her friends have been making plans for Holi, so we are prepared. Good job I brought some old clothes with me! AJ and Rueben have bought paints and balloons and we make paint bombs to throw.

As the oldest person here I open the festivities by sprinkling the coloured dyes over Faezeh, Ailsa and the Dutch boys. And then 'Hai Holi, Holi Hai,' the singing starts. Out in the street Indian women throw buckets of coloured water, painting vivid cotton saris even more vividly. Pink, purple, orange, yellow, red, blue dyes quarrel or harmonise with the existing tints. Everyone is dancing, playing with colours, some of the craftier youngsters have filled water pistols with the dyes and there is no escape. We are covered from head to toe in all shades of the rainbow, plus a few other colours which might have come from somewhere else in the solar system. Ailsa and the Dutch boys are

MONKEY ON MY ROOF

just as colourful. The fun goes on for hours.

Around four o'clock — wondering if the conductor will allow us on — we stand at the bus stop. The driver and the bus conductor are both covered in dye, 'Never mind, it's Holi!' the conductor smiles.

Another wonderful day.

*

On Thursday, Ailsa and I are off to Matheran with the Dutch boys. Faezeh won't be able to come with us, she has a college exam. We've finally managed to cut through the Indian head-nodding and red tape and get train tickets. We will catch the six-thirty train to Neral Junction, then the toy train up the mountains.

Matheran is a small Indian Hill Station, which according to the Lonely Planet is very quiet and peaceful. No vehicles of any kind are allowed within the town, no cars, vans, wagons or motorbikes. The only transport is man-drawn rickshaws and ponies. It's likely that we will be the only Europeans because Matheran isn't on the tourist trail. Sounds like heaven after the madness of Pune!

MONKEY ON MY ROOF

29

A toy train is meant to carry passengers up the hill between Neral Junction and Matheran, but the track has been washed away by the monsoon. In the heat of the sun we walk nine kilometres up a hill steeper than any mountain in Britain, and stagger into the first hotel we come to.

The hotel is pleasant, set on a hill at the side of the forest. A courtyard contains the usual tables, sun umbrellas and chairs, and there is a play area with garden swings and ping-pong tables. Monkeys are everywhere. They swing from the trees, stand on the balconies to peer through windows, jump up and down on the roofs. A row of washbasins set up in the courtyard holds monkeys' drinking water from the taps. They are clever enough to turn the taps on, but can't be bothered to turn them off.

'Keep your doors and windows closed,' the owner tells us.

'Why?' AJ asks.

'Monkeys come in rooms. Steal your things.'

Ailsa and I dump our bags in our room, sit outside at a table and order toast, marmalade and coffee. The boys settle for chapattis with tomato sauce. A monkey swinging between two trees snatches AJ's chapatti and grabs the bottle of ketchup.

His face a study of surprised delight, AJ shakes his fist and shouts, 'Hey, that's mine!'

The monkey seats itself on a branch of the tree, shakes the bottle of ketchup, unscrews the top, chucks the bottle top over his shoulder and pours ketchup on the chapatti.

Rueben is convulsed with laughter.

'Too clever, this monkey,' Ailsa says.

'Definitely a candidate for MENSA,' I tell her.

MONKEY ON MY ROOF

I pass my plate to AJ. 'Here! Have some of my toast.'

The monkey grins and chatters at us as it eats the chapatti.

We leave the monkey to enjoy his ill-gotten gains and walk through the trees to the unpaved track that leads to the town. A rickshaw passes, one man straining his back to pull, two others at the back pushing to stop it slipping back down the hill. On a parallel path among the trees a line of black, grey and roan horses canter. Scarlet blankets embroidered in gold with the names of their owners lie under the horses' saddles. Young, handsome men sit straight-backed in the saddles, they sing as they ride.

*

The Union bank is the only one in Matheran. Stepping inside is like entering a time warp. White-washed walls going a bit grubby, a fan turning lazily on the ceiling, grimy wood- grained floorboards that stick to my shoes as I walk. A desk behind a dark wooden counter where the manager sits. The counter is open to the public; no security screens get between the smiling tellers and their clients. This is how banks must have been in England in times past. In times more innocent. The manager invites me behind the counter, pulls out a chair for me to sit, and sends one of the tellers to fetch chai.

'Aren't you afraid of bank robbers?' I ask him.

He shrugs and smiles, 'How would they get away?'

'Well yes,' I say, 'being three thousand feet up a mountain without any transport would make that a bit difficult!'

There isn't any network coverage for my mobile up here in Matheran. The manager lends me his mobile while he sorts out the paper work. I text Mark to let him know I'll be out of reach for the

MONKEY ON MY ROOF

next ten days.

Outside at the ice cream parlour AJ and Rueben say they want to trek to Shivaji's Ladder and Charlotte Lake. While they're gone, Ailsa and I hit a few shops, then we hire a rickshaw to take us to Porcupine Point.

*

Back at the hotel, the mattresses in the room I share with Ailsa smell of stale urine. The one I am sleeping on is so solid that each time I turn over, a corner of it rears up and whacks me on the backside. Ailsa is just as uncomfortable. Soundproofing is not a priority in this hotel; the walls are so thin we can hear Rueben and AJ snoring in the next room. Neither of us sleeps too well.

Next morning Rueben and AJ leave for Bombay, so Ailsa and I are looking for another hotel. We find a pretty place at the very top of the hill. Long, low wooden terraces face each other across flower gardens tended by Dalit women; a veranda with benches set under the windows runs the full length of each terrace. The rooms are clean and bright with comfortable beds.

Two women run the hotel; this makes Ailsa happy. It worries her that some of the waiters in our previous hotel had been looking at her lustfully.

We unpack and go outside to sit on one of the mosaic-topped benches set against our room. On a platform to my right an Indian man sits on a small terrace. He stands and stretches, big muscular body, long, curly red hair, a broad, fleshy face. The kind of face which, if painted blue, wouldn't look out of place impersonating a God in a Hindi movie. He is staring at Ailsa. There's no mistaking the look of sexual intensity on his face.

MONKEY ON MY ROOF

'Hello, I'm Jerry Junior,' he says.

Ailsa, who has been facing the other way talking to one of the women gardeners, hadn't seen him until now. She gives a screech of alarm, and murmurs, 'If he's Junior I wouldn't like to meet his big brother.'

Carrying a bottle in one hand, Jerry Junior bounds down the steps. 'Have a drink. Have some port.'

The invitation is aimed at me but his eyes are pointed in Ailsa's direction.

Ailsa keeps *her* eyes downcast and shakes her head. 'No way!'

'Thanks, but we don't drink alcohol,' I tell him.

'Port is not alcohol,' he says.

I laugh, 'Who are you trying to kid? I wasn't born yesterday.'

Ailsa edges past him and goes in the room.

Jerry's eyes follow her. 'What wrong with her?'

'She's tired. It's been a long day.'

He looks me up and down, 'I like older women.'

My patience is wearing thin, 'Oh you do, do you?' I say. 'Well this older woman isn't interested. Now sod off and leave us alone.'

Looking for the entire world like a little boy, Jerry Junior hangs his head in apology, 'I'm sorry. I'm sorry!'

Despite his size, he is nothing but a big pussycat!

Earlier, in the market place, I had bought a brightly woven friendship bracelet, intending to give it to Ailsa. My fingers creep into my pocket of their own accord to wrap around it.

I can always buy Ailsa another.

Taking the bracelet from my pocket I say, 'Okay, okay, no need to cry. I accept your apology.'

MONKEY ON MY ROOF

He watches solemnly as I tie the bracelet around his wrist, 'Now I am your brother.'

'Yes,' I say, 'so you have to behave yourself!'

Jerry Junior has become a friend.

MONKEY ON MY ROOF

30

For the last few days, Jerry and his friend have been showing Ailsa and me around the local beauty spots. We view Vishalgad and Prabal forts at Louisa Point where a waterfall cascades majestically through mystic forest. Monkey Point is crowded with red-and-black-faced monkeys. The four of us shout our names into the pure fresh air and listen to our voices echoing back one, two, three, seven times, becoming softer and fainter until finally fading away into silence.

On Mahatma Gandhi Road, Jerry waves and calls, 'Hello, bousarn, how goes it?' to the men sitting outside the shops and ice cream parlours.

'What does bousarn mean?' I ask Jerry.

Jerry and his friend speak at the same time.

'It means friend,' says Jerry.

'Brother, it means brother,' his friend says.

This word "bousarn" is not hard to pronounce, it's simple for me to call a greeting when Ailsa is off trekking and I walk alone. The men sitting outside the shops laugh delightedly when I smile and pronounce my new word.

This morning, breakfast in the dining room, coffee and chapattis with Jerry's sister and mother.

Jerry comes in, 'Hi bousarn, how are you today?' I say.

His mother gasps and drops her coffee cup.

'Sally!' Jerry's sister is shocked. 'Do you know what that word means?'

'Oh Dear God,' Ailsa shoulders are shaking in that familiar signal which means she's trying not to laugh, 'whatever have you been saying?'

MONKEY ON MY ROOF

'Oh! Er...Friend? Brother?' I say hopefully, I'm cringing inside.

Jerry's sister shakes her head, 'Who taught you to say that?'

Their mother gets up and leaves the room.

I look pointedly at Jerry.

'My brother is a very naughty boy,' Maria glares at Jerry who is sneaking quietly towards the door.

'What does it mean?'

Maria shakes her head again.

'Tell me what it means,' I insist, 'I'm entitled to know. I'm the person who's been using it all over Matheran.'

Blushing and embarrassed, Maria mumbles something about sperm at the bottom of a condom before it is thrown away!

*

The unpaved path is lined with trees and infested with monkeys. Monkeys can smell a banana from a hundred yards. Every day, no matter how careful we are to wrap our fruit in newspaper, we get mugged. This morning, dressed in our oldest jeans and off-white tee shirts, Ailsa and I are prepared for them. However, the monkeys are curiously absent, scared away by the noise of drums and bugles from men dressed in red khurtas — a sort of long collarless tunic type shirt.

Behind this band of musicians, his eyes heavily outlined in kohl, a barefoot young man — cream coloured satin Mughal suit embroidered in gold, enormous jewel flashing in the centre of a cream satin turban — rides a white horse. But this isn't any old horse. This large, haughtily strutting, four-legged equine is a wedding horse. Every hair on his silvery coat shines in the sunlight;

MONKEY ON MY ROOF

all four hooves are polished to ebon black. A richly embroidered blanket hangs below a saddle and bridle ornately decorated in red and gold.

The rider is the groom. We stand and watch as two men lift the groom down from the horse and carry him shoulder-high inside the marquee.

'His feet mustn't touch the ground,' a man close by tells us.

Two women making their way inside see us watching, 'Come join the wedding,' the younger one says.

'We're not dressed for a wedding,' I reply.

'No matter,' the older woman says. 'Everyone is welcome, please come.'

'Yes Sally,' Ailsa says, and pulls me by the hand. 'Come on,' she's laughing, 'don't be a fuddy-duddy.'

Inside the marquee, rows of chairs face a stage. A fire is burning in a brazier on the stage, and the bride and groom are sitting cross-legged facing one another. Small beads of sweat sit on the groom's face. The bride is dressed in red and gold, I can't see her face, a veil covers it; but sitting beside that fire her face must be as red as her dress.

Ailsa and me are given packets of coloured rice and shown to a seat. Thinking the rice to be small sweets I start to tear the packet open.

A woman sitting to my right nudges me, 'Not yet,' she says. 'You throw rice when the sadhu comes.'

'How will we know when to throw?'

'Watch what I do,' our neighbour tells us.

The sadhu (priest) arrives, prayers are said in Sanskrit. Everyone throws rice. The bride and groom place garlands of flowers around each other's necks. The sadhu ties their hands

MONKEY ON MY ROOF

together with a silk scarf.

Intoning a mantra, the couple stand and walk around the fire brazier.

'This is Agni which is holy fire,' the woman sitting next to me says.

Ailsa asks, 'What are they saying?'

'He is telling how much he loves her.'

The bride's veil is lifted, she looks solemn and scared. The groom is smiling; he places a gold necklace around her neck. They are still walking around the sacred fire; I lose count after the fifth circuit.

After the ceremony, ice cream and cakes are served. Amid much frivolity, the bride and groom are taken out to sit in a rickshaw. The drums and bugles start up again, men and boys dance suggestively, twisting their torsos, thrusting their groins in front of the rickshaw as it is pulled around the town.

Ailsa stares after them, 'The bride looks terrified,' she murmurs.

'The music and dancing will go on all night,' the woman who had been sitting next to me says, 'the rickshaw will be pulled around town all through the night.'

'All night?'

'Yes, it makes good luck for potency.'

'Potency!' I protest. 'Those poor kids will be too exhausted to procreate!'

*

However, I'm wrong about that, because this morning, like a blueprint of the young girl's virginity, a buoyant banner, a white

MONKEY ON MY ROOF

sheet spotted with blood hangs from the window of a house at the side of the path.

MONKEY ON MY ROOF

31

At Neral Junction the train only stops for a few minutes, there isn't time for us to find our carriage. Helplessly we watch as the train starts to pull away from the platform. A tiny woman; no more than four foot six and three quarters, jumps down from a coach, grabs our bags, chucks them on the train then grabs me with one hand and Ailsa with the other and chucks us after them. She tows us over the baskets of fish and fruit that always seem to stand in the passageway of Indian trains and hauls us into the nearest carriage.

In the next carriage men are peering lecherously through rusty iron bars streaked with rusty blue paint eyeing the women.

A woman occupies every seat in the carriage we have been dragged to.

The tiny woman pushes us into a seat and sits down next to me.

'You'll be safe here,' a young woman holding a baby that looks about six months old says from the seat opposite, 'this is the Ladies Carriage.'

'What a good idea,' I say, 'what a pity we don't have the same thing in England.'

One of the women asks us where we have been staying.

The tiny woman who chucked us on the train understands more English then she speaks, and points to Ailsa's sandaled feet, which are stained red, 'Matheran. Matheran!'

Matheran is famous for its red dust.

Another woman points at my hair, still speckled with pink, purple, green and blue dye.

'Holi. Holi!' the little woman says.

Everyone laughs — even the men listening through the bars

MONKEY ON MY ROOF

of the fenced-off carriage.

Snacks and fruit are passed around. I end up clutching the baby with one hand while trying to peel a banana with the other. The baby is nuzzling at my breast. 'Hey up,' I say, 'you'll get nothing from that. The well's run dry.'

Once again everyone laughs.

'Let me hold him,' Ailsa says.

She takes the baby from me cradles his head on her arm, the baby stops nuzzling and looks up at her with that wise old man stare some young children have. In one of those rare unforgettable moments, Ailsa and the baby's glances meet in perfect accord. The child frowns as if to say, "I know you from somewhere," and falls asleep.

Attention caught by this tableau, the rest of us hold our breath. The carriage is silent, finally one of the women asks, 'Do you have children?'

'No,' Ailsa says softly, 'but I love this one.'

'When you have your own child you'll be a perfect mother,' one of the older women says.

'Thank you,' Ailsa answers gravely. She doesn't tell them that she'll never be able to have children of her own, and it's not my place to inform them of that fact. Looking at her holding the child I can't help admiring her guts.

Half an hour later, the railway carriage is alive with good-humoured bantering and laughter.

A loudspeaker blares, gobbledygook gobbledygook...

It's always hard to understand loudspeaker gibberish. Never more so than on railway trains. I strain my ears, but if the announcement had been in English it would still have been Double Dutch to me. A woman sitting on my left gasps and lifts both hands

MONKEY ON MY ROOF

up to her face.

The laughter stops.

'What did they say?'

'A bomb,' one of the women says, 'we must get off train. It finish at Dadar station.'

Dadar is the station before the one Ailsa and I need!

'Let's hope this is only a scare, a false alarm,' I say, thinking of the damage I'd seen bombs do in Delhi.

After the cool hills of Matheran, Mumbai is sweltering, the air stifling. We wander around the roads until we find a police post. The policeman asks our destination, and notes my mobile number. He hails a taxi, writes down its number plate and tells us to phone him when we reach our hotel. He'll be checking that we've reached it safely he says.

MONKEY ON MY ROOF

<u>32</u>

The hotel is the grottiest I have ever seen, but *it is cheap*; two hundred and fifty rupees per night.

Anke, the German woman we met on the train to Pune, is here already, staying on the floor above us. We arrange to meet for dinner around seven o'clock. We will be staying in the same hotel for a few days before we go our separate ways.

There's an air conditioning unit fitted in the window of our room. I turn the AC on, switch it to the coolest setting; the unit explodes spectacularly and I jump back as a flame shoots towards me narrowly missing my face. Dense black smoke along with millions of tiny red winged insects fill the room. The flame dies away quickly, but the insects cling to the walls, the bed, my hair; they are up my nose, in my ears. The black smoke billows around my face, gets in my eyes and blinds me. Deaf and blind, fringe and eyebrows singed, I stagger back and fall on the bed screaming.

My screams bring the manager to our door, 'What happen?' he asks.

'Your bloody AC unit blew up,' Ailsa says, 'what kind of hotel is this that the AC units blow up. Doesn't anyone ever clean this place?'

'Is very good hotel,' he answers in injured tones, 'top class hotel. Win many awards for cleanliness.'

This statement is so blatantly false that it makes us laugh, 'Maybe the cockroaches and rats agree with you,' Ailsa tells him.

He shrugs.

I gesture at the beds, which are covered with dead and wounded insects, 'Well what are you going to do about it? We can't sleep here.'

MONKEY ON MY ROOF

'I find you another room.'

'Please make sure it's clean,' Ailsa says.

He nods, and calls a room boy.

The room boy tells us that there's an internet café two doors up from the hotel. We can check our e-mails while our room is being cleaned.

Matheran with its clean pure air and mountain trails had been a sorely needed haven. An escape from the modern world, a distraction from the constant harassment of internet and mobile phones. Yet Ailsa and I have come to realise that being out of touch with family and friends is more a disadvantage than an advantage.

At the cyber café, we settle ourselves at the chipped Formica desks

A whole string of e-mails awaits my attention.

There are three from Mark.

He's booked his plane ticket, obtained his visa and will be arriving in Nepal the week after me. Mark is determined to trek to Everest base camp despite my warnings about the constant stream of TV and press news telling of riots in Nepal

I reply and tell him there is still a lot of trouble in Nepal but I will meet him at the airport.

Beside me, Ailsa is talking animatedly to Greg on Skype.

My daughters have e-mailed wanting to know where I am and what I'm up to. I write a round robin describing Matheran and saying I'm on my way to Nepal, and send it to each of them.

The French girl I met in Palolem has sent two e-mails, she says her Nepalese boyfriend will not talk about their relationship, but he has asked her to go to Kathmandu and meet his mother.

It's always difficult to get men to talk their feelings through I reply, but asking you to go to Nepal and meet his mother must

MONKEY ON MY ROOF

show that he cares in a big way. Take the advice Gosh gives out, I say: sit back and watch the movie.

An e-mail from the Irishman who stayed in the room next to me tells me not to worry about internet in Nepal. It's cheaper and far more widespread than in India, he writes; but mobile phones are not so clever, because the king plays God sometimes with the communications.

I reply with a thank you.

Back at the hotel, our new room isn't much better than the first. I eye the AC unit with one eye and the ceiling fan with the other and debate whether to find another hotel.

Ailsa notices me looking at the AC unit; she grins and crosses her eyes, 'Why don't you switch it on, Sally?'

'No way am I risking what's left of my eyebrows,' I tell her, 'the fan will have to do.'

Then Anke arrives to show us the way to the restaurant.

Outside, murky pollution has bruised the sky yellow, black and blue. Traffic whizzes past, cows, people running dodging cars, lorries and rickshaws. Blue haze of exhaust fumes, constant blowing of horns, dogs barking, the smell of burning incense mingling with the stink of shit from a rubbish cart as it trundles past.

On the broken pavement a line of wheelbarrows are selling spices, fruit and vegetables. Behind them, neon signs shout "VENUS" and "CUPID" above the doors of bars. No prizes for guessing the kind of patrons these bars cater for! This district might be nothing like the tourist hot spots in Colaba district with its shops, restaurants and massage parlours, but men here still have to fulfil their desires.

Very few westerners are to be found in this part of Mumbai.

MONKEY ON MY ROOF

An old woman, a fruit seller, leaves her barrow and shyly touches my arm; she giggles behind her hand, and says something in the local language.

A man walking past tells me, 'She touches you to bring her good fortune.'

I smile at the fruit seller.

My mother would take my sister and me to catch the bus to the Pier Head to take the Royal Daffodil or Royal Iris ferry across the Mersey River to New Brighton. She would point to the sailors and tell us that if we touched the backs of sailors' collars it would bring us good luck.

There was never any shortage of sailors, or their collars, in the port of Liverpool when I was growing up, but the jury is still out on whether touching their collars ever brought me any luck.

Putting my hands together I say, 'Namaste, Didi. Good luck to you.'

Didi, older sister. A word of respect. Though it's likely she is much younger than me.

Anke squeezes the old woman's hand for a moment.

She has a nice way about her, this Anke, a lovely warm smile. It draws people to her.

Back at our grotty hotel, we say goodbye to Anke. She goes to her room to pack her suitcase and pay her bill; in two hours, she leaves for the airport. Home to Berlin.

MONKEY ON MY ROOF

33

Next morning the taxi driver we've hired takes us on a tour of Mumbai. At the Mahatma Gandhi house in Laburnum Road, we look at the pictures and statues, read the framed letters on the walls, letters Gandhi wrote to Churchill, Hitler, and Roosevelt imploring them to stop the war. Then it's to the Tower of Silence where the Parsees leave their dead to be devoured by vultures. The taxi driver tells us that the vultures are dying with some kind of disease; fewer and fewer vultures come to the Tower of Silence.

'It make big problem for Parsees,' he says.

At the Gateway to India, we take photos, debate whether or not to go to Elephanta Island. Decide to take one of the small motor launches for a trip around the harbour for a couple of hours. Then we walk up the magnificent central staircase in the Taj Mahal Hotel to have high tea in the Sea Lounge.

According to legend, Jama Tata — the richest man in Bombay — was so incensed when he was refused admission to Watsons Hotel — which was restricted to whites only — that he vowed to build a hotel where people of all nationalities and colours would be welcome. He's succeeded spectacularly.

What a place!

There are no words to describe the luxury we see all around us. The tables in the Sea Lounge are all filled. Black, brown, yellow and white people sit together talking and laughing.

As Tata wanted. As it should be.

A pianist tinkles the keys of a grand piano. He plays semi-classical music as the waiter brings sandwiches, cakes and scones to our table.

'So much food,' Ailsa says.

MONKEY ON MY ROOF

'Make sure you eat it all up,' I tell her, 'this is going to cost an arm and a leg.'

Gazing at the white tablecloth, which is set with more cutlery than I have ever seen before, I can't resist saying to the waiter, 'I'm hard pressed to know if I should eat my cakes with a knife and spoon or fork, or stuff them in my mouth sideways.'

'Don't you dare,' Ailsa says, but she's smiling when she says it.

When the bill arrives, it's for the same price as a week's lodging in Palolem.

Back at our hotel Ailsa tells me she doesn't want me to come to the airport, and when I protest, she takes both my hands in hers, 'No Sally! No Sally! We will both end up in tears. I don't want you to remember me with tears on my face, and I don't want to see your tears.'

I watch as she folds tee shirts into her suitcase, 'Promise me you'll write,' she says, 'send lots of e-mails.'

I nod, 'Yes if you like.'

She folds the blue silk shirt she'd bought from the market in Chaudi, 'I want to know where you go, what you do.'

'I promise.'

I follow her downstairs when she goes to the reception desk to pay her bill.

Nothing on this earth can stop me from walking down the steps of the Hotel to catch a last glimpse of her and wave goodbye as her taxi speeds her away. Home to Scotland, home to Greg.

It's eight o'clock and I'm starting to feel hungry. Cakes are all very well, but they let you down after a couple of hours. The restaurant I ate at last night might not be the Taj Mahal but the food is good. I'll have dinner there.

The old lady who touched my sleeve for luck is still on the

MONKEY ON MY ROOF

roadside selling fruit. When all her fruit is sold or packed away she'll be sleeping there tonight; her charpai is stashed under the wheelbarrow. Charpai — a kind of bed, four short legs, a sagging woven fibre base attached to the frame, no mattress or pillow.

The old woman smiles at me, 'Namaste.'

I smile back at her as I walk past; then a few yards further on remember that tomorrow I leave for Kathmandu. Will breakfast be available at the hotel? Maybe not! It might be a good idea to buy some fruit. Leaning on the walking stick that Ailsa bought me — I carry it with me everywhere I go whether I need it or not — I turn back, take my shoulder bag from my shoulder with the intention of taking out my purse.

The pavement is crowded. A man in his twenties is coming towards me. Seeing me he breaks into a run. I'm not alarmed; it isn't unusual in Bombay to see men running in the cool of the evening.

Then...

'Whaaa...'

The running man has snatched my bag from out of my hand! Now he's dodging through people on the pavement.

Adrenalin kicks in, flooding my body with heat; my passport, money, plane tickets are all in that bag! I can't let him get away with it! A group of teenagers fall out of a bar slowing him down. Holding it by the spike, I stretch my walking stick out as far as it will go, snag his ankle with the hook. Holding the stick with both hands...I HEAVE.

The thief crashes to the floor in front of the old woman's wheelbarrow and drops my bag.

The old woman picks it up.

Lying on the pavement the thief yells, 'Leg is broken, leg is

145

MONKEY ON MY ROOF

broken! I want compensation!'

'Compensation!' I say, and raise my walking stick, 'No chance! You're lucky not to get a thrashing.'

A crowd is gathering; most of them just arrived. They haven't seen what happened, haven't seen him steal my bag. What they *have* seen is one of their own lying injured on the pavement with a foreigner standing over him holding a stick.

The old woman with the wheelbarrow is trying to tell what happened but the shouts from the thief drown her voice out.

The thief shouts again that his leg is broken, that he wants compensation.

People in the crowd are eyeing me with hostility, I try to push through but they're closing in on me. The situation is getting out of hand.

Desperately I raise my voice, 'Compensation,' I say, 'You'll get compensation when I call the police. You thief, you dog, you, you, you Bousarn!'

Suddenly everyone in the crowd is laughing.

It's that word that does the trick, the swear word I learned in Matheran from Jerry Junior. The crowd think it hysterically funny coming from the mouth of a foreign woman.

The thief gets to his feet.

'Nothing wrong with your leg, bousarn,' I call after him as he slinks away.

The old fruit seller and I smile at one another as she hands me my shoulder bag.

I buy apples and bananas, 'My luck was in when you touched me,' I tell her.

She doesn't speak English, but she has no trouble understanding the five hundred rupee tip I hand her for her help.

MONKEY ON MY ROOF

*

In the restaurant, head bent, I study the menu which is hand-written on a piece of cardboard. I'm sitting at the same table as last night. Apart from clutching my bag tighter against my shoulder, I take no notice when someone sits down opposite me.

After a while he speaks, 'Can I have the menu when you've finished with it.'

There's no mistaking that faint Welsh lilt or the touch of surprise in his voice.

I can feel myself blushing like a teen-age girl as I exclaim, 'Stephan!'

'Hello, Sally! What are you doing here?'

'I thought you'd left Mumbai,' I try to keep my voice cool, but the smile on my face betrays me. 'Never mind me. What are you doing here?'

Stephan is smiling back at me. His smile tells me that he is as pleased to see me as I am to bump into him. 'I eat here most days,' he says, 'the children's home I help out at is only two streets away. How long are you here for?'

'My visa expires in a couple of days so I'm off to Nepal in the morning to renew it.'

He takes my hand, curls his fingers around mine, 'Nepal! Really? Is that wise? It's getting to be dangerous with the rioting there,' he says.

There's a sense of satisfaction on hearing the note of concern in his voice, seeing the look of worry on his face.

'I know,' I say. 'But my husband arrives there next week. He's planning to trek to Everest base camp.'

MONKEY ON MY ROOF

'Your husband!'

'It was a last minute decision of Mark's,' I say. 'Didn't you know I was married?'

'No. I thought you were joking.'

'Doug should have told you.'

He shakes his head, 'I assumed... because you're travelling alone...'

'I need this year for myself.'

Need it so that I can understand the things going wrong in my life, going wrong in my marriage, going wrong in myself.

'One year only out of more than thirty, is that too much to ask?'

Stephan takes my hand again, 'No, of course it isn't.'

'But I've already had six months, and another six to come,' I say miserably, 'so how can I begrudge Mark his few weeks holiday?'

'You can't,' Stephan says. He squeezes my hand, 'All you can do is to sit back and watch the movie.'

Our food arrives. We smile at each other, he lets go of my hand. We eat in silence. Then he escorts me along the road. On the steps of the hotel, he kisses my cheek when he says goodbye. In my room, I stand in front of the mirror.

Stephan's kiss is etched on my cheek. I lift a hand to touch it.

It tingles all night.

My mobile plays its little tune, Ailsa is calling. 'Thought I'd give you a ring,' she says,' I'm stuck in Frankfurt for the next two hours while we change planes.'

'Poor you! What a drag.'

'What you up to?'

'Nothing much, just been saying goodbye to Stephan.'

MONKEY ON MY ROOF

'Stephan?' she says. 'What's he doing there?'

'Helping out at an orphanage around the corner.'

'Now isn't that handy?' she says. 'The Stephan from the party. The Stephan who turned up at the German Bakery in Pune.' There's a smile in her voice, 'How long has this been going on?'

'There's nothing going on, as you put it. We just keep bumping into each another.'

'Really?' she says sardonically, 'You just keep bumping into each other?'

'Yeah,' I protest picturing her crossing her eyes in that comic way she has, 'nothing planned... not by either of us.'

'Really,' she says again. 'And are you sure it's not accidentally on purpose?'

MONKEY ON MY ROOF

PART TWO

INDIA - HIMALAYA SUNSET

Scratched on the stony windows of the sky
To rasp rough music from sun-singing space,
You turn your brutal backs and ice-cold lie
To tempt the next contenders in the chase,
Content to know that maybe they will die
Where avalanche and snowfall leave no trace
In ice, crevassed – they come to satisfy
That passion that your siren call inspires.
Let not some paltry man-made box enclose.
Their bones. Peaks, ridges, pinnacles and spires
Are epitaphs enough for those who chose
To turn their feet away from cottage fires.
They went where sunset turns your peaks to rose
And darkness cannot quench man's bold desires.

© David Lythgoe

MONKEY ON MY ROOF

34

3rd April 2006
Dear Ailsa,
By now you will have arrived home, unpacked your stuff, hugged Greg until he screams for mercy, and done your shopping. At this very moment, you are most likely slouched on the settee in front of the fire with a glass of wine in one hand and a slice of haggis in the other singing, "I belong to Glasgow, dear old Glasgow town."

What was that you said in Bombay? Oh yes! 'Promise you'll write,' you said, 'send lots of e-mails!'

Of course, you've never been to Nepal, so just to completely wind you up I'm going to tell you all about it. Don't say you didn't ask for it.

So: Kathmandu airport such as it is… just like Manchester airport — but more exotic-looking with armed soldiers on guard. The Nepalese only give tourists a two months visa. Mark will be here for six weeks so a two-month visa will have to do us both.

The pollution is appalling, worse than Bombay. Thick yellow smog hiding the stars, making them invisible in the black night sky. There was only one taxi at the rank, and the driver was asleep. I woke him up and told him to take me to the Lotus Guest house right by the Boudhanath Stupa, which Gosh my Reiki master told me is a holy Buddhist temple.

'No madam, no madam. Is too far,' he grumbled sleepily. 'I take you to hotel in Thamel.'

Thamel, the district where the Nepalese king lives in his pink palace. The district of hotels, shops and restaurants where foreign tourists can spend their money. A hotel in Thamel is bound to be expensive.

MONKEY ON MY ROOF

Taxi drivers earn commission for taking tourists to certain hotels. Even though I'm ridden with guilt at begrudging those few rupees when he has so little, lives so poorly, I told him, 'No, my guesthouse is booked. Boudhanath is not so far.'

'Where is your husband?' he asked.

That question again!

'My husband is waiting for me at the Lotus Guest House in Boudhanath,' I answered. Okay so I told a lie! But come on; it's more a fib than an outright lie. Mark *is* arriving in a couple of days.

'Lotus Guest house. I not know this place.'

No way was I going to let that driver escape! Do you blame me? This was the only taxi around. Might not be another for hours.

'That's okay, I have a map,' I said firmly. 'The Lotus is behind the monastery at the Stupa.'

At last he opened the door got out of the taxi; said hopefully, 'Is double fare night-time?'

Happy and excited to be in Nepal, not bothering to barter, not minding that he was ripping me off, I handed the taxi driver my suitcase jumped in the back seat said, 'Okay! Challo, let's go.'

It might surprise you to know that cabbies in Kathmandu don't take a test to get "The Knowledge" the way cabbies do in London; and the driver got completely lost!

We drove for a long time around the dusty unpaved streets. Rats scampered over the bodies of beggars who had curled up to sleep on the broken, rubbish-filled pavements. When my driver stopped to ask directions from one of these beggars, my fertile imagination had the two of them in league with the Maoists. By the time the security guard at The Lotus Guest House had opened the big metal gates for the taxi to drive into the courtyard, I'd seen myself kidnapped, beaten, raped, ransomed, killed, and cremated!

MONKEY ON MY ROOF

Not necessarily in that order.

Inside the courtyard — in complete contrast to the streets outside — a terraced garden with flower beds and green lawns shone clean and neat in the moonlight. The taxi driver lifted my case from the trunk, I paid him three hundred Nepalese Rupees — about Two Pounds fifty in English currency, so he hadn't ripped me off — and a monk appeared to show me to my room. This Guesthouse is part of the monastery run by Buddhist Monks.

I can hear you laughing all the way from Scotland! Who would have thought it, eh; me, Sally, ending up in a monastery. Still it's better than a nunnery I suppose.

My room is lovely, a carpeted floor, two soft beds with bedside tables and big fluffy duvets, a wardrobe, a TV on a stand — satellite TV in Buddhist monasteries, whatever next? Pretty curtains hang at the windows, even in the bathroom.

No need for me to hang a towel over the window to stop people looking in. Not a bit like our bathroom in Matheran. How could we ever forget Jerry Junior peering at you through the window as you stood on a chair to hang a towel over it? 'That'll stop the barmpot,' you said, 'I catch him watching me taking a shower again, and he'll be walking round with a Glasgae smile.'

The bathroom is tiled in pink, with a washbasin, and shower. Best of all — Oh thank you, God — there's a western toilet with a proper seat and a lid! I won't have to squat over a stinking hole in the ground!

Hugs from Sally X

*

MONKEY ON MY ROOF

5th April 2006
Dear Ailsa,
The sky this morning is blue, the sun is shining, the temperature a lovely seventy-five degrees Fahrenheit. The street outside — which though kind of smelly doesn't seem to me to be as dirty as it was the night before — has a medieval feel to it, an atmosphere of times gone past.

When I walked through the gate which leads to the Great Stupa, I could feel the whole of my body, from the soles of my feet to the top of my head, opening in a smile. I'm going to like it here!

According to legend, the Stupa contains the remains of Kashyapa Buddha — whoever he was, there are so many Buddhas around I've lost count! Multi-coloured prayer flags flutter around the dome. A central tower topped with a kind of umbrella with a frill around its bottom has the avatar's eyes painted on all four sides. The eyes follow me as I do a Kora, a meditation walk three times clockwise around the Stupa — this is such a zany place! Red robed Buddhist monks spinning prayer wheels walk one hundred and eight times around the Stupa, while other monks, in red robes and with shaven heads, sit at tables outside cafés taking photos and talking into mobile phones. Tibetan men and women prostrate themselves reverently on the flagged ground. And Nepalese women — who seem much more emancipated than Indian women — give the eye back to Nepalese men.

The roof top terrace at the Stupa View Restaurant was crowded. I parked myself in a spare seat next to a Buddhist monk and ordered fruit salad and toast for breakfast.

The monk smiled at me.

Private citizen or monk, there's nothing in the world to make a person feel loved and welcome like a smile from a Tibetan Buddhist.

MONKEY ON MY ROOF

'Where you from?' the monk asked.

'I'm English, by way of India.'

'Now you by way of Boudhanath,' he said.

We sat and looked at the view of the Stupa and he explained how it embodies all of the four elements. The base signifies the earth, he said, the dome is water, the spire symbolises fire, the umbrella represents the air we breathe.

He didn't ask, "Where is your husband?" but I found myself telling him that Mark would be arriving in a couple of days.

'He's planning to walk to Everest Base Camp,' I said. 'I'm so worried. My husband isn't getting any younger, and given his age I think he's being a bit ambitious.'

The monk smiled serenely and told me, 'His holiness say: "Happiness is not ready-made. It comes from your own actions."'

'His Holiness also says that "not getting what you want is sometimes a wonderful stroke of luck,"' I reminded him.

The monk was surprised, 'You meet Dalai Lama?'

'No, I only read his wise words.'

My anxiety is because of Doug. You know what Doug is like, don't you Ailsa?

Doug told Mark that he had been to Base Camp. "It's so easy," he said, "there's nothing to it. Base Camp is a walk in the park," he said.

And Mark believed him! He hasn't sussed yet that Doug is the biggest bullshitter on this planet, not to say the rest of the universe! Only last year Doug told me how he'd helped the Dalai Lama escape from the Chinese when Tibet was invaded, and how he'd been standing on the steps of the hotel but wasn't quick enough to disarm the man who killed John Lennon.

Given that His Holiness escaped from the Chinese in 1959,

MONKEY ON MY ROOF

that Lennon was shot in 1980, and Doug was born in 1972... do I need to say more? Doug is a lovely guy, I love him to bits, but now I take everything he says with two pounds of salt.

    Wish you were here. Sally X

*

6th April 2006
Hi Sally,
Just a quick mail to let you know that I'm home safe, and missing you already! How long are you staying in Nepal? I want lots and lots of mail from you telling me all about that geriatric gap year you are always joking about! Told Greg all about you, he loves you for the way you took care of me. It's snowing here. Scotland! Snow in April! I miss you and I miss the sun. I have been a bit down lately; I guess this is how it's going to be for a while.

    Lots of love Ailsa.

MONKEY ON MY ROOF

35

So Ailsa's feeling down!
We can't have that now, can we? I type quickly.

6th April 2006
Hi beautiful Ailsa,
Snowing! What is snow? I've forgotten! How are you? Hope you are recovering from the journey and the shock of the cold weather back there in Scotland. It doesn't seem the same without you here snoring in my room. And just to stop you getting too jealous, I thought you might like to know what happened this morning:

5.00AM	Wake up to a monkey running across the roof tiles.
5.01AM	Crows attack monkey, who retaliates by tearing off roof tiles to throw at crows.
5.03AM	Dogs start barking at monkeys and crows.
5.06AM	The guesthouse manager comes out and climbs on roof with firecrackers to scare monkey away. Monkey stops throwing roof tiles at crows and throws them at the manager instead.
5.08AM	The manager climbs back down from roof.
5.10AM	Sacred cow wanders into garden. Dogs stop barking at crows and monkeys to bark at and chase sacred cow.
5.12AM	The manager returns and climbs on roof again. This time he has louder fireworks and it sounds like WW3 has started. Monkeys surrender and leave. Crows fly away. Dogs and cow scarper.
5.14AM	All is quiet, I turn over to go back to sleep.
5.32AM	Bread man parps the horn on his bicycle 45 times in quick succession.

MONKEY ON MY ROOF

5.35AM	Get up and go to loo. Wash a cockroach down plughole in washbasin.
5.50AM	Rescue baby frog from drain in bathroom floor.
5.55AM	Put baby frog out in garden, and am bedazzled by sun rising.
6.00AM	Grope my way back into bedroom, climb longingly back into bed.
6.15AM	Monkeys return to roof, dogs start barking, the manager climbs ladder, etc, etc
6.20AM	Sod it may as well get up.
7.00AM	Sitting alone on sun terrace reading.

It started to rain about half past ten tonight; not a lot, just enough to make me scuttle off away from my guesthouse to this internet café and write to you. Still, I can put up with a few drops of rain now and again when I think of you shivering back there in Glasgow. I wish you could have been here at five'o'clock last night when the manager stopped me as I was going out the gate. I was hurrying to Om Shanti — which is a restaurant just up the street, a rustic place where a curtain hangs Tibetan-fashion over the doorway, rushing to get there while there was still time, before the lopsided wooden tables and chairs filled up...

'Where you going?'

'I'm off to Om Shanti,' I told him.

'Lama Dance in Monastery,' he said, 'very special. You should watch.'

Dinner or Lama Dance?

He stared at me as I dithered, 'Three times you eat each day,' he told me, 'Lama Dance happen only once in ten years.'

I smiled, 'Really? Then there's no contest!.'

MONKEY ON MY ROOF

He ushered me through the monastery gates, fetched a chair.

In the courtyard young monks — little more than boys — sat lotus position in a circle. Inside this circle another was drawn with white chalk, inside that a smaller circle contained four chairs and four figures wearing masks and costumes; they were chanting and singing. An orchestra was formed of men in bright costumes holding drums, pipes and conches.

Tapestry curtains hung over the monastery doors, a figure in costume wearing a gold mask danced through them. Another and another followed him until there were twenty dancers, each one in a different costume and mask.

Some of these dancers were holding spears, others held flags, and several waved swords aloft. They danced on one leg on the white chalk circle, spinning around and around while the people in the centre circle chanted and sang. Drums drummed, pipes played, conches blew, dancers in red, green, purple, orange, yellow, blue and white swirled, spinning, as if in a mandala. Oh Ailsa, I wish you could have been here to see it, it was utterly enthralling.

And I sat there on my chair among those monks in their red robes and wondered which dancer was the Lama? Was it the one in green or the one in blue? Finally, one by one, they danced alone in front of the monastery curtains before disappearing inside.

All except one! He was dressed in red and gold, and was the only dancer to wear black leggings. He danced one-legged around the circle, never a step out of place; and the monks applauded.

I told the manager: 'Thank you, that was well worth missing dinner for.'

He smiled back at me and said 'Ah' to show he understood.

Cheer up Ailsa Darlin, don't allow yourself to get down, sit up and smell the roses.

Love from Sally X

MONKEY ON MY ROOF

36

When I got up on Thursday morning it was to hear my mobile playing its annoying little tune. *At eight in the morning.* I felt like chucking the damn thing on the floor and jumping up and down on it, but couldn't summon up the energy until I'd had my first cup of coffee. Good job I didn't because it was Sheila phoning, 'Surprise! Doug and me are staying in Thamel,' she said. 'Why don't you join us for Nepalese Sunday Lunch?'

'Okay,' I told her, 'See you one o'clockish?'

Sheila and Doug are in Kathmandu to renew their Indian visas, I haven't been expecting to see them in Nepal, but nothing can surprise me after watching that Lama Dance.

It doesn't take long to get to Thamel, but I needed to shower, wash my hair, put on lipstick. A girl has to do what a girl has to do. Trouble is what this girl has to do takes longer as the girl gets older. So I was a bit late starting out, and there was a police cordon across the main road in Thamel. My taxi was stopped, the police officer looked at me, frowned, gestured, said something to the driver, walked away.

'What's happening?' I asked.

'You have to get out, I can't go any further,' the driver said.

'But I don't know the way,' I wailed.

He pointed, 'Go right, past the cordon, cross the road, turn left, then right, then left again. Is not far.'

Did my driver say turn left, then right? Or did he say right, then left? Everything was quiet, no one around to ask. I was in a narrow cobblestoned residential street, all windows and doors closed; and I was completely lost. Not knowing the district; is it so surprising I couldn't find my way to Sheila and Doug's hotel?

MONKEY ON MY ROOF

Stumbling on the cobblestones, I walked around a corner into a square. Suddenly from out of nowhere, the square was full of people. Almost as if waiting for me, a riot broke out, bricks and stones being thrown at armed police in combat gear. The air was thick with tear gas, not to mention the odd bullet!

Nearby was a KLM travel office. I dived through the door. The Nepalese courier grabbed me and pulled me behind the counter to crouch down beside her. We cowered, afraid to pop our heads above the counter for what seems like hours — but was really only about fifteen minutes — until things quietened down.

Then the courier plugged in a kettle, took a tea caddy, tea strainer and mugs from a cupboard, and made tea. We drank tea smiling at one another with relief. After what was happening outside neither of us ever expected to drink another cup of tea again! The courier walked me to the door, and pointed the way to The Blue Horizon Hotel where Sheila and Doug are staying. Outside in the square everything was quiet again. No blood, no broken bodies, just a few stones and bits of brick lying around on the cobbles, and a spent cartridge or two. It looked as if nothing out of the ordinary had happened.

*

9th April 2006
Dear Ailsa,
How's it going with you and Greg back there in sunny Glasgae? Everything ok with you both? Mark was supposed to arrive at ten o'clock yesterday morning, but wouldn't you know it his plane was delayed. A security guard with a rifle showed me the way to a scruffy little café next to the airport; a kind of Nepalese greasy

spoon. I spent four hours sitting there drinking chai with the airport workers and taxi drivers who all thought it hilarious to teach me how to swear in their language. The swear words came in very handy every time another airport worker arrived and said the plane been had been delayed for another hour.

Four hours later there he was: Big Mark, tired, nervous and expectant. He let go of the luggage trolley to give me a hug. No way! Not with all those armed police surrounding us! Touching in public between the sexes is against Nepalese law!

I had to push him away, 'Wait until we get to the guest house.'

Then the driver arrived to hustle us to our taxi and there wasn't time to explain. Mark gave me one of his hurt puppy looks. Oh God! I hope he isn't going to start sulking! Mark's sulks can last for days.

More later. Sally X

MONKEY ON MY ROOF

37

My husband's journey of a lifetime is turning out to be a bit of a disaster. There's a curfew from 11am until 4 pm, and armed police are on the street to enforce it. Never mind about trekking to base camp, we're stuck here, can't even leave the guesthouse. It isn't only the Bandh (what the Nepalese call a strike) that stops us from moving to the mountains. Mark has the Kathmandu Squitters — which is ten times worse than Delhi belli — he daren't move away from the loo! We could be stuck here for months without any money. The banks, moneychangers and ATMs are all on strike.

Still, it was pleasant enough to escape yesterday and sit with my newspaper in the garden away from Mark's long suffering sighs and groans, his dashes to the bathroom, the smell of his farts and shit.

The manager passed by, 'What will we do about the bill if we can't get money from the cash machine?' I asked him. 'We need what money we have for food and water.'

He understands, he won't chase me for the bill, 'No worry, Sally,' he said, 'Pay when Bandh finish.'

We smiled at each other and I made my way towards our room to see how Mark was doing.

The Lama from the next room was sitting in his wheel chair on the terrace. He stopped me to have a chat. We talked about Buddhism and the monastery at Dharamsala where The Dalai Lama has made his home.

'I'm going to Dharamsala for the teachings,' I told the Lama.
'We go Tibet next week.'
How the Dickens will he get to Tibet?
Imagine! Young monks stumbling along the mountain trails,

MONKEY ON MY ROOF

carrying the Lama over the Himalayas in his wheelchair. Carrying him shoulder high with those red and yellow robes a sure target for Chinese soldiers!

'You can come Tibet with us,' the Lama said.

No fear!

'I can't; when the strike finishes my husband and me are going to Pokhara,' I said, 'I'm really only in Nepal to renew my Indian visa.'

The waiter from the Banyan Tree in Palolem is in Kathmandu, he was meant to come to our guesthouse today and take us for an outing in the Kathmandu valley. A message on my mobile said he dare not break the curfew. It's too dangerous for us to go outside the Stupa, we are stuck here in Boudhanath.

Oh well, every downside has an upside, at least the King has stopped playing silly beggars with the networks. Now I can use my mobile again! And I've just heard that the curfew has been lifted for a couple of hours, so I'm off away to the internet café.

*

12th April 2006

Hello my dearest Sally,

Thanks for the e-mails, it's lovely to hear all your news. Do you still live at the same guesthouse? Is that monkey still throwing roof tiles at the manager? I'm still laughing! I miss India, the warm weather, the palm-trees, the sand between my toes, the fabulous sea-food, I even miss Matheran and Jerry Junior, but most of all I miss you. I've just decided to give you the job of my Mum full time; you seem to know exactly what I need to hear, and how to pick me up when I am down.

MONKEY ON MY ROOF

I have some news. For the last two weeks I've been worried sick thinking something was wrong because of stomach problems. I was afraid it might involve a scalpel — that hospital is beginning to feel like a second home. It's hard to keep quiet when all you want to do is shout and scream, and it's hard not to feel bitter. The Doctor told me it could be an amoeba — that's worms to you and me — I've imported from India. Just to be sure, I had to have tests. I nearly asked you to send me some distant healing, but wanted to wait for the test results.

The good news is everything is okay! My test results came back clear this morning. The Doctor was wrong about the worms. Now he says it was something I ate! He says my scar has healed so well, that there is no reason why I can't go swimming.

On Saturday, there was a works party with old friends that I haven't seen for a while. Good friends but not friends that I hang out with a lot. It was nice, but at the same time awful, as if I was the freak show of the evening, "Look there's the girl who had cancer and can't have children." For the whole night I had to talk with everyone, even people I don't know very well, about my illness. I know it's their way of caring, but it made me depressed. I'd had enough after a couple of hours and went home.

Last night Greg and me had a long talk, we shared a bottle of wine, then one thing led to another — you know how it is when you get tipsy — we ended up making love on the floor. Pleasure and pain all mixed up together. I asked him how he could still love me after my operation.

He says that it makes no difference to him that I can't have kids of my own; IT'S ME HE LOVES, AND IT DOESN'T MATTER TO HIM THAT I CAN'T BEAR HIS CHILDREN, and anyway he says we can adopt a couple of kids! So now I'm

165

MONKEY ON MY ROOF

dreaming of small black- haired babies from an orphanage in India or China. Greg wants to meet you. We are talking about getting married next year, and spending the honeymoon in Goa!

Tomorrow we are taking a couple of days for ourselves without telling anyone! Greg has booked us into a hotel, a belated Christmas present he says. The hotel is like a health club, it has a swimming pool, Jacuzzi, sauna, and a gym! Should be so cool! Me and Greg swimming! Drinking champagne in the Jacuzzi! Working out in the gym together! Taking a shower and sauna together! I can hardly wait!

Keep spraying that can of Hit around. Stay away from riots and tear gas, and from fast motor scooters. And watch out for sacred cows when you're crossing the road. I will think of you and send you all my happy thoughts!!!

Feel hugged and kissed! Ailsa.

MONKEY ON MY ROOF

38

14th April 2006
Dear Ailsa,
I'm sooo flattered that you want to give me a full time job as your Mum. But Ailsa darling, you already have a Mum. You only ever have one Mum; please think about settling your differences with her. Out here, the Indian children call me Auntie. How about I adopt you as my niece? Call me Aunt Sally if you like; just don't go shying any coconuts at me! How are you? Have you started treatment yet? Sorry if I sound nosey, I don't mean to be.

A belated Christmas prezzie, what a wonderful idea! Greg sounds like a lovely man, I'm sure he'll make a fantastic father, and you'll make a great Mum! I can imagine the two of you, strolling around Glasgow town with a pram full of those babies you're dreaming about.

Darling, when you go to parties I think you should just tell your friends that you don't want to talk about your cancer. You should be able to enjoy yourself without being reminded of such a traumatic event in your life. Your friends are just being kind but it's you that has to deal with it not them. Tell them, 'Enough already, let me enjoy the moment!'

As for me, well it's getting a bit hairy here in Kathmandu. The police have stopped all traffic in and out of the town centre because of a political strike, which will last for the next four days...

This morning, on the main road outside the Stupa, police with riot shields had set up a roadblock. A tank was there pointing its guns at Buddhist monks who were breaking the curfew to walk up the road and implore the soldiers not to shoot their own people or anyone else for that matter. Luckily, the soldiers take heed. No

MONKEY ON MY ROOF

one obeys the curfew, and who can blame them. If the English government were to impose an all-day curfew on us in England I'd be out there throwing stones too, and sod the consequences.

Sally X

*

There's a tank outside in the street again, so Mark and me are staying safely in our room. I'm lying on my bed trying to reading a book, but what with our room door open, sun shining, birds singing, and people passing to and fro on the terrace, it's hard to concentrate.

Mark's stomach has settled down, so he's sitting on the end of *his* bed to watch Manchester United play on TV. Man U is Mark's team. He never misses a match.

One of the young monks who attend to the Lama has just walked past on the terrace.

Now he's peeping in the door, 'Ah football!'

Next minute he's sat on the bed next to my husband, and Mark is smiling at him as if to say: Ah, another Man U supporter! They both watch the game.

A second young monk is peeping inside, his eyes on the TV.

Now he's sat on Mark's bed next to the first monk.

A third monk has arrived, sits at the bottom of *my* bed.

Our room is beginning to look like a Buddhist convention.

The sound of Man U supporters roaring and shouting bursts from the TV. On the screen, a player dodges towards the net. Excitement is building, I put my book down on the bedside table and sit up.

My husband is leaning forward, face alight with anticipation,

MONKEY ON MY ROOF

the footballer kicks the ball, and Mark jumps to his feet, 'Goal…?'

Then…

The third monk to arrive (obviously not a Man U supporter) reaches across, picks up the remote control and switches channels.

'Wha…Wha…Wha…' Mark stutters, 'What did you do that for?' His face doesn't know what to do with itself. He snatches the remote from the monk, switches channels back again, but it's too late; he's missed the goal!

The monk explains that he thought the Tibetan National Football Team — the Forbidden Team — was playing today.

My husband has never heard of the TNFT! He is not a happy bunny. 'From now on that door will be locked when I'm watching TV,' he tells the monks as they slink guiltily away.

MONKEY ON MY ROOF

39

Ailsa and I have been phoning each other back and forth a couple of times a week. I haven't had an e-mail from her and it isn't my turn to phone, but I call her anyway.

'My friend, the girl I told you about with ovarian cancer,' Ailsa says, 'is taking a Reiki course soon and then we can practice on one another.'

'That's good.'

'It always makes me feel better when I do Reiki.'

'How are things with you?'

'I'm okay, just a bit of back ache because of the operation.'

'Back ache?'

'Nothing for you to worry about.'

Something is wrong, I can feel it.

'You'd tell me if there was. Wouldn't you?'

'For Goodness sake…' she brushes me off, and prattles on: 'Are there parties in Kathmandu?'

'Yeah,' I say sardonically, 'I'm dancing every night.'

'Don't you wish you were back in Goa? The party season will still be buzzing in Palolem,' she says.

'You can say that again! The only parties in Kathmandu are with tanks and rifles.'

'Even so,' she says in a rush, 'It's cold here. Snowing! Wish I was there with you!'

'I won't be here much longer,' I say, 'soon as this strike is over me and Mark will be off to Pokhara.'

*

MONKEY ON MY ROOF

22nd April 2006

Hello Sally,

Forgive me for not telling you when we spoke on the phone yesterday but I have bad news! For two weeks I've had a really bad backache. The Doctor says I have a tumour as big as a golf ball. It's really aggressive since it has been growing so much in such short time. He thinks that I'm looking at radiation five times a week combined with chemotherapy once a week, also a new operation. I'm heartbroken. It feels overwhelming, I don't know how to manage, I'm angry and afraid and tired all at the same time. I don't feel that I have the strength I need to fight it. Jesus Christ! I cannot believe I'm writing this. Is this really happening to me?!! It feels like I just want to wake up from this ridiculously bad dream.

    I just want to get married, and have a nice house with a big garden for my kids to play in.

    Why should it be so hard??!!

    I'm sorry for just blurting this out to you.

    I'm soon going to the hospital to do an MR and a lung x-ray.

    Thank you for being there for me. It seems like we both have a journey to make. You to travel around India. Me to travel... I don't know where...I can't say it, can hardly think it.

    x Ailsa.

*

So that's what it is!

    The sun is still shining, the birds are singing, horns blowing, people laughing. The world uncaring, carrying on its business as usual: as if nothing had changed. While here, staring at me in black and white from the computer screen in the internet shop, are those words: *tumour* and *chemotherapy*. I can hardly believe what I'm reading, don't want to believe it.

MONKEY ON MY ROOF

*

22nd April 2006

Oh Darling, what can I say?

We always knew somehow didn't we? When we spoke on the phone the other night, you trying to hide your trouble and me pretending not to hear what was in your voice. No wonder you are angry and afraid and tired, God knows how I'd feel in your place. I can see you sitting there going quietly mad, being brave, so as not to worry everyone. Don't be so fucking brave! Shout and scream if you want, you can shout and scream at me on the phone, I won't tell anyone, I promise; any time day or night doesn't matter, call me, I'll keep my phone switched on and fully charged for you.

So yes, we do both have a journey to make. My journey will hopefully take me to a place where I can make some kind of sense of what is left of my life. Yours, my darling Ailsa, will be the hardest journey, because now you have to fight. To fight with all your courage, every inch of the way. How I wish that we could swap, or at least do our journeys together.

Being here in Kathmandu makes no difference; my thoughts are always with you. If you need me just let me know, I will be there.

Keep your spirit up.

        Missing you. Sally X

MONKEY ON MY ROOF

<u>40</u>

Mark wants to move to Thamel. The sound of drums and conches coming from the monastery at four o'clock in the morning wake him up he says. Personally, I think the reason is more that my husband can't wait to get away from the monk who switched TV channels during the Man U game, but I'm willing to go along with him to stop him sulking. He deserves to enjoy his holiday.

Funnily enough, Mark hasn't realised yet that his sulks don't affect me the way they once did. Once upon a time, I'd have walked through fire not to have to endure that icy coldness on his face. Now his petulance is like water off a duck's back. A couple of times lately I've caught him studying the new thinner, suntanned, more confident me. The look on his face makes it plain he thinks I've been having an affair while I've been in India. But it's not Mark's style to ask me outright.

Anyway why should I reassure him that my marriage vows are more important to me than his are to him? But I can't help comparing his sulkiness with Stephan's laid-back attitude. Nothing seems to faze Stephan. A meal together in Bombay and — of its own accord my hand creeps up to touch my face — a kiss on the cheek doesn't count as an affair.

Does it?

It seems like the Bandh is finally over, though the night-time curfew is still on. Mark has managed to stop a taxi and get the driver to take us to the centre of Thamel — the tourist section of Kathmandu.

The streets are quiet with a kind of uneasy calm, not helped by the soldiers and armed police everywhere we look. Seeing the tanks and soldiers hasn't stopped Mark from going through the

MONKEY ON MY ROOF

gates of Tridevi Marg to book a room at The Blue Horizon Hotel which is only a stone's throw from King Gyanendra's hideous pink palace. This is the hotel where Sheila and Doug are staying, though they aren't in at the moment. The hotel has a room vacant, and the rate is reasonable — 400 nrps per night, which works out at about three quid, half the price of the one in the Lotus Guest House. But I'm going to miss the manager at the Lotus Guesthouse, not to mention that old Lama and his young monks.

'No dining room on premises,' the manager tells us, 'you eat on the terrace.'

Mark isn't concerned; he's spotted the restaurant serving food in a pretty garden next door.

'We'll take the room,' he tells the manager and pays the deposit.

'When will you arrive?' the manager asks.

'Not until tomorrow because of the curfew,' I say. 'We have to collect our luggage from Boudhanath.'

We head for Freak Street, where the last time I met her Sheila told me, 'Every shop in Freak Street is scented with incense. You can buy anything in the shops on Freak Street. Embroidered clothes and pashminas. Mandalas and Buddhas…'

'Oh just the usual tourist junk then,' I'd teased.

'You'll see!'

She was right, I do see. I see the bright pennants flying above the tiny, fascinating stores, the ornate Nepalese woodcarvings, the garish Tibetan masks lavishly placed around shop doorways. I see bicycle rickshaws with their colourful leather hoods. Children running twirling prayer wheels.

But I don't see them for long.

From somewhere nearby comes the sound of a mob chanting,

MONKEY ON MY ROOF

and the sound is getting closer. A stone flies through the air. Suddenly, women are running snatching children off the street; shopkeepers are throwing goods inside shops and bolting doors.

Mark keeps on strolling, hands in pockets, head in clouds, blissfully unaware that the events he's read about in the English newspapers and seen on TV are only the tip of the iceberg. The things happening to the Nepalese people are sickening. Even hospitals are not safe here. Doctors giving their services free are beaten when they protect their patients. Yesterday at a first aid compound, a patient had his eye gouged out with a lathi — a bamboo stick — wielded by a police chief, and I don't want the same kind of thing to happen to us!

I grab Mark's arm, 'Run!'

He shakes me off, 'Don't!'

Why is it always me who has to take care of him? Isn't it the man who is supposed to be the protector?

'For God's sake run!'

I grab his arm again to drag him around the corner of the street.

A taxi stops, the driver leans his head from the window, 'Get in. I help you.' I pull the taxi door open and dive in dragging Mark with me. The driver floors the accelerator and takes off like a bat out of hell.

To avoid the riots our ride back to the Boudha involves a detour into parts of Kathmandu I've never seen before, and don't want to see again. At a crossroad, our driver is forced to make an emergency stop when we come across hundreds of people fighting armed police who are using tear gas. With stones, whizzing past the windows we speed in reverse up a narrow street filled with rubble. It all makes for an exciting life, but it's a relief to get back to the

MONKEY ON MY ROOF

relative safety of the Stupa, and the Lotus guesthouse.

MONKEY ON MY ROOF

41

Hurrah! Guess what? Today the curfew has been lifted! The King has stopped playing silly beggars with the communications system! My phone is working again and the roads are full of traffic!

It's three o'clock in the afternoon here, nearly nine in the morning in England. Round about now the street where Mark and I live in Knotty Ash will be filling up with four-wheel drive off-roaders as parents deliver their offspring to the High School at the end of the road. Mums, and the occasional Dad, will be sitting high up in their vehicles treating innocent passers-by to suspicious glances, and glaring at any residents who have the presumption to back their own vehicles into the road.

Later in the day, there'll be the hullabaloo of schoolchildren jostling along the street as they make their way home sweeping any person unlucky enough to get in their way off the pavement. Four-letter words, and fists flying. Girls in navy blue skirts short as curtain pelmets, with blouses tied above the midriff to show off belly-button jewellery. Boys with spiked hair, pierced noses and eyebrow rings; and that's only the first formers!

Was I like that when I was young?

I remember having to walk the mile and a half home from school, summer and winter, carrying my heavy schoolbag; but that was okay, most of my friends were in the same boat. Maybe there was the occasional fight, but a passing adult would soon put a stop to it. Nowadays teenagers are a lot more aggressive, and BIGGER.

It must be around nine o'clock in the morning in Glasgow, the kids will have passed Ailsa and Greg's place to get to school. Except that is for those little sods bunking off to play truant.

Mark and me have moved to Thamel. When we arrived with

MONKEY ON MY ROOF

our luggage the beggar children left the tiny fire they'd made at the side of the road and came running — one of them turning cartwheels. They wouldn't let us through the gate into Trevendi Marg until we'd given them a rupee each. No school for these poor kids, no chance of *them* ever being able to play truant.

'Their parents sent them to Kathmandu to get them away from the Maoists,' Sheila says. 'Under the belief that it's better to beg than get shot.'

We are on the terrace drinking coffee.

Mark and Doug, maps spread out on the table, are organising a two-day white water rafting trip, and Sheila and I are grinning at one another, because we're planning some retail therapy while they're gone. I need some warmer clothes for Dharamsala. Reportedly clothes are cheaper and better quality in Nepal than in India.

Because of the curfews we haven't had much chance to shop, and we mostly eat at the restaurant next door. Tonight Mark wants to sample the French food served at one or two of the restaurants before Doug and he go on their rafting trip. Loves his food does our Mark.

Talking about those French menus has sparked Mark off. He's just given an enormous belch.

Sheila nearly jumped out of her skin! 'I've never known anyone to belch as loudly as Mark,' I whisper to her. 'Sometimes I think he does it on purpose to annoy me. He's always doing it. His father was the same. Sitting on the settee with Mark in an armchair on one side of me, his Dad on the other, was like being in a cinema with smelliophonic sound.'

Sheila is laughing, 'I'm not surprised.'

Mark looks up, 'I'm going to the internet shop. Got to check

MONKEY ON MY ROOF

what gear I'll need for white water rafting,' he says.

I stand and stretch, 'I'll come with you.'

*

25th April 2006

Ailsa darling you are never out of my thoughts, every day I pin your photo on my room wall, concentrate intently, perform the ceremony that Gosh taught me, and send distant healing.

Mark watches me. He thinks I've gone barmy!

What are you doing I wonder? Are you getting ready for a doctor's appointment? Have you started your treatment? I've been trying to phone you but a mechanical voice keeps telling me I can only make emergency calls. Of course, that doesn't mean anything. The way the communication system is in Nepal...

TaTa for now.

100 hugs from Sally X

26th April 2006

Dear Sally,

It's been a while and I'm sorry for that. My phone is out of credit.

I'm not feeling very well I'm taking nine tablets a day. On Thursday I had my first chemotherapy session, and it made me so sick, couldn't keep any food down. Now I've been given tablets to stop the sickness but they're not working.

No good news, I don't know what to do, I feel...angry, hurt, and bitter all at the same time. Why me? What have I ever done to deserve this? Everything around me is blackness, I'm filled with blackness. A black hole a black pit has opened up and swallowed me and I can't get out. Oh, God I'm just telling you all my bad

MONKEY ON MY ROOF

things, I'm sorry for that. The only good thing around me is Greg. He wants me to go the clinic for a Reiki session and a massage tomorrow. I can't be bothered. What's the use?

    Missing you Ailsa.

27th April 2006
Dear beautiful Ailsa,
It isn't surprising that you aren't using the phone or computer, starting Chemotherapy is tough. People in the know have told me that anti sickness pills are very good. They should stop you vomiting. Try to persevere with them. Please come back from the blackness, many people love you so don't let yourself become bitter. Okay it's all right to be angry, anger can help. Of course you are angry and hurt, but try not to be bitter.

    The one thing I have learned in all my years is that bitterness colours everything around with blackness. It steals all the joy from life. Try to believe that you have a lot of joy waiting for you. Don't let the blackness swallow you my dear. Live for the Now. Try to enjoy some moments each day, even if it's only in the sound of your favourite song played on that radio station you told me about…Smooth Radio. Or a friendly smile from a stranger in the street. As for you telling me all the bad things, who else would you tell them to. That's what friends are for!

    Hopefully you'll soon feel better. Greg, bless him, has the right idea. Reiki and massage is good. I'll still send you distant healing, I feel closer to you when I send Reiki.

    Mark used to let me practice my Reiki on him. Reiki helped him relax he said, though whether he was only saying it to please me is a matter for speculation, and it did nothing to cure his flatulence, he's still as smelly as ever!

MONKEY ON MY ROOF

Mark is here in the cybercafé sitting next to me at the first computer as you go in the door. A moment ago he let out an enormous belch. A Nepalese woman strolling past on Tridevi Marg glanced through the door at him and pulled her face.

Now as I sit reading your e-mail Mark's bodily functions no longer have the power to embarrass me. I realise there are other more important things.

100 HUGS and much much love from Sally.

MONKEY ON MY ROOF

<u>42</u>

Here in Kathmandu the monsoon is starting. A couple of days ago there was a big thunderstorm, it rained cats and dogs all day. Now the air is cleaner, the pollution has cleared perhaps because of the rain or because there's been less traffic on the roads. Or does everything look brighter because of the good news in the Kathmandu Post... parliament has been reinstated! The curfew still stands but everyone, both the Nepalese and us Westerners, breaks it. Manish, that waiter from Palolem, finally made it to our hotel yesterday and took us to Durbar Square.

'Durbar is word for Palace,' he told us, 'the kings of Nepal were crowned here in Hanuman Dhoka Palace.' Then he grinned, 'King in Thamel now. King Gyanendra not stay long in Palace now.'

No prizes for guessing whose side he's on!

We toured temples, photographed two- and three-tiered pagodas, inspected a statue of a sort of oriental angel with the face of a Buddha.

Manish took us to Kumari Bahal, a red brick, three-storey building with carved windows. The Kumari Bahal is where the living virgin Goddess of Kathmandu lives until she reaches puberty and gets to be an ordinary girl, able to have fun with boys.

'Did you hear that, Mark?' I asked a bit wickedly, because I've stopped all that eggshell walking around his sensitivities. 'Fun with boys. What kind of fun could that be do you think?'

Mark gave me one of his hurt puppy looks, heaved a sigh and said, 'What are you trying to say?' in an injured tone.

'Just joking. Just joking,' I said imitating his injured tone.

And we carried on walking around what must be the most

MONKEY ON MY ROOF

beautiful courtyard in Nepal.

There's a small Stupa carrying the symbols of Saraswati, the goddess of the arts, and I touched it for luck — I still have that poster of Saraswati Ailsa bought for me in Chaudi. It's rolled up inside my suitcase. I'm planning to take the steam iron to it when I get home to England before I hang it on the wall.

Then along the street people started shouting to one another, there were a few scattered cheers. King Gyanendra has given up his powers, and now is King in name only!

At Freak Street, we left our passports with an agent for him to get Indian tourist visas.

'Your visas will take a week to come through,' the agent said.

'If I can't get to the Nepalese mountains,' Mark said, 'I'll go to India.'

'It might not come to that,' I told him.

Sharing a room with him is like sharing a cage with a stressed-out, angry wildcat. He paces, sighs, scowls at me as if this whole situation, the riots, the curfews, the cancelled trip, is my fault. Then there are those subtle snide remarks at which he excels, 'Just joking, just joking,' he says, but we both know that's not true.

*

30th April 2006
Dear Ailsa,
Ailsa dear, thinking about these e- mails I wonder if I should still keep on sending them? I've been asking myself: doesn't Ailsa have enough to think about without worrying about replying? If you want me to stop, I won't be offended; though I'll miss these

MONKEY ON MY ROOF

sessions in the cyber café, it seems to me they bring us closer.

Now for my news if you can bear it.

Wouldn't you know it! Shittt!!! The Bandh has started again! Another curfew to stop us from leaving the soddin' hotel. The newspaper is full of talk of food and essential supply shortages.

This morning the manager stopped us as we passed his desk, 'No breakfast, no supplies,' he said, 'trucks can't get petrol, no fuel for cooking from Sunday.'

Mark groaned, 'What will we do?'

'Go supermarket buy dried food,' said the manager.

'That's if the supermarket isn't boarded up, and the curfew is lifted,' I said.

The curfew is meant to be lifted at eight o'clock tonight... but who knows?

'Never mind. It wouldn't hurt for us both to lose some weight,' I told the manager.

Mark groaned again.

'Every cloud has a diet sheet in its silver lining,' I told him, but like Queen Victoria he was not amused!

'That's scuppered our shopping trip,' Sheila said, 'we can't shop till we drop if the shops aren't open.'

My husband is totally pissed off. The man organising the rafting trip came round earlier this morning saying, 'No fuckin' way,' in Nepalese, English and Hindi.

Mark has no chance of white-water rafting.

          Feel yourself hugged by Aunt Sally X

MONKEY ON MY ROOF

43

It's the first day of the new month, I forgot to say 'White Rabbits' when I woke up so there'll be no good luck for me this month! In the internet shop there are e-mails from each of our daughters. Lisa writes that she's bought a computer. Now she doesn't have to book a time at the local library to read my e-mails. Jayne is doing extra shifts at the hospital she says because a lot of nurses are off with spring flu. Emma is busy revising. I send a round robin to all three assuring them we are both safe.

Deliberately I've left Ailsa's e-mail until last. The symbol of that little white envelope stares at me, I stare back afraid to click the mouse and open it. Is it good news, or bad? My finger takes on a life of its own, refusing to push down on the computer mouse as it floats the white arrow over the computer screen.

I stare at the screen, gulp, swallow, say a little prayer, please God don't let it be bad news.

Hasn't she suffered enough? Finally I open her mail.

*

30th April 2006
Dear Sally,
Got home yesterday after being in hospital for the last couple of days. Had to see a new specialist. He seems a lot more hopeful. Now I've had chemo straight into my abdomen to shrink the tumour before he operates. Came out of there crying sweating and feeling as if my ovaries are being pulled out through my backside. Hope it's worth it, keep your fingers crossed for me.

My phone is still not working. Frustrating. I'm still feeling tired and sick from the chemo, but I'm hanging in there. Greg is

MONKEY ON MY ROOF

taking a Reiki course this weekend and will practice a lot on me — great! Is everything all right with you? Please keep sending your mails, I love to read them.

Imagining your arms around me. Ailsa.

*

This sounds bad, worse than before. Desperately I fumble around for words…

What to write? What to write? How to answer her mails, those hidden cries for help. Help is out of my reach. Ailsa, the daughter who doesn't belong to me, but as close to my heart as if she were one of mine. Her mail sounds desperate and optimistic both at the same time… Humour may be the way for today. Just hope I'm right.

*

1st May 2006

Darling Ailsa,

Your new specialist seems a gift from God. Hold on to that thought! By the way do you remember how crying, sweating, and feeling like your ovaries are being pulled out through your backside is the normal course of events in bloody Goa after eating the fish curry? Okay okay I know you have the pain without the gain, no paradisiacal beach, no sunbed and umbrella, no warm sea, no smiling waiters bringing cocktails to compensate. *And* no disgustingly smelly fly and spider ridden Indian squat toilets and cow shit all over your flip-flops.

Still I wish to God you were here with me to enjoy those smelly fly and spider ridden squat toilets. Keep your pecker up darling. It won't be forever, and then you can get back to a normal

MONKEY ON MY ROOF

life. Good luck to Greg and his Reiki course. The more I hear about him the more I like him!

Here in Kathmandu armed soldiers and police are everywhere. At the crossroad yesterday, a tank was pointing guns towards the Pink Palace. When Sheila and me went out into the street last night a young soldier, who looked no more than twelve years old, shouted, 'Curfew! Curfew!' Jabbed his rifle at us, and prodded us back inside. Twenty minutes later he wandered off to urinate behind an armoured car so we took the opportunity to sneak through the Trivedi Marg gates like a couple of giggling teenagers and escape into the street.

It was eerie when we did get out, like being in a ghost town. No people, no traffic, the streets spookily silent. Shops were shuttered. Rats and stray dogs foraged for food in mountains of rubbish — the rubbish-collectors are under curfew too. Everything stops when there's a Bandh: telephones, post, internet, banks. Even the beggar boys are in hiding. When there's a curfew, nothing moves except cows, dogs, and soldiers. At least without traffic on the roads the pollution isn't so bad.

But this morning the curfew was lifted! Doug and Sheila have gone to the airport. Today they fly to Delhi.

Mark and I went to Freak Street to check up on our visas.

'Your passports and visas will be here on Monday,' the agent said.

On the way back we walked into a demo. The violence spilled from Durbar Square into Freak Street. This time Mark needed no urging to run.

100 hugs and Love from Aunt Sally.

MONKEY ON MY ROOF

44

6th May 2006
Dear Ailsa,
It's been a few days since I've been in touch; it couldn't be helped, the internet café was shuttered and my mobile was out of credit. How are things with you? Can I uncross my fingers before they go into spasm? Did the chemo work? Are you feeling any better? Don't worry if you can't manage to answer my mails, I'll just keep writing them in the hope you can find the strength to read them.

I have news…the riots are really over at last!

The internet café owner was locking his shop up. My mobile phone was fully charged and topped with credit, raring to go; I shoved it in my pocket and went back to the hotel, where the manager — like everyone else in Kathmandu — had heard the news. He closed the reception desk, grabbed me around the waist and waltzed me around the entrance hall hollering, 'Party we go party!'

So we went party. Wow! What a party. The Nepalese sure know how to let their hair down.

Mark was already there, beer in one hand, chapatti in the other.

'Hey! Don't just stand there guzzling beer, get your things packed,' I told him, 'There's not much time left if we want to get to Pokhara.'

Pokhara is where he's been planning to start his trek to Everest base camp.

Mark didn't move. 'It's hardly worth going,' he said, 'I'm flying home in eight days.'

'Eight days,' I declared, 'is enough time to get there, book into a hotel and set up your trek.'

MONKEY ON MY ROOF

Mark crammed the last piece of chapatti in his mouth and mumbled despondently, 'Not enough time to do what I came out here to do.'

Being stuck in a hotel for coming up to five weeks is not much of a holiday is it? No wonder he feels so miserable. Who wouldn't be miserable not being able to do the one thing they want to do. It doesn't seem fair on him that I'll still be here in Nepal when Mark, frustrated, disappointed and upset, is back home in England.

When his hand was free of chapatti — I caught hold of it, gave his greasy fingers a little greasy squeeze, 'Okay, so there's not enough time to get to Base Camp. But you could still go trekking.'

He shook his head.

'Five day trek?'

He shook his head again, said, 'It's sixteen hours on the bus to Pokhara. There won't be time for a trek. I don't want to go all that way just to sit by a lake just to contemplate my navel.'

I laughed, 'Sixteen hours? Someone has been pulling your leg; the bus doesn't take that long! Anyway there's an airport at Pokhara. We could fly. Be there in an hour.'

'Fly?'

'Yes! Think about it. No riots, no curfews. All that clean, clear air. The mountains, the Himalaya breeze gliding across your face. A friendly Sherpa to carry your backpack. Birds singing, green grass, flowers, aching muscles…sore feet… Whatever would the neighbours say if you went back without breaking those climbing boots in?'

Mark lifted his head; he was smiling, 'Okay. Okay. Okay! You've talked me into it.'

Keep your pecker up Ailsa darling we are all praying for you.
    Love you, kisses and hugs from Aunt Sally

MONKEY ON MY ROOF

*

Pokhara airport, one of the worst landings I've ever experienced! Sixteen hours or no sixteen hours, I'm definitely getting the bus when we go back to Kathmandu. It's been raining heavily ever since we got here. Last night the thunder rolled and echoed around the mountains, I couldn't sleep so I sat at the window and watched lightning shoot silver streaks, like strobe lights across Fewa Lake.

Mark has gone away on a five-day trek. The Ghorepani Poon Hill Trek.

'This our bestseller. An easy trek with beautiful mountain scenery,' the man in the agency told us.

'Easy?' Mark was disappointed, 'I don't want easy.'

'There's plenty of walking along streams and forests,' the agency man reassured him, 'that's if you're looking for a few days close to nature?'

'How high, what kind of altitude?'

'Some high climbing.'

'What about altitude sickness?'

'No risk of sickness on this trek.'

'I'll have to think about it.'

While Mark was thinking I opened my purse, 'Okay,' I said and took out the money, 'we'll take it.'

'Both of you?'

'No, just my husband. I'm not crazy enough to go trekking in the rain.'

Now I'm beating my brains out wondering if he'll be okay up there in the mountains. It's been raining cats, dogs, and sacred cows for the last few days, so I'm hoping that there aren't any landslides. There is talk of the Maoists holding tourists to ransom. Has he

MONKEY ON MY ROOF

enough money to pay the Maoists? Will he fall, break his leg; or even his neck? Will I have to arrange a Hindu funeral?

Oh for goodness sake! Why am I being so stupid? He's only going to be away a few days.

*

The rain has stopped, the sun is shining, and I'm off for a walk around the lake. Got to see how far I can walk. Not very far as it turns out. I only manage three miles, maybe four. Hot, sweaty, thirsty and with aching feet, what better excuse do I need to stagger into this small bar at the side of the lake and sink a well-deserved pint of cool cool lager.

Shaded by a tree thick with lilac blossom, a group of Nepalese fishermen are sitting on the terrace at one end of a long wooden table; I sit at the other end to sip my lager. Crimson bougainvillea and blue morning glory bloom extravagantly around the terrace. The bar has a pool fed by a stream and waterfall; Koi carp swim under the small bridges. The owner of the bar gives me some fish food and the Koi feed from my hand.

'Where you from?' one of the fishermen asks.

'England; Liverpool.'

'Liverpool?'

'It's near Manchester.'

'Ah Manchester United,' he smiles.

Everyone in Asia seems to know of Manchester United.

'David Beckham,' another man says.

All the fishermen smile and nod.

'His wife calls him Golden Balls,' I tell them.

'You met him?' the bar tender asks.

MONKEY ON MY ROOF

'I wish! No, his wife won't let me near him,' I say.

The fishermen are full of stories about the Maoists. How they attack factories and police outposts, ransack and destroy property, how they set off explosives that kill many people.

'We have civil war,' the bar owner states, 'many people die because of Maoists.'

'They take children from schools to be soldiers. Teenagers and children, eight, nine and ten years old. And if school resist they beat the teachers,' another fisherman says.

I tell them about the beggar children in Kathmandu. Tell them of the hundreds of children who have fled their homes scared of being kidnapped by the Maoists. Now they live on the street, half-starved, afraid to go home, afraid to stay, afraid of the police, so they sniff glue to add a little pleasure to their lives; to help them forget their fear.

'They are sent to Kathmandu by their parents to keep them safe from the Maoists,' I say; '"Go find work," their parents tell them, "find work in bar. Dish wash, sweep floors. Not get shot."'

'But now,' I declare, 'there are so many of these kids there isn't enough work to go round.'

Then I tell the fishermen the other side. Tell them of the hospital patient who had his eye gouged out with a lathi wielded by a police chief.

The bar owner and the fishermen nod their heads. They've heard stories like this many times before.

One of the fishermen asks, 'Where you stay? Which hotel?'

'The Hotel Shikara,' I tell him.

'Long walk back in hot sun. I row you back across lake,' he offers.

The distance around Fewa Lake to the bar is roughly four miles.

MONKEY ON MY ROOF

'That's kind of you.'

Purple and red butterflies flutter by, kingfishers dart for fish, blue flashes above the still water as he rows me across the lake. He lands me on a stretch of pebbles near to my hotel.

'How much?' I ask.

He smiles, 'Name Ragish. Tell David Beckham him come visit me in Pokhara.'

MONKEY ON MY ROOF

45

20th May 2006

Hi Dear beautiful Ailsa,

How are you? How is my brave soldier? Have you had your op yet? Sorry I haven't been in touch, believe me it isn't because I haven't been thinking of you. It's because the chaos isn't over yet in Nepal.

    Don't get me wrong, Nepal isn't all doom and gloom. When Mark and I got back to Kathmandu, we were on top of the world. Actually on top of the world! A mountain flight with Buddha Air.

    The plane was small, but passengers had their own window seat. What can I say? How can I describe it? Anything I say will have been said before, will be a cliché, but life is full of clichés so here goes…

    Everest seems to go on forever, like a monochromatic movie stretching high and wide, the largest, longest, highest mountain in the world; it's like flying over the Grand Canyon except that Everest is black and white instead of the hot purple and crimsons I remember from America.

    Seeing it made me wonder how that Supreme Being felt when He created it! Did He have a Godlike giggle as He said to Himself, "This will show those humans just how small they are and remind them who's the boss!"

    'Almost as good as trekking,' Mark said, leaning over from the seat behind me.

    'Yeah!' I told him. 'Now you can tell Doug Base Camp is just a walk in the park.'

    Love and Light, hugs and XXXXs from Sally.

MONKEY ON MY ROOF

*

Mark came back from his five-day trek like a dog with two tails, talking fifteen to the dozen like an excited schoolboy. It was good to see him happy for a change; almost like the man I used to know. The night before he left to go home to England, he made love to me as if we were newly married. Like on one of those early days, when he borrowed his Dads Austin 7 to take me out for the day. On those days when we were so hot for one another that we had to stop the car in the nearest country lane. Engine still running, windows all steamed up, not waiting to get onto the back seat, bonking furiously in the front, with me not knowing or caring if I was being bonked by Mark or the gear lever.

We don't make love anymore; at least not what I can call making love. What we do is to have the odd bout of sex in a perfunctory kind of way, mechanical on his part, dutiful on mine.

That night was an exception, and because he was flying back the next day, I started to think: Who knows what tomorrow may bring? If he had said, come home with me Sally, I need you, I love you, I'd have been right there.

But...'Goodbye old girl,' was all he said. There was that faintly ironic expression on his face again when he looked at me. It makes me cringe inside, puts me in mind of how my mother used to look at me after she and Dad split up. Like in those long ago days when I was a kid when she was always shouting, 'You're no bloody good, just like your bloody father; just like him. You'll never be any good.'

So I told Mark, 'You're not so young yourself old boy.'

We didn't part on very good terms!

MONKEY ON MY ROOF

*

25th May 2006

Dear Ailsa,

Got an e-mail from Mark this morning telling me that he's saving all the ironing up for me now that he's home again. So I've-mailed him back to tell him that I'm suffering from Alzheimer's and can't remember where we keep the ironing board. Better if he does the ironing himself I told him or I'll stay in Asia for the duration!

I've decided to stay in Nepal until the end of May anyway. Seems daft to go back to India when I still have a couple of weeks Nepalese visa left.

Good Luck darling and 100 hugs. Love and Light from Sally
XXX.

*

29th May 2006

Dear Ailsa,

My Nepalese visa expires tomorrow, I'm booked on a plane to Delhi. Don't know whether to be glad or sorry to be leaving Nepal. It's been interesting...to say the least!

Decided to take one last trip before I leave; to Swayambhunath Monkey temple which is a mixture of Buddhism and Hinduism. The old Lama from Boudhanath was sitting in the Gompa — a kind of meditation hall in a temple — where the monks were having a ceremony.

There's a Tibetan refugee camp near here so the Monkey temple was swarming with Tibetan refugees as well as monkeys. The Tibetans were all trying to sell me singing bowls, and the

MONKEY ON MY ROOF

monkeys were trying to steal the camera Mark brought me from England.

'Sally,' the old Lama wheeled his chair towards me as I fended off a monkey with one hand and a prayer bowl with the other, 'nice to see you.'

'So you haven't gone back to Tibet after all.'

'Stay at the refugee camp three days. Then go Tibet,' he said.

We smiled at one another, 'I'm flying off to Delhi tomorrow.'

'Back home to husband?'

'No! Dharamsala, Darjeeling, Rishikesh or Amritsar? Who knows? The world is my lobster.'

We said goodbye and I rushed back to the hotel to pack. Now I'm all set to go.

Keep hanging in there dear Ailsa. My fingers are crossed for you.

Love and light from Aunt Sally X

*

30th May 2006

Thanks darling Sally for your loving support.

I've just come back from the hospital, it's spread to my liver and another place. I start to take poison next Thursday. No good news.

Now I don't feel like shouting or screaming. I was so worried because I just knew something was not right and that it might involve a scalpel. When I found out, for the first few hours I just didn't know how I felt, my head was going ten to the dozen and my imagination had already reached the stage of having my legs

MONKEY ON MY ROOF

amputated from MRSA before I got home! How stupid is THAT! Now all I feel is a kind of calm. It might not stay that way, but at least the questions aren't spinning around in my head. Sorry about the way I jabbered on at you when I phoned yesterday, but keep the lines open ok! Please keep those e-mails coming. Greg loves to read them too.

Love you, Ailsa.

*

Ailsa's news isn't unexpected. Still... when I sit in that narrow booth, and read those unbending words on the computer screen standing so innocently on that blue Formica desk... it seems to take a long time for my brain to absorb the text. Finally, I wipe the tears from my face and type.

*

2nd June 2006
My darling Ailsa,
No need for thanks. I won't dare to say I know how you feel and NO you're not stupid for thinking of MRSA, if I were in your shoes I'd be thinking of head amputation never mind anything else! You can jabber at me whenever you feel the need; the lines will always be open for you. I can imagine how you feel. No, scrub that! It's a lie! I cannot imagine! Couldn't ever imagine. All I can do is pray that the treatment isn't too hard for you, and send you distant healing every day.

Try to keep a smile on your face and stay positive.
Love and light from Aunt Sally X

MONKEY ON MY ROOF

46

With his sly crafty face and with only one tooth in his ugly mouth, the taxi driver taking me from Delhi airport to the Para Ganj looks a bit of a ruffian. Not that I care: after seeing off the thief who tried to steal my handbag in Bombay I feel more than capable of dealing with him should he cut up rough. So I jump in the back seat of the taxi.

The sun is so hot that omelettes could be cooked on the pavements — that's if a pavement could be found that was clean enough to cook an omelette on. All I want is a cold shower, a cool drink, and a cigarette. At this moment the first two are out of the question. But I'm no saint; I needed something to help me through the Nepalese riots! There's a pack of ciggies in my bag so I ask the driver, 'Is it okay if I smoke?'

The driver turns around in his seat and pulls something wrapped in cellophane from his pocket, 'You like smoke mine? Ganga, Hashish?'

'No! No!' Horrified, I take out my pack of Silk Cut, 'I'll smoke my own.'

He grins at me with his one tooth, leans across with a cigarette lighter, watches me light up, takes the lighter back, extracts a home-made cigarette from the glove box puts it between his lips and sets light to it. The sweet smell of cannabis fills the taxi.

The engine roars into life and we're off with the car lurching and swaying along the main road. Only then do I realise that the driver is completely stoned.

It's too late to find another taxi!

Nervously, more to stop him from falling into a stupor than

MONKEY ON MY ROOF

anything else I tell him about the last time I was in Delhi and the monkeys stealing bananas from a barrow.

'Monkeys,' he says, 'you like see monkeys?'

A cold shower and a cool glass of lemonade are a lot higher up my list of priorities than seeing a few monkeys. 'No, thank you very much,' I tell him, 'I'd rather go to my hotel.'

Despite my protests, he swings the car around a corner and says, 'I show you many monkeys, madam.'

Narrowly missing the trees on either side of the path, we wobble into a wooded park. The driver is right: there are monkeys. Monkeys in abundance.

Hairy red bottoms scoot along the paths and swing through the trees to mob people for bananas. A wheelbarrow piled with bananas is set in a cleared patch. These monkeys don't need to steal! People are actually buying bananas to feed them.

The driver stops the taxi, and we get out. I take some photos to please him before getting back in the car. He puts the key in the ignition and turns it. There is a grinding noise from the starter motor. He turns the key again. The car won't start. He gets out of the car, takes a can of oil and a plastic bottle of water from the boot, opens the bonnet and feeds the engine.

Night is starting to fall. Shadows from the trees are getting deeper. As if to mock us the sound of engines echo from the cars and motor bikes of those who only moments before were feeding the monkeys.

The driver gets back in the car and turns the key. The car still won't start. Our eyes meet in the driving mirror and I wonder if he feels as nervous as I do. He's beginning to look even more of a ruffian to me.

I lean over between the two front seats and ask, 'What about petrol?'

MONKEY ON MY ROOF

'Petrol okay,' he says, and plucks at the clump of grey whiskers growing from a wart on his chin.

'What are we going to do?' I wail.

He starts to shake his head, and then gazes at a big monkey standing on the path. All at once his one tooth gleams as his face lights up in a smile, 'I know what to do, madam!'

He walks to the barrow, buys a bunch of bananas and hands them one at a time to the big monkey. Then he climbs back in the driving seat, turns the key in the ignition and the engine roars into life.

'It started first time!' I say with amazement.

Once again his tooth gleams in a grin, 'Yes. I pay the monkey toll and road tax to Hanuman!'

Hanuman the monkey God!

When we get to my hotel the driver apologises for the car breaking down. He won't take a tip. Not a ruffian after all!

The hotel in Delhi is the same one I stayed in last October and everyone is very kind, but the temperature is forty-four degrees. People are dying. I figure that the best thing to do is to get myself to Dharamsala double quick. I hope to be there by tomorrow evening. Then on to McLeod Gang and Manali.

*

All the trains to Pathankot — the nearest station — are fully booked up. I blow the expense and splash out on a taxi. A young Sikh wearing a Day-Glo lime green turban drives the taxi. He has a full set of teeth and no warts on his chin and either doesn't speak much English or else thinks it beneath his dignity to make conversation with a woman. On the other hand his grave smile and reserved manner make me think that perhaps he is only shy.

    The silent Sikh (during the whole journey he speaks only once) drives me through Haryana and part of the Punjab, where the scenery is unmoving and unremarkable like his conversation.

MONKEY ON MY ROOF

47

The bed in my guesthouse room at Dharamsala has no pillow, a questionably stained bare mattress and only one threadbare blanket. There are mouse droppings on the windowsill. The whole room looks dirty. It reeks of old pee and fresh incense.

The incense smell is coming from the three sticks of Nag Champa stuck in the soil of a dying aloe vera plant sitting in a pot on top of the cistern of the western-style loo in the bathroom. The pong of old pee comes from the damp, rotting floorboards around the lavatory. The aloe vera plant hasn't seen water for weeks. The toilet bowl hasn't seen a lavatory brush for decades, and there is cockroach lurking on the rim. An old paint tin, meant to serve as a bucket, has a pink plastic jug hanging from the edge. As I pick the jug up to knock the cockroach away, a rat runs across the filthy bare floorboards.

It's eleven o'clock at night, too late to find another guesthouse. Tomorrow morning I'll get myself off to McLeod Ganj to finding something better.

*

Sixteen of us! Monks and nuns in maroon robes. Tibetan women in their national skirts and aprons, Indian women wearing saris or shalwar kameez, men carrying cages full of chickens and ducks, and me — the only westerner — sprawl on each other's knees in a ten-seater Maruti van. A narrow road winds along mountain passes with an abyss dropping down to the chasm below. I clutch frantically at the back of the seat in front of me where an Indian baby regards me gravely from over his mother's shoulder.

A Tibetan woman sits on one side of me. She is trying to sell

MONKEY ON MY ROOF

me a string of prayer beads. I shake my head; No! To reach my purse I would have to let go of the seat in front. Nothing on this earth can persuaded me to do that! In any event I won't be able to let go. My fingers have gone into spasm.

Each time the van twists around a curve in the road my stomach lurches and I want to throw up. When it reaches a bend in the road and gets too close to the edge a Buddhist monk sitting with one buttock on the seat and the other on my knee pats my back. He speaks very little English so it's difficult for me to tell whether he's patting my back to comfort himself or me as we both close our eyes imagining the van going over the edge of the cliff. On my right a smiling nun desperately fingers her prayer beads and mumbles a mantra.

At last we are at McLeod Ganj. The nun tucks her prayer beads up her sleeve, stops mumbling the mantra and is first down from the van. I am right behind her. She helps me totter down the steps, 'Where you staying?'

'I haven't got anywhere yet,' I tell her, 'I'm looking for somewhere clean.'

The nun smiles, 'Try the Om Hotel,' she points towards a gravel path running along the side of the mountain. 'You'll like it there.'

I hardly hear her.

Men, women, children are all around me. Monks, nuns, walking the narrow streets, spinning prayer wheels, counting the beads on wrist malas — a sort of Tibetan rosary — lips moving silently — *Om Mani Padme Hum* — a mantra.

Tibetans are everywhere outnumbering the Indians two, three, four to one. This isn't India, it's Little Tibet!

MONKEY ON MY ROOF

*

The terrace at the Om Hotel leans out over the Kangra Valley.

To shade the tables and chairs a yellow plastic awning is put up every morning and taken down again in the evening. Tibetan men stretch and balance on the parapet over the long, dizzying drop down into the valley. It makes me giddy to watch them.

From a small monastery a hundred feet below a steady murmur of prayer echoes. The vibration of singing bowls hums in the air and I can see monks in red robes heating pans of water on fires.

That nun couldn't have been more right. I do like it at the Om Hotel!

*

Seems like the monsoon has started. Rain is lashing down, it hits the cobblestones so violently that it bounces straight back up, only to lash down again turning the road into a watercourse. Even the waterproof I finally managed to buy in Kathmandu can't keep the wet out. My skirt is soaking wet, and the leather in my shoes has stretched with the damp, they now slip around as if they are three sizes too big. Hard to believe that only this morning I was sitting on the terrace in the hot sun teaching conversational English to a Buddhist monk and a young Tibetan guy.

Because of the monsoon, my arthritis has been playing up, so yesterday I went to see a Tibetan Doctor whose name sounds like some kind of disease. Doctor Tzetze Dongdong is over ninety years old and his face shows every day of his age, unlike his robust body, which is straight and strong. When he took my hand to feel my pulse a jolt of energy coursed up my arm. He prescribed a Tibetan

MONKEY ON MY ROOF

medicine that tasted like it had been mixed with water from the drains; I had the trots all last night!

This morning, though, I feel great, no need to spend the morning on the terrace in case the trots come back! The roads are slippery in the rain, and one can't see the potholes when they're filled with rainwater. I need a new walking stick, this one is splitting half way along its middle. On my way to see Doctor Dongdong yesterday I had it repaired by the carpenter in the bazaar. He only charged me twenty rupees but I don't know how much longer it's going to last.

Lisa my eldest daughter is interested in Buddhism. When she was a teenager it was all Take That and the Spice Girls, now it's Buddhist chants and hippy dresses. I've promised her some CDs, mantras, photos, and wise Dalai Lama sayings. Now I'm off to the post office with her parcel. Lisa is the one who looks like her Dad, curly black hair and brown eyes.

The middle one Jayne is mousy brown and blue eyed like me. She's the serious one of the family, always with her head stuck in a book arguing with her dad about politics. My youngest Emma has my mother's red hair, and the temper to go with it. An old woman living in our road once glared at me as if I'd done something wrong and said, 'All your children have different hair colours.'

I couldn't resist winding her up, 'Yes,' I replied, 'but Mark lets them all call him Daddy.'

The steps to the post office are high, set back behind a four-foot-wide trench. The trench is full of water and like all trenches in India the water is full of rubbish. Orange peel, used condoms, vegetable leavings, and sewerage float on the top, and because of the smell I suspect a few dead cows and monkeys are lurking somewhere under its surface.

MONKEY ON MY ROOF

I have to jump over the trench to reach the steps. With intrepid courage, I tuck my parcel and walking stick under one arm, hold my nose with my other hand, and leap. Yanking my skirt away from the clutches of the beggar woman sitting on the platform beyond, I brush three fleas, five mosquitoes, and a dead cockroach from the hem of my skirt, and scale the heights of the steps to the post office counter.

Registered post is the only option if I want my parcel to arrive without falling into thieving hands. It usually takes twenty minutes to register a parcel; everything at the post office has to be done in triplicate. The British taught India about red tape so it's no use complaining.

Hope my daughter appreciates the effort!

MONKEY ON MY ROOF

48

14th June 2006
Dear Ailsa,
How are things? I wish I could be there with you. Remember my dear that I'm thinking of you. The Tibetan woman who owns the hotel gave me some blue tack so that I could put your photo on the wall of my room. Don't know if you can feel it but I'm still doing Reiki for you.

When I do my Kora around the monastery, I visualize your face, say the mantras and do the symbols. I was a bit embarrassed when I first started, but nobody here takes any notice, they are all too busy doing their own thing. Anyway; what better place can there be to send healing from?

Love and light and 100 hugs from Aunt Sally.

*

The Dalai Lamas Complex is roughly a mile away from my guesthouse. Not long after I got to McLeod Ganj I sat on a window seat in the restaurant there to eat my lunch. The young Tibetan man who runs the restaurant chatted to me as I ate.

'What a wonderful display,' I exclaimed as we watched a thunderstorm flaunt itself over the valley as if in competition with the mountains, 'it almost has me believing in God.'

The Tibetan smiled. 'His Holiness will be teaching next week.'

'Really?'

He nodded. 'Yes.'

I laughed, 'That should sort my beliefs out.'

MONKEY ON MY ROOF

My intentions hadn't included the Dalai Lama's teachings when I came to India... but suddenly it seemed like a good idea. I asked, 'What do I have to do to attend the teachings?'

The Tibetan man showed me around the temple complex and pointed me in the direction of the Dalai Lama's security office. 'Go quickly now if you want to get into the teachings.'

Luckily for me the security office was open, and I was able to get a security pass.

This is the reason I've been sitting in a rain shower on a plastic chair in the temple yard for the last few days...

On the first morning I sat in the Foreigners section, all squashed up like a sardine in a can trying to maintain the lotus position on a cushion. But some of the westerners in the Foreigners section are so precious, seeming to regard themselves as more Buddhist than Buddha himself. So now I've escaped to sit with the Tibetans in the big yard where no-one snarls at me if I should dare to bump into them or knock over one of their books by accident.

A nun with a huge kettle is pouring cups of tsampa tea; a monk hands the tea around. A young Tibetan woman gives me her baby to jiggle on my knee while she fills a plate with biscuits. Our mouths full of biscuit crumbs, the baby and me smile at an old man — Grand-dad perhaps — who is looking on with beaming approval.

I have a lot more fun in the Tibetan section. If those precious westerners were to sit among the Tibetans... if they could see the smiling faces, the good-humoured budging up to make room for one another, the sharing of books, the young mums jiggling babies, they would realise what Buddhism is all about!

'Ahhh,' a collective reverential sigh springs from the throats of the thousands of people gathered here. Trying not to drop the baby I stand and crane my neck over the heads of the people

MONKEY ON MY ROOF

bowing and prostrating. A bent old man in yellow and red robes has arrived surrounded by a host of security personnel — the Dalai Lama is sheltered from the drizzle by a huge umbrella. I'd expected a taller, stronger person, but his presence brightens everything around.

I bow as he walks past. Is it my imagination, or just before my head dipped in its awkward bow, did His Holiness smile? Was that impish, good-natured smile for me? I'll never know for sure, but one thing I am sure of: like an image from a digital camera, that moment will stay with me for the rest of my life.

There are no musical instruments, only human voices for the singing. After the prayers, the Dalai Lama begins the teaching. He is teaching "The Way of the Bodhisattva", a book written over one thousand years ago by Shantideva, an Indian Buddhist scholar.

The teaching is in Tibetan; I hand the baby back to its mother and put my headphones on to listen to the English translation on a pocket radio.

Over the radio someone — a westerner — is asking: 'If I ever break an important vow, can I take it again?'

'No! Once it's broken, it's broken,' His Holiness replies seriously. Then he smiles, 'If you piss on the ground, can you put it back?'

The young man beside me is laughing, 'His Holiness tells funny story.'

Why do I always get a terrible urge to go to the loo at the wrong time? Today is the last day of the teachings, at any moment the Long Life Blessing will begin and I'm desperate. The toilets are down a passageway at the other end of the yard…I can't wait any longer.

My young Tibetan friend smiles at me when I come back,

MONKEY ON MY ROOF

'You've missed the most important part of the ceremony,' he says, 'you've lost your chance to live to a hundred!'

But I don't really mind. Yesterday was the Bodhisattvas ceremony.

> "For as long as space endures
> And for as long as living beings remain,
> Until then may I too abide
> To dispel the misery of the world."

Now I have to be nice to everyone, stop having bad thoughts about people, and mustn't use bad language.

I don't want to live to be a hundred anyway...

'What is your name?' I ask the young man.

He looks embarrassed. Then he tells me his name is Huang.

'Huang,' I say, 'isn't that a Chinese name?'

'I'm not Chinese.'

'Oh?'

'I was brought up as Chinese, but I'm Tibetan by birth.'

My puzzlement must be showing on my face but I don't like to ask.

He tells me anyway.

'Nine years ago my father died of a heart attack,' he says. 'The day after his funeral my mother called me to her room and told me that I wasn't really her son. I'd been adopted, she said. Taken from my natural parents at two weeks old by the Chinese after they invaded Tibet. My adoptive parents couldn't have children of their own so I'd been given to her and my father. I had no idea until then.'

'How awful! What a thing to be told when you've just lost

the man you thought was your father.'

'It wasn't easy,' Huang says, 'but he was a good kind father to me, and I loved him.'

'What about your adoptive mother?'

'She kind too. The best of mothers. I know it hurt her to have to tell me, but she thought it the right thing to do. '

I ask, 'Did you ever find your natural parents?'

'No, and I don't suppose I ever will now. All I know is that they lived in Lhasa.'

'Your English is very good,' I say.

'Yes my adoptive parents had money. They paid for my education.'

We smile at one another and settle down to listen and learn.

MONKEY ON MY ROOF

49

A prickly feeling at the back of my neck has me looking around, and there he is, the man who keeps following me. The first time I saw him was during a power cut last week. I've got used to the power cuts, don't mind them anymore. It's pleasant to sit on the terrace in the moonlight, to drink tea and talk to the American guy who stays in the room next to mine and anyone else who happens to be around. At least it *was* pleasant until those two men, a Westerner and a Tibetan, walked up the steps onto the terrace.

The Westerner was wearing a full-length black wool overcoat. It smelled of old rancid sweat and stale urine, the rest of him smelled like shitty underwear. He asked the American guy for a cigarette.

The American gestured at the packet on the table, 'Help yourself.'

When the man leaned over the table to pick up the packet his hand brushed against my arm and every hair on the back of my neck stood up.

As if sensing my reaction the man turned to look at me, 'Who are you?'

'This is Sally,' the American told him.

Eyes locked onto mine, the man said, 'I'll remember you.' The tone of his voice was menacing.

Then he gave the Tibetan one of the cigarettes and they both left.

I shivered, 'Who was that?'

'That's Herman,' the American said.

'I don't like the way he looked at me.'

My companion frowned, 'You should keep well away from

MONKEY ON MY ROOF

him,' he said seriously, 'he kinda has… problems…'

I didn't ask what kind of problems, sometimes it's better not to know; but I was still shivering when I went to bed.

That same man was on the rooftop terrace again the next morning. He and his Tibetan friend walked up the stairs while I was giving the monk and the waiter their English lesson. Already at eight o'clock in the morning the temperature was in the high eighties.

Without a word the waiter, the monk, and me got up and left.

Going down the stairs I held my nose.

'He smell like he gone to the toilet in his trousers!' the waiter said.

The monk was shocked. 'You mustn't say that.'

I laughed, 'Not even if it's true?'

I'm not laughing now; every morning he turns up on the terrace again, still wearing his black floor-length wool overcoat. He doesn't speak, just sits at the next table and looks at me.

A dark stare.

The man obviously has problems. Maybe he didn't have a happy childhood, perhaps I remind him of his mother? Last night I found him lurking in the dark on the patio outside my room; I brushed past him and fled down the stairs to the indoor café where there is light, music, and laughter. Now he's taken to following me along the street.

When I see him goose bumps break out on my arms. I've tried telling myself to ignore him, it's not as if I haven't met weirdoes before. They are all over the place in India. But this guy terrifies me.

MONKEY ON MY ROOF

*

I'm in the internet shop when my mobile sings and the screen lights up: Ailsa calling.

'Hi Ailsa' I say, 'I've just been e-mailing you.'

'Hello Sally,' her voice is husky, she sounds tired, 'keep sending the mails, Greg prints them out and I read them in bed. I thought I'd better give you a call while I still can.'

'That bad is it darlin'?'

'It's not exactly a bundle of laughs.'

'Is the treatment working do you think?'

She coughs, a dry painful cough, 'Sometimes I think it is, and sometimes I'm sure it isn't…if it wasn't for Greg,' she coughs again, '… I don't know what I'd do.'

What can I say? Oh God why is this happening to her? To Ailsa of all people.

'He'll always be there for you.'

'Yes. I'm having my operation next week,' she says between coughs. 'He's taken all his holiday time from work to look after me.'

'Have you told your Mum and Dad?'

'No.'

'You should let them know, Ailsa. Think about it, apart from anything else Greg could probably do with their help.'

And we say goodbye.

*

2nd July 2006

Dear Ailsa,

Thanks for the phone call, it was lovely to hear your voice again,

MONKEY ON MY ROOF

even if it was a bit croaky!!

You would love it here in Himmala Pradesh. Of course, this is the Himalayas and the scenery is spectacular, even more so I think than in Nepal. There are many treks for people who are interested in trekking. Who knows; you and Greg? Maybe when you've recovered from your operation — because you are going to recover, don't you doubt it.

Anyway, thought I'd tell you about the young monk who stopped me in the street a while back and asked if I'd help him with his English. Of course I agreed, and he arrived with an English fairy tale book and joined the waiter — who is also trying to improve his English — and me on the terrace. Their English is good, it only needs a few corrections in pronunciation here and there.

In the afternoons I've been teaching conversational English to some of the young Tibetan refugees at LHA, a voluntary charity in the centre of town. And there's a nightly drop-in English conversation class, where anyone can just come along and chat with newly arrived refugees and monks. So, if you should come across any Tibetan monks who talk with a Scouse accent you'll know who's responsible!

Missing you. HugsOOO and KissesXXX from Sally.

MONKEY ON MY ROOF

50

Serendipity. It's happened again, that happy accident!

I'm sitting on the terrace pretending to enjoy my coffee. Pretending; because that crazy man Herman is sitting at the next table putting the frighteners on me.

Then, from behind me, I hear that unmistakable voice saying my name; 'Sally.' That lovely lilt in his voice.

'Nice to see you, Stephan,' I say, and grip the edge of the table to restrain myself from jumping up and grabbing hold of him.

I attempt to lift one hand and I point to the seat opposite me, 'Sit down why don't you,'

He's been staying at the Tushita Meditation Centre doing a Vipassana course, Stephan says.

'A ten day meditation. I had to sit all day watching my breath. Wasn't allowed to smoke, drink alcohol, read, write, pray, chant, or count beads.'

'Sounds grim!'

He smiles, 'And absolutely no sex!'

Before I can stop myself I ask, 'Get much of that do you?'

And could have bitten my tongue off.

Stephan laughs, those grey-green eyes crinkle, 'Not enough.'

'Isn't it funny,' I say, 'how we're always bumping into one another? I'd no idea you were going to be here.'

He turns his head to look at me, looks quickly away, says quietly, 'I'll be sorry to leave.'

'When are you going?'

'Not for a few days. Thought I'd stay for the Dalai Lama's birthday celebrations. Then I'm catching the bus to—'

I put my hand across his mouth, 'Don't tell me!'

MONKEY ON MY ROOF

Taking my hand in his he says, 'You're right! If we are meant to meet again it will happen whatever we do.'

'Yes,' and I find myself thinking: What will happen then?

Fight it as much as I can the chemistry is there. Stephan feels it too. I can tell by the way he *doesn't* look at me. From the corner of my eye I sneak a secret glance at him when I think he isn't looking, and catch him sneaking a secret glance at me.

It's a dead giveaway.

'But there's always tomorrow,' he says, 'I'm thinking of a day trip to Amritsar. Fancy sharing a taxi with me?'

I can't answer; a movement behind him has caught my eye. Herman is leaving his table.

He pauses next to me, polluting the space around us with his smell.

Stephan stands up, 'Did you want something?'

Herman doesn't answer; just stands there staring at me. That dark stare.

'This is a private conversation,' Stephan says, 'we don't want company.'

Herman doesn't move.

'I suggest you leave,' Stephan's voice is steely.

Herman turns his head and looks at Stephan, takes a step towards him.

Stephan straightened his shoulders, and I hold my breath.

'While you still can,' Stephan says.

His voice is soft, but there is no mistaking the threat in it.

Herman doesn't mistake it either. He hesitates for a moment, then turns on his heel and walks down the stairs.

Phew! Now I can breathe again.

'Do you know that man?' Stephan asks

MONKEY ON MY ROOF

'No,' I say with a shiver, 'But he's always hanging around. I feel as if I'm being stalked.'

Stephan frowns, 'If he causes you any trouble I'll sort him out.'

'My hero,' I say sardonically, 'fat chance if you're away again in a couple of days!'

Stephan laughs, leans across the table and catches hold of my hand, 'Now how about that trip to Amritsar?'

'Only if we go Dutch!'

'If you like.'

The waiter comes with the menus.

Without looking at me, Stephan asks 'What do you fancy?'

You! I fancy you!

Thank goodness he is looking away and can't see my face. I've never been much good at hiding my feelings.

'This scenery is amazing,' I say, pretending to watch the eagles swoop and soar over the Himalayas.

'There's a kind of cultural evening on at the school tonight,' Stephan announces. 'Would you like to go?'

I nod my head. Who knows when we'll meet again?

'Meet you here at half seven,' he says.

*

Shoes covered in the nauseous mess that runs down into the drains, Stephan and me dodge the cars, vans, motorbikes and cows on our way to the school. We slip and slither down three or four hundred steep stone steps, greasy with banana skins and dog poo.

There aren't any chairs in the schoolroom so we squat side by side on a pallet covered by a brown sack. A big black dog

MONKEY ON MY ROOF

wanders in, he sits next to me on the sack. From the corner of my eye I watch his back leg come up to scratch his neck. When he's finished scratching, the dog puts his leg down and lowers his head. It's easy to tell this dog is male from the way he is sniffing at his privates.

We are supposed to be watching a programme of dancing and singing, but it's just one man playing a Tibetan guitar and singing Tibetan songs.

'Tashi is singing a Tibetan love song,' an assistant tells us and starts a translation.

This dog sitting next to me appears to like the love song, because now he's panting and dribbling as he licks his testicles. Stephan seems to like the song too because now he is holding my hand. In my opinion even if it were in English, Tashi's song has no chance of reaching the top ten. Or the top million for that matter.

On the sack next to me, the dog has stopped scratching at his testicles and is sniffing at my crotch. Some children are peeping round the door to get a look at the foreigners; others are running in and out of the room. The assistant stops translating the love song to shoo the children away.

I nudge Stephan, who is watching the dog and laughing.

'Time to go,' I say.

Enough is enough,

It's pitch dark outside. Those steps seem even steeper in the dark. Stephan has a torch and holds my hand as I puff my way up.

When we reach the top he offers me a cigarette.

'No thanks,' I say. 'All I really want is oxygen!'

He laughs and catches me in a bear hug, 'Oh, I'm going to miss you!'

'Me too,' I say.

220

MONKEY ON MY ROOF

'I'd better see you to your room.'

'What for...?' I give him a questioning look.

'In case that crazy guy is hanging around?'

He hugs me again outside my room, his breath smells of mint toothpaste, his skin smells of the cologne he uses as aftershave and his hair of coconut oil. He kisses my cheek, the same cheek, the exact same place he kissed in Bombay, 'Are you going to let me come in?'

Desire blazes through me and I shudder... but what about that promise I made to myself?

The promise that I'd be faithful as long as Mark and I stayed married. Promises aren't meant to be broken. What kind of person breaks a promise to herself? Just because Mark's been unfaithful doesn't mean I have to be. Do I want to turn into one of those angry women who talk about revenge fucks on daytime TV shows? No way! Revenge seldom seems to do those women a blind bit of good. I've never believed in revenge myself.

Still... Pulling away I put my hand up to my face, to that spot on my cheek. The place still burns and tingles, I can feel myself getting hot. Afraid to look at him I turn away. It's ridiculous! Oh God, I shouldn't be feeling like this.

'Behave yourself,' somehow I find the strength to push him away, 'we hardly know one another.'

And walk alone to my room.

MONKEY ON MY ROOF

51

Amritsar! What can I say? It's dirty, dusty, smelly, a dazzling display of colour in the markets, the streets vibrant with so much life that the beggars have enough get-up-and-go to smile at us and give a blessing; even when we haven't any small change to give them. This is real India.

The Golden Temple is built of white marble crowned with gold minarets, the floors are tiled with what look like semi-precious stones. We have to take our shoes off and bathe our feet before we can enter.

The Sikhs are proud of their temple; happy to see us there, they queue up to show us around. A group of young children ask us to take their photos. Young girls and boys shake our hands; shyly show their parents how well they can speak English, 'Hello. How are you? Where you from? Can I take your photo? Will you take my photo?'

'My God, Sikh men are so BIG!' I say to Stephan, 'Look at the size of that man there.'

Stephan laughs, and points to men and boys bathing in the lake surrounding the Golden Temple, 'Must be something in the water.'

'Hmm, you may be right,' I say as I watch a group of Sikh women who are as slim and delicate as all the other Indian women we've met, 'I don't see any girls bathing in their holy lake.'

A Sikh man hurriedly pulls on his clothes and dresses his young son. 'Please will you take my son's picture?' he asks shyly.

The little boy stands ramrod straight by his father's side, as smart and proud as any soldier. How can we refuse?

The Golden Temple is beautiful, quite stunning. But it's the

MONKEY ON MY ROOF

people who worship there — the tall black bearded men, incongruous in their bright turbans and underpants, dunking their young sons in the lake; the slim delicate women wearing the colourful shalwar kameez; the giggling teenagers, the wide-eyed children, the sentries with their spears ready to prod anyone showing disrespect to the Guru — that Stephan and me find the most interesting.

It's half past two in the afternoon, and we haven't eaten since breakfast. There's a queue at the food kitchen — food is given free to visitors at the temple.

Stephan says, 'We'll go eat at the restaurant outside.'

But... 'No lunch. The kitchen is closed,' a waiter says.

Disappointed, we turn to leave, the waiter calls us back, and 'I'll get the staff to cook for you.'

The Shahi Korma and chapatti's that we eat are the best I've ever tasted.

We pay the bill, and I say, 'Can you imagine a restaurant kitchen being opened for us in England? They'd let us starve first.'

'Food always tastes better when served with kindness,' Stephan said.

I laugh, 'Yes. Particularly when it's so cheap!'

Seventy-five rupees including the tip for the two of us.

A rickshaw took us to see the changing of the guard at the Pakistan border. One of the guards lifted the chain to let us through to the Pakistan side, and somehow or other we end up in the VIP box with all the dignitaries. Thousands of people were clapping, chanting, dancing and singing. The party had begun!

The guards arrived, magnificent stately men, all of them well over two metres in height, slim and handsome in their khaki uniforms. On their heads, huge hats crowned with red feathers

MONKEY ON MY ROOF

shaped like peacocks' tails.

Music, hundreds of people on the bridges and towers chanting, 'Hindustan, Hindustan, Hindustan!'

Hindustan: The land of the Hindus. Guards parading. Men rushing down to the parade ground. Guards pushing them back into the boxes. Women running waving a large Indian flag, dancing daringly in front of the Pakistan guards, 'Hindustan, Hindustan, Hindustan!'

I clutch Stephan's hand.

More women run down with a Pakistani flag, taunting the guards, daring the Indian women to stop them.

The guards march away lifting their legs high.

The party is over!

In the taxi on the way back to McLeod Ganj I say, 'Whew! What a performance! Thank you Stephan. I wouldn't have missed it for the world.'

He puts an arm around my shoulder and kisses the top of my head. I drop off to sleep with my head on his shoulder.

*

Ailsa is never out of my thoughts, each day I pin her photo on my room wall, to send distant healing. When was the last time I heard from her? Whenever I phone or send a text a mechanical voice tells me I can only make emergency calls. She hasn't answered my last e-mail. Of course, that doesn't mean anything. It's likely she hasn't received it.

Still...

On my mobile I call up her number.

Her phone rings for a long time then... 'Ailsa? It's me Sally.'

MONKEY ON MY ROOF

'No this is Greg,' sleepy voice, Scottish accent.

My hand flies to my mouth. Why is Greg answering her phone? What am I about to hear? Was she...?

Somehow I find the courage to ask, 'What is it? What has happened?'

'Ailsa's in hospital. She had another operation yesterday.'

Not the worst news then; but bad enough.

'I've been there all night, just got back,' he says. 'It was touch and go, but... you know Ailsa...'

'Yes,' I choke out, 'She's one of the strongest, bravest people I've ever known.'

'She told me to tell you that her mother and father have been at her bedside the last couple of days. She wants you to know she's forgiven her parents.'

'That's good to hear.'

'Sally? You know we were planning to get married this year?'

'Yes.'

'Whatever arises... I want that to happen. What do you think about Ailsa and me having the wedding at the hospital?'

Sniffing back a tear, I tell him, 'I think it's a brilliant idea, wish I could be there.'

Beep, beep, beep, the out of credit signal sounds on my mobile, I just manage to say, 'Love to Ailsa. Let me know how it goes,' as my mobile switches itself off.

MONKEY ON MY ROOF

52

Yesterday was the Dalai Lama's Birthday celebrations; Stephan and me had to be at the Temple for half past eight to meet the waiter from the Om Hotel who'd promised to show us around. We couldn't find him and were beginning to think he'd let us down when a young Tibetan guy with a long black ponytail arrived.

He asked, 'You Sally?'

'Yes.'

He only knew about twelve words in English, Stephan doesn't speak Tibetan, and my Tibetan is limited to "Good Luck" and "Please sit down".

'Friend sent me,' black ponytail said, 'Sister come Delhi.'

He found us a place under the awning; somewhere we could put our cushions out of the rain. After a while my back started screaming at having to sit on the floor and my knees had gone into spasm from forcing them into the lotus position, so Stephan and me sneaked off by ourselves and watched the dancing and singing while sharing a monk's umbrella.

Everyone, despite the rain, was laughing and happy, having fun. A sadhu who told us he was a Karate Guru showed Stephan some of his karate kicks, while I chatted to a Danish woman who invited me to stay with her in Pune.

Stephan said cheerio to the Karate Guru, smiled at the Danish woman and took hold of my hand, 'Let's find a café. I need a drink.'

'Okay.'

That was when I saw Herman in his long overcoat. The weirdo had been lurking around all day. It was making me nervous. I pulled Stephan's hand to make him walk in the opposite direction;

MONKEY ON MY ROOF

a party is no place for a confrontation; especially a party in monastery.

'What you doing?' he said, and laughed. Then he looked at my face and stopped laughing.

'What's the matter?'

'Nothing, nothing,' I said distractedly. 'Let's go this way.'

'No!'

Stephan had already spotted Herman coming towards us, and Herman looked as if he was burning for trouble.

'Out of my way,' he brushed past Stephan and made a grab for my arm.

Brave now because Stephan was standing beside me, I gave him a push, 'OH SOD OFF!'

And Herman raised his arm, fingers already curled into a fist, 'I'm to going kill you.'

Stephan jumped in front of me, grabbed Herman by the arm, twisted it behind his back.

'You're killing no one,' Stephan growled, and forcing Herman down onto his knees, gave his arm another twist, 'You heard the lady, now sod off.'

He let go of Herman and leaving him kneeling on the floor, put his arm around me, 'Let's go and get that drink.'

Expecting Herman to come after us, I looked back but he'd got up and was disappearing into the crowd.

'Wow! You certainly don't need a Karate Guru,' I said. 'That's some accomplishment you have there, where did you learn how to do that?'

'I was in the police force remember,' he said, 'that kind of training never leaves you.'

A couple of minutes later there was a commotion behind us.

MONKEY ON MY ROOF

A policeman shoved his way through the crowd.

'What's going on?' I asked a woman standing near.

'That crazy man's been arrested,' she said, 'he attacked a woman and some children.'

Another policeman arrived to say that they would deport the man back to Germany. 'We need to speak to his mother,' he said. 'Do you know where she is?'

Stephan and me looked at one another.

'He has a mother?' we said.

MONKEY ON MY ROOF

53

Back at the guesthouse my mobile chirps its little tune: Ailsa calling.

Scientists tell us that e-mail messages travel for light years through the ether into outer space. I've often wondered if the same is true of mobile phones. Are there life forms from another planet somewhere out there listening to what we humans say to one another? Are they pondering how to lend a hand with our education, or are they amused by our stupidity? Are they listening in right now; smiling at human insecurities? At this very moment are they preparing to decode Greg's and my speech patterns?

Because it can only be Greg on the other end of the phone. Ailsa can't possibly be out of hospital yet, and mobile phones aren't allowed on hospital wards.

I bite my lip and press the green button on the keypad. Will it be good news or bad?

'Sally! At last!' a voice says. 'I've been trying to reach you.'

'Hello Greg,' I answer slowly, 'what's happening? How's Ailsa?'

'Don't worry,' there's a smile in his voice; 'Mrs. McDonald is holding her own!'

'Mrs. McDonald... who's Mrs. McDon...'

For a second I don't understand. Then...relief flows upward from my feet to my face, sweat prickles, my eyes sting, try to form tears but the smile already forming on my lips won't let them.

'Oh! Wow! You got married then? How was it? Did she wear that dress she'd bought? Did her Dad give her away? How is she? How are you? How long will she be in hospi...'

'Hey. Slow down! Slow down!' He's laughing, 'One

question at a time.'

'Just tell me!'

'Okay. The wedding. Yes Ailsa did wear her wedding dress, and her Dad gave her away. Pushed her in a wheel chair to the hospital garden, and her mother cried like all mothers do at weddings.'

'They let you do that then? Get married at the hospital?'

'The admin staff people at the hospital were fantastic. Couldn't have been more helpful once Ailsa's oncologist had a word with them. We decided on a Humanist wedding. You can have a humanist wedding wherever you like. Write your own vows as long as you let the registrar know in advance.'

'Oh lovely,' I say doubtfully; because I don't know much about humanist weddings and am not even sure if they are legal.

Almost as if he's read my mind Greg says, 'Scotland legalised humanist marriages last year.'

I ask the question I've been afraid to ask, 'How did Ailsa's operation go?'

'Her oncologist says chemotherapy has cleared the spots on her liver, and the tumour on her spine is a low grade one.'

'Tumour low grade! Oh Greg, that's really wonderful,' now I'm crying for real.

'Her specialist says that there's definitely hope, because Ailsa's young and in fairly good health to start with, and to just take it one day at a time.'

'Tell her Aunt Sally sends her love,' I choke out.

*

MONKEY ON MY ROOF

14th July 2006

Hi Ailsa or should I say Mrs. McDonald?
Don't know if you'll get to read this e-mail, but maybe Greg can print it out and read it to you in hospital? Anyroad, here is the latest news from your India reporter.

In a couple of days I'll be travelling to Manali. By bus! Ten hours up the valley and over the mountain trails to the other side, I'm not looking forward to it I can tell you. Arrival in Manali will be five o'clock in the morning, the monsoon is in full flood, and if there isn't a room free I'll be in deep you know what!! Oh well, it all adds to life's rich tapestry.

I'm travelling with the American man who has the next room to mine at the guesthouse, and an Australian woman. We were supposed to be going on to Ladakh together, but I've had second thoughts about that.

The American; his name is Burt, is from New Orleans. He came out to India to get his head around what happened in that hurricane last year when all those people died. He's about fifty years old and has a great sense of humour with casual throwaway lines that crack me up a lot of the time. He and I are quite sceptical of the beautiful souls around here.

On the other hand, Chris the Australian woman is one of those beautiful souls. When she arrived she had gorgeous hair, long and wavy, a rich chestnut brown, two days later she had it all shaved off!

'What did you do that for?' I asked her.
'I want to be a Buddhist,' she said.
'The Tibetans are all Buddhists, but you don't see them shaving their heads,' I told her.

Now Chris is walking around like a nun in mufti. But it

MONKEY ON MY ROOF

doesn't stop her from wearing makeup. Can't say I blame her though, she has the most amazing eyes, a kind of cerulean blue with a green line around the iris. Is this the sign of a truly spiritual Being do you think? Or is she an Alien from another planet?

Last night she was in the restaurant talking to Ahni, an old nun: 'Hello cheeky face, haven't you got a cheeky face then? Go on, give me a cheeky smile.'

Talking to Ahni as if she's two years old! Any minute now I told myself, and it'll be Coochie, Coochie, Coo!

The Tibetan staff started laughing and calling over, 'Go on Ahni! Give her a smile, show her your lovely teeth!'

The poor old nun only has two yellow teeth, which are stuck in the bottom of her jaw like walrus tusks.

Yesterday I told Chris and the American that the altitude would be too much for me so I won't be taking the jeep with them to Ladakh.

Now that I've taken my vows I have to remember that the main tenets of Buddhism are Compassion, Patience, and Endeavour; but if Chris tries that Coochie Coo business with me I'll forget about the Compassion and the Patience... and Endeavour to throw her off the bus!

Oh Damn! Guess who's just come to sit beside me at the next computer?

Must be my punishment or a test of my patience.

I'll get back to you from Manali.

        Love Light and lots of Laughter from Aunt Sally.

MONKEY ON MY ROOF

54

Tired and fed up, I slither and slide along the narrow puddled path which runs three hundred yards along the side of the mountain to our guest-house in Manali old town. The bus trip was tough, squashed up into a space that even pygmies would find uncomfortable.

The pungent perfume of cannabis is everywhere. Those spiky green leaves sprout from roof tiles, burgeon wildly from window ledges and push up from the gutters under the eaves of houses and shops. Inhaling the scent makes my rucksack feel lighter and I smile recalling a place and time four years ago.

It's a sunny Saturday in August. I'm sitting with my best friend Dawn drinking coffee and looking at some old photos in the leaky conservatory in our bungalow in Knotty Ash. Dawn and me are alone, Mark is at work, our two eldest daughters have moved into a flat of their own, and the youngest is in France on a school trip.

'The problem is,' I confided to Dawn, 'we never have any fun anymore. Mark is such a workaholic.'

'You look as if you're having fun here,' she said, and handed me a snapshot of Mark and me roaring with laughter at a one of his works do's.

I glanced at the photo, then I put it down on the bamboo coffee table that had come with the conservatory settee and chairs. 'That was ages ago. Now even when he isn't working he can't relax. He's much too buttoned up... too square.'

'Okay, so he needs to relax,' Dawn said. 'So get him some tranquilisers.'

'Don't be daft! The doc won't prescribe them without seeing

MONKEY ON MY ROOF

him, and I can't get him to go to the doctor.'

Dawn grinned, 'I didn't mean prescription tranquilisers. How about I make you a couple of spliffs? That should relax him.'

'Do you think so?' I'd said sceptically, 'Mark has never smoked a cigarette, never mind a spliff!'

'Well maybe it's about time he did!'

'Hmm,' I said, 'the way things are…anything's worth a try.'

After dinner that evening I'd poured Mark and me a glass each of Shiraz, opened the envelope Dawn had left, pulled out her funny fags and asked Mark, 'Want to share one of these with your wine?'

He'd taken some persuading but finally he'd agreed.

An hour later we were tearing each other's clothes off, and making love anywhere that had a surface: the floor, a chair, the dining table. With Mark's naked buttocks rising and falling between my legs, I gazed over his shoulder to the other side of the room at the fuchsia plant which was standing in a pot surveying us from its position on the windowsill. The fuchsia nodded its petals at me.

Lying on our shaggy hearthrug with my head in the grate, every perception polished to perfect awareness, I murmured, 'He's watching us.'

Mark stopped nuzzling at my neck, he lifted his head, 'Who's watching us?'

'The plant. The fuchsia.'

Dropping his head to run his tongue across my breast Mark mumbled, 'Take no notice and he'll go away.'

On the other side of the room, as if to contradict my husband's words, the fuchsia craned its pink and purple head, stretched out a long green stalk and peeped over Mark's shoulder to

MONKEY ON MY ROOF

inspect the rhythmic plunge, the in-and-out thrust of our thighs.

I'd been overcome with laughter.

Mark reared his head up and gasped, 'What you laughing at?'

'The plant! The plant! He's watching us. He's watching what we're doing,' I choked.

'Let him watch,' Mark said, 'he might learn something!'

It didn't put Mark off his stroke, we went on all night. I must say, for a man whose only idea of foreplay is to turn the bedroom light out, my husband excelled himself that night. Seven hours of unadulterated bliss, the best sex I've ever had! Pity it's never happened again!

Maybe…I smile to myself imagining Stephan's long humorous face, looking at my naked body, crinkly eyes becoming serious, turning smoky with desire. No! I can't go there. Mustn't go there…

'What are you smiling at?' Chris asked.

I pointed to the side of the mountain, which was covered with those green distinctive plants, 'All this cannabis! Everyone here must be stoned. No wonder they all walk around with smiles on their faces!'

Pulling a leaf from one of the plants I crushed it between my fingers and put it to my nose, 'Why should I be any different?'

Chris and Burt both laughed.

If only they knew!

MONKEY ON MY ROOF

55

15th July 2006
Dear Ailsa,
How is married life treating you? Okay, it's only been a couple of days since last I e-mailed, and you're probably sick and fed up reading the damn things, but I'm not going to stop. At least not until you beg me to on your bended knees. Here is my latest instalment.

Our guesthouse is lovely, with a view of mountains covered in pine trees and apple orchards — not to mention cannabis plants. There is a river down below. From my room I can hear the water as it rushes over the rocks. Tonight it can sing me to sleep; it won't have to sing for very long.

The weather this morning was pleasant, not too hot with a nice breeze. Chris and Burt left for their trip to Leh last night and I was running short of money. There's an ATM in New Manali, so I decided to have lunch at my favourite Punjabi Restaurant.

The walk through the Pine forest to New Manali is lovely, five rupees to enter the gate into the park — which is bordered by a high wall on three sides and a river on the other — and take the short cut instead of paying thirty rupees for a rickshaw. Seemed like a good deal to me.

The pines are almost as tall as the redwood trees I saw in California; the scent of the pines was everywhere. Small butterflies the colour of English bluebells fluttered among the ferns and wild flowers, the air was filled with bird song, the river murmured dreamily nearby as it tumbled over the rocks, and the sounds of traffic passing on the road got fainter and fainter as I got deeper into the forest.

Moss-covered rocks on the sides of the path had notices

MONKEY ON MY ROOF

painted on them. "Resting Place," a large reddish rock stated in black letters painted on a yellow background. It dominated a group of smaller rocks, which were just the right size and height for me to sit on. There were no man-made picnic seats and tables; Indians don't believe in improving on nature unless it's to do with something electronic, the latest mobile phone or I-pod for instance. Further along the path another rock told anyone who wanted to know, "A forest is the border between Earth and Heaven."

A lovely walk.

After I'd drawn my money at the ATM in Manali and eaten lunch, I looked around the Gompa, took photos in the Temple and bought myself a hat in the market. It was getting on for two o'clock, time I was making my way back. To walk back through the Nature Reserve I thought, would be pleasanter than taking a bus or rickshaw. The path is paved and there are steps on the steeper parts. So much easier and a lot safer than walking on the road dodging rickshaws, sacred cows, snake charmers, and crazy Israelis on souped-up motorbikes. Or should that be souped-up Israelis on crazy motorbikes?

The sky was looking a bit overcast; nothing to worry about, it wouldn't start to rain for hours I told myself. There was another path that I hadn't explored. A notice board read, "This way to the Peasantry!" Okay I know Indian notice boards are often misspelled, but Peasantry? Was it a bird sanctuary or a tribal village? Intriguing!

Ignoring the light shower that had started to fall I turned my feet onto this new path which meandered around for roughly two miles before ending up at a collection of cages. The cages housed a few scrawny, stir-crazy pheasants running back and forth, throwing themselves at the wire mesh. There was no sign of any peasants,

MONKEY ON MY ROOF

pleasant or otherwise.

That light shower had turned into a heavy downpour. Majestic and beautiful as pine trees are, they don't provide much shelter from the rain. I hadn't an umbrella or a raincoat and I was getting soaked but it seemed silly to walk all the way back to the entrance in the rain. The paved path to the exit near the river bridge couldn't be far away. Could it?

Big mistake! Will I never learn? Given my lack of direction and poor knowledge of geography, I should have known better! Stumbling over rocks, I waded through pine needles lying so deep on the boggy ground that they covered my ankles and got caught in the hairs on my legs. Trying to remember the last time I had my legs waxed, I gingerly lifted them as high as my knees would allow.

Oh my God! From the corner of my eye I could see something moving, slithering along the ground. What was it? A snake? A scorpion? The Indians say there aren't any snakes here in North India, but only last night I was woken up at two in the morning by one of the girls in the room next to mine. She'd stood on a snake while on her way to the toilet. Okay it was only a harmless grass snake, but that was no consolation to her at the time. Poor girl thought she'd trodden on a cobra!

I'd been walking in circles for hours; the forest didn't seem so lovely anymore. Rain was coming down harder and faster, I couldn't see where I was going, my hair was plastered to my head and water was dripping from my nose. I'd have given my right arm for a hot drink and one of those warm peanut butter biscuits, the ones Sanjay makes at the Coffee House. As soon as I'm back on the main road, I told myself, I'm going to stop at that Coffee House. I'll order three cups of coffee and half a dozen biscuits.

At last there was the gate! Through the heavy metal bars, I

MONKEY ON MY ROOF

could see the lights of shops, horns were blowing as buses and rickshaws passed by; but the soddin' gate was locked! Only four thirty and it was locked! That gate was supposed to stay open until five. A huge steel padlock hanging from the bars and no one around to turn the key! I felt like weeping with frustration.

'It's okay,' An Indian man passing on the road on the other side of the gate said and pointed to where the barbed wire was broken through, on top of the eight-foot wall, 'You can get out through there!'

'What me?' I showed him my walking stick. 'I can't climb up there!'

'Go the other way towards the river. The fence is broken, the wall not so high. It will be easier for you to get through,' he reassured me.

I thanked him and stumbled away in the direction he indicated.

He was right, there was a fence, and it was lower. But not by much! To cap it all, huge nettles were growing in the crevices along the wall. If I slipped trying to climb that wall I could fall down into the river below, and the river was in full flood over jagged rocks.

Imagining myself slipping and falling, my broken body smashed on the rocks below, I stared at the wall and the river. The wall and the river stared back at me. The more I stared at them, the more dangerous they seemed. The rain was still pelting down, the rocks getting slipperier.

The only thing for it was to walk the path back to New Manali! But by the time I got there the other gate would be locked and I'd have to spend the night in the forest with the mosquitoes and scorpions, plus heaven alone knows what kind of other animals lurk here by moonlight. Are there tigers in Manali, I wondered?

MONKEY ON MY ROOF

Does India have wolves?

No way! I lifted my knee as high as it would go, but still couldn't make it to the top of that damn wall.

Luckily, a driver stopped his rickshaw and got down, 'Don't worry, Ji. I'll help you!'

He climbed over and together we gathered rocks and piled them up against the wall like a set of stairs. He held the barbed wire down so that I could climb through. Soaking wet and stung by nettles, I felt like kissing him! Indians! I love them! They always find a way of putting right the problems they created in the first place!

Next time I go in that forest I'll take a map, or at least an umbrella, and perhaps a folding step ladder and a pair of wire cutters.

Lots of you know what; combined with hugs from Aunt Sally X

*

19th July 2006

Hello Dear Aunt Sally.

Just thought I'd let you know that I'm writing this e-mail from my own computer! In my own living room in my own flat! There's a glass of Irn Brew on the table next to me, and Greg is sitting on the settee watching footie on TV with the sound turned down. Yesterday I saw my specialist; he says I'm doing great. Good News to tell you at last! I can hardly believe it.

Let me know how things are with you.

Feel yourself hugged by Mrs. Mc Donald

MONKEY ON MY ROOF

<u>56</u>

24th July 2006

Hi Ailsa Darling,

WHOOPEE, HURRAY, YOU'RE OUT OF HOSPITAL AND HOME AGAIN! It's wonderful to hear you're doing so well. You clever girl! How is Hubby? Do you think you'll get to like married life now that you're an old married woman? It's so lovely to think of you and Greg being married.

Sorry for the delay in writing. This blinking computer keeps crashing, and I'm working from memory. My typing skills have never been very good. The keyboard being in Hebrew doesn't help much either.

Talking of which, Manali is full of Israelis who just love to play scratchy techno music at full volume all day and all night, and they don't even invite me to their parties!

So as you can guess it's a bit noisy here at night. I've moved my room down the path to the Brahma Guest House and Laffing Buddha restaurant. It's cheap; one hundred and fifty rupees a night, and even has a wardrobe for my clothes and fly screens on the windows, hot water too! But no sleep for the last three nights. I'm beginning to wonder is it worth it?

The monsoon is here and it rains every day, no sun, no beach, only mountains. Just my luck to be stuck in a monsoon when there's a heat wave in Europe. My family keeps texting and e-mailing, complaining about how hot it is, and according to the BBC news there have been power cuts in London because too many people are using air conditioners!

I've heard that motorised rickshaws are being used as taxis in Brighton. I'm losing my tan. Can't wait to get back to Goa in

241

MONKEY ON MY ROOF

September, swim in the ocean and sit on the beach getting all my wobbly white bits as brown as a barbecued chicken. Tomorrow I'm moving to Shimla, hopefully it will be quieter there, and maybe the computer keyboards will be in English!

Love and Light and 100 hugs from Sally.

*

What a journey! The road to Shimla is narrow with a long drop down one side of the mountain to a winding river. Through the windows of the bus, I watch the Himalayas scrape the sky on both sides of the valley, the views are amazing. Small houses cling to the side of the mountains. The gardens are bordered with hedges of pink bougainvillea and flowerbeds of hollyhocks and lilies. To further brighten the landscape the Hindu Temples are painted in Day-Glo shocking pink, with edges outlined in sky blue, golden yellow and lime green.

The air is warm, silky-smooth against the skin, and smells strongly of the cannabis which grows wild in the valley. There are hedges of the stuff everywhere, it nudges its way between the hollyhocks and roses, grows in the fields among the ripe corn, climbs half way up into the mountains, pokes out of every rocky crevice, lines the gutters in the dirty streets of every little town we pass, and spreads over roof tiles and fences. The scent clings to my clothes and hair.

With that long drop to the river on the one side and the huge rock formations on the other, meeting a coach or a lorry coming down the mountain towards our bus is hair-raising. There's hardly enough room for one vehicle never mind two! We'd barely travelled ten miles when there was a standoff between our bus

MONKEY ON MY ROOF

driver and a lorry driver. Both drivers beckoning the other to reverse out of the way. Sitting at the window, I closed my eyes and prayed that the driver of my bus wasn't the one who would have to reverse towards the precipice. Eventually after much horn blowing, hand waving and shouting, the lorry driver gave in; just in time to miss the rocks that fell down the mountain onto the road in front of the bus!

Gingerly — offside wheels slipping and sliding on the edge of the road (a car had already plunged over the side into the river) — our driver edged his way through the rocks. On the ravine side of the bus male passengers hung out of the windows shouting advice to the driver at the top of their voices in a mixture of Hindi and English. On the other side, the side nearest the mountain, the female passengers — including me the intrepid explorer — leaned sideways with the hope of keeping the bus balanced as we prayed. The sound of horns blasted from the jeeps and wagons behind us; whether in encouragement or condemnation…who could tell?

Then we were clear! Safely on the other side of the rock fall, and suddenly the road looked a lot wider than it had when we were driving the other way! All I can say is that the bus driver must have had the patience of saint; either that or one of those 3000-odd Indian gods was looking out for him.

*

Mock Tudor buildings, sandstone Christian church, and grey stone courthouse with turrets! Shimla is as English as a tailcoat on an Eton schoolboy. If it wasn't for the big red monkeys swinging from the trees to mug people for their bananas I'd think I was in England.

Over the escarpment, deep velvety green valleys are filled

MONKEY ON MY ROOF

with pine and neem trees, with small houses dotted here and there. Eagles swoop through the fluffy clouds that twist around the mountains, the clouds coil their way through the windows in my hotel room like wisps of steam. Unfortunately, so do the monkeys if I forget to close my window.

Lakkar Bazaar at the top of the forked path leading from the White Hotel in Shimla sells the same kind of tourist junk as any other Indian bazaar. I love Indian bazaars, the vibrant bartering voices, and the energetic bustle. I'm smiling at the friendly banter between two stallholders as an Indian man walks towards me over the broken cobblestones. He stops, and stares, his eyes wide, 'You have grown into a beautiful woman, Bebeji,' he says.

Poor guy must need glasses. Or else he's drunk!

I smile and say, 'Thank you.'

The man puts the box of fruit he is carrying down on the ground and bends to touch my feet.

'Hey! What are you doing?' I exclaim.

No one has ever bent to touch my feet before.

He doesn't answer, just squats silently over my feet, gazing up at me with tears in his eyes.

'Don't do that,' I say. 'What's the matter? Please! Please, get up!'

Now he's sobbing and talking at the same time, the words spluttering out in rapid Hindi.

I don't know what to do, 'Get up. Getup! Why are you crying?'

People are staring.

A woman smiles at my red face, 'Don't worry, Ji. It's a mark of respect.'

Her words make no difference. Imagine! A strange man

MONKEY ON MY ROOF

babbling in a foreign language, touching my feet and weeping.

There is a stall selling souvenirs at the side of the road, I appeal to the owner, 'What is he saying?'

'He says he was your servant when you were only three years old! He dressed you and fed you. His mother was your ayah, your nursemaid; you were like his own sister.'

The weeping man is looking up at me as he touches my feet.

'No, no. Tell him he's wrong,' I protest.

'He says you don't remember because you were a baby at the time.'

'Look at me!' I tell the stall keeper, 'I'm over fifty! How old is he?'

'He says he's forty-eight.'

I stoop and put my hand on the weeping man's bony shoulder, 'I was already six years old when your mother gave birth to you,' I say gently, 'you've mistaken me for someone else.'

The man stands up. Wiping his eyes on his sleeve and speaking in English, he says with dignity, 'No, Ji! I know who you are.'

He takes a mango from his box and hands it to me, 'And I know how very much you love to eat mangos, Bebeji!'

Then he bends to touch my feet again, says, 'Namaste,' and walks away.

The stallholder asks, 'And do you love mangoes?'

'Yes, as a matter of fact I do.'

With a gesture from his hands, he says, 'In another life then.'

'Perhaps,' I respond slowly, because for one tiny moment there, when the weeping man's eyes and mine had first met, there'd been a spark, a connection between him and me.

It's happened before, that spark. It happened when I first met

MONKEY ON MY ROOF

Mark: me and Dawn rocking to the Kinks at the Cavern Club and Mark tapping me on the shoulder drawling, 'Wanna dance?' in a fake Yankee accent.

Dawn and me had stopped bopping and I'd turned around.

He was tall with black curly hair, brown eyes, and eyebrows not quite meeting across the bridge of a snub nose. Good looking in the way I liked. So I said, 'Yeah,' letting him know I could do fake Yankee too and Dawn faded away.

He bought me a drink at the bar and when our eyes met he dropped the fake Yankee accent and said, 'Can I see you home?'

Love at first sight, I'd thought romantically. I'm older now and know better. Now I know that a feeling of déjà vu can be caused by a chemical reaction between ones brain and ones hormones.

But with that skinny, bony Indian? No way! Though after what has just happened, perhaps it isn't hormonal. Perhaps that's the reason Stephan and me…

MONKEY ON MY ROOF

57

From behind me someone says, 'What are you doing here? I thought you were in Manali!'

Am I dreaming? It can't be him. Can it?

Shading my eyes from the sun, I turn — and, as if my thoughts have conjured him up, there he is standing on the cobbles. The sun is behind him, a rucksack pulls his shoulders back, but there is no mistaking that tall, slim body, that curly hair or those grey-green eyes crinkled in that smile.

'Stephan!'

He opens his arms, 'Don't just stand there with your mouth open! Come here and give me a hug!'

'What are you doing here?' I ask from the circle of his arms.

'I've just got here. From Ladakh.'

'Ladakh?'

'You should've been there, it was amazing. I met a couple of people you know while I was there…Chris and Burt.'

'So that's why you thought I was in Manali. Oh, Damn! You've just got here, and I'm leaving in the morning!'

'Do you have to go?'

'Afraid so, my train ticket is already booked and paid for.'

Stephan kisses my cheek, 'Meet me on the Mall tonight. At least we can eat together.'

I nod; seems like we'll always be fated to meet and leave, meet and leave …

*

Indian women parade along the Mall, looking like Paris fashion models in their finest outfits. It wouldn't do for me to join the

MONKEY ON MY ROOF

parade in my scruffy old denims. So I'm wearing *my* best shalwar kameez, the only outfit I possess that's in keeping with the fashions here. My Indian friend Eliza in Palolem had it made for me from one of her old saris. The tunic fits me perfectly but her tailor forgot to line the trousers and my legs show through the material when the light is behind me.

When we meet, Stephan's gaze lingers on my legs, 'Nice outfit!'

In the evening the Mall and Scandal Point is a seething mass of humanity. The boys, like boys everywhere, eyeing the girls; the girls giggling behind their hands and fluttering their eyelashes in that seductive way eastern girls do so well, and to my horror I find myself giggling behind my hand and fluttering my eyelashes; just like one of those seductive young maidens.

In silence Stephan and I walk hand in hand, we stop to buy corn on the cob, which is being roasted over an open fire on the pavement. The vendor sprinkles the cobs with lime juice. Stephan wipes some juice away from my chin with his finger, and puts his arm around me.

Hawkers stroll along the Mall selling huge sticks of fluffy pink sugar candy; beggars sit against the fence to sell bangles and black magnetic snake eggs that hiss when thrown up in the air. Young children are lifted onto the horses and ponies that parade up Scandal Point and the Ridge, the smell of wood smoke is everywhere. Honeymooners feed each other with Puri Bhaji they've bought from a stall on the pavement.

When darkness falls we watch as the lights are switched on in the thousands of small houses strung along the ridges. The Himalayas are crowned with brilliance as if garlanded with a giant tiara; as if decked out with precious jewels, purely for Stephan and me.

MONKEY ON MY ROOF

In a passageway outside the White Hotel Stephan takes me in his arms, 'Can I come to your room?'

I can smell the sweat on his skin mixed with the aftershave he uses, for an instant I let him hold me, let him press his lean, hard body against me. Then somehow I find the strength to push him away, 'No, Stephan. No. Not yet.'

'You're a hard woman, Sally.'

'I'm a married woman, Stephan.'

If only he knew how, within myself, I'm groaning quietly, imagining his lips on mine, knowing they'll taste of corn on the cob and lime juice. Imagining his body...

'When you talk to him on the phone, will you tell your husband about me?'

'There's nothing to tell, is there?' I say, lying through my teeth.

'You're right,' he answers, 'there's nothing to tell.'

We look into each other's eyes both knowing this isn't true.

I say helplessly, 'I have to go now. Goodnight.'

'Oh, this isn't goodbye, Sally. We'll meet again.'

It's hormones, just hormones I remind myself. Good job I'm not romantic anymore. Good job I'm off to Pushka tomorrow!

MONKEY ON MY ROOF

58

There are times that I ask myself: Why are you doing this Sally? Why are you travelling, why aren't you at home with your family? The arrangement was for you to suss out how it would be to live through the monsoon. You've done that, grown the mushrooms in your armpits, the mould on your shoes, lived inside the steam iron. So why stay? Go home you silly sod, stop being so damn obstinate. Just because you said you were staying away for a year doesn't mean you can't go home early.

Then something like this happens.

Pushka, five o'clock. Soon it will be sunset. On the side of the lake, around the base of a tree, young boys sit cross-legged with drums in their laps ready to beat the sun out of the sky. On the waterside, backpackers, hippies, tourists and pilgrims fill the tables. I park myself on the top step facing the ghats and watch an old man sitting at the bottom puff away on his Bhang, a blissful smile on his skinny, shrewd face. He's seen me, knows I'm a soft touch, and asks gently, 'Ten rupees for samosas and chai, miss?'

'It was only five rupees yesterday,' I say indignantly.

'I have to eat tomorrow also,' he tells me, and rummages in his rags for more Bhang.

I laugh; his head might be full of dope but there isn't much wrong with his logic. I give him the ten rupees.

The old man says something in Hindi.

'He never sleeps,' a young Indian man sitting beside me on the steps translates, 'just sits and smokes all night on the steps — the ghat leading down to the holy lake.'

'Hasn't he got a home?'

'His son has thrown him out because he wakes the house up

MONKEY ON MY ROOF

with his crazy ramblings, howling in the night that he sees ghosts.'

The dozy look in his half open eyes, that serene smile on his face; 'No wonder he can't sleep,' I say, 'he's dreaming all day. Tell him if he didn't smoke that shit he wouldn't see ghosts at night.'

Waving his joint, the old man bursts into Hindi again.

'What's he saying?'

'He says he sees them in the daytime too. He only smokes to help him sleep.'

'Well, it's not working.'

Sunset is incredible, the stillness broken only by the ripples of lazily swimming fish, the sun hanging, hugely red over the lake, a crimson eye reflecting white temples, not a whisper of breeze in the dreamlike air. Priests in white robes chant and throw rose petals on the water as the boys around the tree ready their instruments.

When the sun sets, the music reaches a crescendo and a whistle summons flocks of birds to wheel and swoop over the lake, their wings seemingly in rhythm with the drums. Is it any wonder the old man sees ghosts? It's easy to believe in ghosts in a place like this.

From the bottom ghat the old man has spotted a woman tourist, 'Ten rupees for samosa and chai, madam?'

She looks him up and down and, blonde hair flapping, shakes her head, 'No.'

'Please, madam, only ten rupees.'

'No way,' the woman says.

Gathering his rags around him, the old man removes his ragged red and white turban, he scratches his bristly grey hair, 'Your son is a camel driver, and fucks a camel,' he tells her scornfully.

She gets up to leave, 'You must have met my daughter-in-

MONKEY ON MY ROOF

law then,' she says over her shoulder.

The old man staggers to his feet, opens his bundle, takes out a ragged green pullover and a navy jacket, puts them on over the two pullovers he's already wearing, and dons the dirty white dhoti they were tied in.

This is why you're here Sally, I tell myself: This is why you haven't gone home to England.

I get up and follow the old man. All that talk of samosas and chai has made me hungry and there's a bus to catch.

MONKEY ON MY ROOF

<u>59</u>

I'd been dreading the bus ride over the bumpy roads. But the journey wasn't so bad — if you discount the heat and flies that is. Now it's a different town, Udaipur: and I'm sitting on a different set of steps. Each afternoon ever since I arrived I've strolled down the street from my guesthouse to walk through the stone arches and sit on the steps of this lake where the Palace Hotel shimmers like a mirage in the heat.

Incongruously; a camel rider calls advice to the boys playing cricket on the sandy lakebed with a homemade bat and an old tennis ball covered in string. A young beggar woman, toddler clinging to the ragged green and yellow skirts of her sari, emerges from the bamboo and blue plastic tent that is her home and crosses the lakebed.

The beggar woman and I have become friends. I share my food with her and the old holy man who lives on the boat marooned in the puddle, which is all that is left of the lake.

A mahout shouts 'Hup, hup, hup,' and gently taps an elephant's leg with a barbed stick.

An elephant occasionally walked along the beach in Palolem, its trunk, ears and legs painted with bright designs, a colourful cloth hanging below the howdah on its back. My friend Manju introduced me to the mahout and it soon became obvious to me that the man loved his elephant.

'The mahouts start as boys in the family business,' Manju said, 'they are given a baby elephant early in life. Like brothers the elephant and his mahout will stay together for life.'

Here in Udaipur a different mahout is trying to get *his* elephant down the steps, four steps then a platform and another four

MONKEY ON MY ROOF

steps, all of them steep.

Small eyes as terrified as the faces of the two tourists hanging on like grim death to the sides of the howdah on his back, trunk waving high in the air, the elephant trumpets, swivels sideways, ears flapping and, taking two steps down then two steps back, splashes scalding yellow urine on the steps.

'This is how to do it,' a teenage boy laughs and rides his bike down the eight steps, down to the lake bed and onto something sharp — a piece of glass or a rusty nail; there's a hiss of air, and the front tyre on his bicycle goes flat. The teenager carries his bike back up the steps, as the elephant turns and backs down them.

Passing the boy, the mahout pats his elephant and calls cheerfully, 'Backwards. That's the way to do it.'

The young man from the shop next door to my hotel comes over to speak to me.

'When are you going to come to my shop and see my pictures?' he asks.

'I've already bought,' I say.

'Only look, madam, you don't have to buy. Looking is free.'

'Not looking is cheaper. I've been caught that way before.'

He shrugs and sits down beside me, 'Where you from?'

'England. Where are you from?'

'Here, where else?' he says huffily, then he hears my laugh and realises I'm teasing him. He smiles, white teeth gleaming against glowing tan skin. 'What's your name?'

'You can call me Sally,' I tell him. 'How long is it since there was water in the lake?'

'The monsoon has not been good for the last six years,' he says. 'The water was over the steps and through the arches into the street when I was sixteen. No one played cricket on the lake or rode

MONKEY ON MY ROOF

camels and elephants on it then.'

We munch on bananas and grapes while the boys play cricket, and the mahout parades his elephant. A flurry at the bottom of the steps catches my attention; dried-up leaves and dust twisting and swirling into a tiny whirlwind.

The short hairs on the back of my neck prickle with alarm, 'What's that?' I say.

The beggar woman, big brown eyes staring at the grey dirt as it coils like water going down a drain, clutches her child to her.

Spinning, growing to the size of a man, the dust devil dances along the step towards us.

'Ghost! Ghost!' The young man scrambles backwards up the steps and runs, nearly knocking over the beggar, her child and the holy man who are already half way to the stone arch at the top.

'Don't be stupid, it's only dust,' I call after them.

'No, no, it's a ghost!' the young man insists peering around the side of the archway.

A cold shiver prickles up my spine to join the hairs bristling at the top of my neck; the dust pillar had stopped in front of me. Oh grow up, I tell myself crossly; you're not some little kid to be frightened by a bit of dust.

Then I take another look. It rears wraithlike before me. As if it it's listening!

There are no such things as ghosts. Are there?

Anyway it will do no harm to perform one of the Reiki healing symbols Gosh taught me. Fingers flashing through the air in the ancient sequence of the power symbol, I chant the mantra, wave my arms in a shooing motion, say, 'Go away. Go away,' in the sternest voice I can manage, and whew, it collapses in front of me, dust and leaves falling back onto the dried-up lake bed.

MONKEY ON MY ROOF

'It's okay, you can come back. I've sent it away,' I call.

The young man creeps back shamefaced to sit on the steps again, 'Are you sure it's gone? Many people have drowned here. They don't know they are dead, their spirits get trapped. Ghosts wander this lake all the time. It's bad luck to get touched by a ghost.'

'Believe me, it's gone,' I tell him, 'it won't come back.'

He's still scared, 'Make sure,' he says, and twirls his fingers, 'Do that thing you did again.'

'Okay, I'll do a stronger one, just to satisfy you,' and I raise my arms, chant the mantra and move my fingers.

There's a shift in the ether, a shimmer in the air, my eyes are stinging, a burning sensation as if dust filaments are whirling through my eyelashes.

I close my eyes.

When I open them again, the sun, only a moment ago on the point of setting, is high in the sky. Boats bob on a lake full of water, and the old man I'd seen at Pushka is sitting on the bottom step smoking his Bhang. People — lots of them — crowd the steps, one of them is staring at me. The person staring at me so intently looks very like Mark. But how could that be? Mark is in England... unless he's decided to join me here in India without telling me... some kind of surprise?

He points, and above the laughter I hear his voice. It's my husband's voice, there's no mistaking that soft, purring drawl with its faint Liverpool accent, 'Look, a dust devil!'

'Not a dust devil,' the old man replies as he puffs at his joint, 'it's a ghost.'

It was meant to be the Time and Distance Symbol. Where did I go wrong?

MONKEY ON MY ROOF

Then the world rights itself once more and I'm back on the steps with the young man, the beggar, her child, and the holy man.

Is it true what the old man says? Does it mean what I think it means?

The boys playing cricket. The Mahout and his elephant. The camel rider and his camel. The woman who has a bad opinion of her daughter-in-law. The beggar woman and her child. The holy man. And me? Are we the ghosts the old man sees? Are we phantoms, shadows floating through life? Am I a ghost too? And Mark?

What about Stephan? Someone taps on my shoulder, 'Hello Sally.'

I turn and Stephan is standing there. Alive! No ghost, living flesh! As if he's been summoned by fate through the whirlwind on the lake bed.

He puts his arms around me and kisses my cheek; always the same cheek, always the same spot and I clench my fists to prevent my fingers from taking hold of his face and pulling it around to my lips.

'How long are you here for?'

'I was on my way to find a rickshaw for the railway station when I saw you.'

'Shucks,' I say, unsure whether to be relieved or sorry, 'a short visit then.'

'If I'd known you were going to be here I'd have made it a longer one.'

'Yes.'

We gaze at one another; his eyes probe my blue ones until I look away.

'I'll come with you to the station,' I say.

MONKEY ON MY ROOF

There isn't much room in a rickshaw; we sit crammed together on the back seat. As if in a conspiracy, each bump and bend in the road throws us against one another. His bare arm brushes mine; the skin on his arms is golden brown; tiny hairs bleached almost white by the sun mingle with the hairs on my bare arm. Nerves tingling, aware of his thigh pressing against mine, I can't help myself, and burst out with, 'Oh, I wish you weren't leaving!'

'You only have to say the word... I'll tear up my rail ticket and stay!'

'No,' I say coming to my senses, 'don't do that.'

On the station platform, ignoring the red-jacketed porters, the two khaki clad, gun-toting soldiers and the Indian law forbidding displays of public affection, Stephan pulls me to him, kisses me on the lips. The kiss resonates down my spinal column, waking my body from its long sexual slumber.

The guard gives two blasts on his whistle, 'Don't say goodbye,' Stephan calls over his shoulder as he jumps on the train, 'we'll meet again.'

With a jerk the train pulls away from the station and he's gone; who knows where? We've kept to our pact of never telling each other where we'll be next. But I could find out where he will be easily enough, I only have to cast my eyes up at the overhead display at the side of the platform to know which stations the train is stopping at, which city is its destination... I can't bring myself to do it, it seems like cheating somehow.

Anyway, what would be the point? If one of us had a ticket to the moon the other would either be there already; or be just about to arrive. As sure as eggs are little eggs Stephan is certain to turn up again and what will happen then?

MONKEY ON MY ROOF

Oh why is this happening to me? I can't go on fighting my feelings forever. Falling in love is only supposed to happen to young people, not to people like me. Not to women who've been married to the same man for thirty-odd years.

I don't want this! Don't want to feel like a besotted teenager; that dry mouth seeing his face coming towards me in the street; only to realise it's a passing stranger; that pounding heart when he turns up again out of the blue and the man walking towards me really is him...

The smell of incense lingers in the rickshaw on my way back to Udaipur; there's a small shrine on the dashboard. The rickshaw driver must be Hindu I tell myself. Busy with my thoughts, I gazed unseeingly at the effigy of Shiva. How I wish I wasn't travelling alone!

Then again, if I hadn't been travelling alone Mark would be sitting beside me.

MONKEY ON MY ROOF

60

Ailsa's name lights up on the tiny screen; the hotel restaurant is empty except for me so when my mobile plays its little tune there's nobody here to be disturbed.

'Hello Mrs. McDonald, how are you today?' I say.

'Sally! Guess what,' she says without preamble, her voice high up the scale in exuberance, 'I've just come back from out-patients. My doctor read his notes, pushed his glasses back up his nose, looked at me over the top of them as if he couldn't believe what he was going to say, then he told me he doesn't know what I've been doing but whatever it is, it's working. My check-up is clear!'

'Wow!' I scream, 'That really is good news.'

'Yes, I just couldn't wait to tell you. Me and Greg are over the moon.'

'I'm not surprised.'

'What are you up to?'

Not so long ago I'd been wishing I had someone I could talk to. A lot of the people here in India — yoga, reiki, meditation teachers etc. — are phonies feeding off the tourists. At least Ailsa is sincere, and she is at the other end of the phone.

I tell her everything.

All the bits I'd left out of my e-mails. From when Stephan waved to me on the beach. From the first time we spoke to one another at the party, to the last time I saw him when he kissed me on the station platform.

The telling takes a long time.

'India's a big place, other people I know are travelling India and I haven't bumped into any of them…The thing is Ailsa… I'm

MONKEY ON MY ROOF

afraid of my feelings, I'm attracted to him. And I know he's attracted to me. It shouldn't be happening. I don't want this, Ailsa, it frightens me. I've no control over what's happening. It's as if something is dangling Stephan and me like puppets on a string.'

Ailsa's laughter comes over loud and clear on my mobile phone, 'Oh Sally! Have you only just worked that out?' she says, 'All these months in spiritual India and only now…'

'Damn spiritual India,' I say, 'and damn Shiva for turning me into one of his wanton milkmaids at my age.'

On my mobile Ailsa is still laughing. 'It's no laughing matter,' I tell her, 'I don't know what to do.'

'There's nothing you can do. Just "Sit back and watch the movie," as Gosh says.'

'Gosh isn't Steven Spielberg! I don't know if I'm starring in a thriller or a horror movie.'

Ailsa stops laughing, 'That's just how I felt when I was in hospital…as if I had the starring role in a horror movie,' now her voice is serious. 'Tubes and drugs, and scans, doctors and nurses rushing around.'

'Oh Ailsa,' I say, 'I wish I'd could've been there with you.'

'You know, Sally, I've never considered myself religious, never believed in supernatural beings the way some of my friends do. You might think me naff to say this…but I came to believe while lying in that hospital bed that there's something mystical out there which a person can tap into if they really need to. If that's what people call God it'll do for me.'

'I don't think you're naff, but whatever it is I wish it would leave me and Stephan alone. I've enough problems with Mark as it is. I don't believe in God. But who really knows? I'm not quarrelling with your beliefs.'

MONKEY ON MY ROOF

'Hmm,' Ailsa says, 'where you off to next?'
'Dehradun. Then maybe Rishikesh in the mountains.'

*

6th August 2006
Dear Ailsa,
It was lovely to speak to you on the phone the other day. Your voice sounds so much stronger. And that makes me think that you must be stronger! Strong enough to read my mails! Or is Greg still printing them out, so that the two of you can read them in bed together?

Now I'm in Dehradun. The restaurant at my hotel is closed this morning. Apparently there's another festival. How these Indians do love their festivals! 'Plenty places to eat on Rajpur Road,' the waiter said.

Vikrams — a vikram is a three-wheeled people carrier, bigger than a rickshaw but smaller than a bus — rickshaws, taxis and motorcycles swerved around me, I crossed the road chanting a mantra, praying that I'd reach the other side safely. As far as traffic goes, Dehradun is one of the busiest towns I've been to. It's as busy as Mumbai and Delhi put together. Miraculously nothing has knocked me down yet, but it doesn't seem wise for me to stop praying.

The Moti Mahal Restaurant is; judging by the prices on the menu, the dearest eating-place in town, but I was hungry and two hundred rupees — all of one pound fifty — isn't that expensive. Apart from me there was only one other person there, a grey-haired classily dressed Indian woman wearing a five strand pearl collar and pearl studs to match. She was sitting alone, not eating, ignored

MONKEY ON MY ROOF

by the waiters, no cutlery or crockery on the white tablecloth.

I thought that she was one of the owners, or an owner's wife.

Then the door opened, three elegantly dressed ladies joined her at her table.

Hmm, I told myself, either the restaurant owner has four wives or this is a family party.

The door opened again, and again.

More ladies came in and sat down.

The door opened once more.

Now there were twenty or so ladies sitting around the long table twittering to one another like a flock of exotic birds. Silk and satin saris. Gold necklaces and bracelets. Only wealthy Indians could have the time and money to dress so smartly, to use cosmetics so tastefully. They couldn't *all* be married to the restaurant owner. Could they?

The waiter delivered a cardboard box and a large black velvet bag to the older woman who seemed to be in charge. She opened the box and the women passed it around. One by one they each took something from it and put it on the table in front of them.

Then diamond and emerald rings flashed as slender hands dipped into handbags and emerged with biros.

Was this meeting for some kind of charitable work? I asked myself. A sort of Indian Women's Institute?

The older woman shook the black velvet bag and opened it, 'Twenty two,' she said loudly. 'Two little ducks.'

Huh?

'Eighty eight. Two fat ladies.'

What?

I ask you! Two fat ladies! I might as well have been back in Liverpool crossing numbers off a card at the Gala in Wavertree.

Love and light to you and Greg from Sally X

MONKEY ON MY ROOF

*

Mark's birthday is only two weeks away, and there's a stationers stall in the bazaar that sells birthday cards, the hotel waiter tells me.

In the bazaar I ask three different people the way to the stationers shop. All three of them waggle their heads and graciously point me in three different directions. This polite head waggle seems to be genetically programmed into the Indian psyche. There are times I wish Indians weren't so well-mannered. Just once in a while I'd like one of them to conquer his desire to impress a stranger. To find the strength within himself to look me in the eye and admit he doesn't know. Then tell me to sod off and ask a policeman.

Around a corner I find myself among beribboned camels, huge painted elephants and garlanded horses. Decorated floats carry men dressed as Gods, faces painted blue, faces painted black. Hijras dressed in spangled costumes sing and dance: a hijra is a male transsexual who believes he has a woman's soul in the body of a man. Gurus and Babas — teachers and holy men — march along with their devotees. Hare Krishna's in saffron robes intone mantras, blow huge horns, beat enormous drums, and play stringed instruments.

A shopkeeper tells me, 'It's Shiva's birthday.'

'No, it's Shiva's wedding day, he's getting married,' says a passer-by.

'Seems strange to me that Shiva is getting married on the day he was born,' I say, 'but there again; anything is possible if you are a God!'

A Swami's helper is handing out pink sherbet drinks. A boy

MONKEY ON MY ROOF

from the drapery shop fetches sweet rice and fruit. The boys from the shop have taken it upon themselves to look after me. They stop motorised floats; call out to clowns, drummers and sadhus that I want to take photographs; pull me away from under the hooves of horses, the snap of camels' teeth, the tusks and lashing trunks of elephants.

Three in the afternoon and the rain has started, but monsoon or no monsoon this procession isn't going to stop. The potholes in the streets of the bazaar begin to fill with water. A misty blue haze hangs in the air. The haze smells of smoky exhaust fumes, kerosene and burning oil from frying samosas. It magnifies the smells of elephant dung and camel shit. It brings out the scent of incense, which all the shopkeepers and stallholders burn in front of the small shrines to Lakshmi the goddess of wealth and prosperity. At last the rain clears the air, but by then the boys have pulled me inside the shop.

MONKEY ON MY ROOF

61

Handing me a mug of masala chai a salesman asks, 'Did you enjoy?'

I say, 'Yes, very much. Did you?'

He smiles and nods.

One of the others says, 'He's a Muslim, but we don't mind him joining our festivals!'

Another says, 'We even give him Prasad!'

Prasad they tell me is a sacred food, sometimes in the form of small sweets that must first be offered to Lord Krishna. To receive it is to be given a blessing.

'Hmm,' I say, 'then I must be well blessed; I've eaten a lot of Prasad since I got to India.'

Everyone laughs, even me, even the Muslim, whose eyes, when he laughs, crinkle at the corners in much the same way as Stephan's, and they are a similar colour. When Stephan looks at me his eyes grow darker, the brown deepening almost into black, the green streaks fading into smoky grey.

What the heck am I doing daydreaming about another man's eyes? I should be looking for a birthday card for my husband, that's the reason I'm here in this bazaar. I try to visualise Mark's eyes, but I can't see his face… Stephan's face keeps getting in the way.

*

Ashrams in India aren't always what I expect them to be. They don't always consist of humble compartments where devout disciples sit in tranquil meditation before twisting themselves into yoga positions and chanting mantras. Oh no, not on your Nellie!

Take Mohyal Ashram just outside Haridwar for instance,

MONKEY ON MY ROOF

where I'm staying there at the moment. It's more like a five star hotel than an ashram, though there is a yoga and meditation hall where chanting seems to go on all through the night. Marble floors, mirror and glass dining room, a winding marble staircase, even an elevator all in marble and glass. My room is decked out in marble and glass too, with a huge built-in wardrobe. There's a balcony overlooking the garden. And, wonder of wonders, the bathroom has hot water and a real shower stall with a curtain! All this, including three meals, for 450 rupees (about five pounds) a day.

The funny thing is that when I arrived and was shown my room I had a sort of dizzy spell, and had to lean against the wall for a few moments until it passed. The heat and travelling perhaps? Or possibly the altitude?

Or was it my intuition telling me to take a different room? Perhaps it was warning me about the black ants, which infest every surface in my room! Ants so tiny they are capable of dancing the tango in my mobile phone and performing a pasodoble in my digital camera. At bedtime last night I laid my glasses down on the bedside table oblivious to those specks of dust covering its surface. This morning I put my specs on again and suddenly my eyes and ears are full of ants!

They are everywhere! Even in the bed! They don't bite, but they itch like mad. They seem to have made their home in the drawer where I keep my clean knickers, I'll leave it to your imagination where it itches the most! What with those pesky ants and the chanting from the meditation hall sliding through the bones of my ears like a medieval ritual, I didn't get a wink of sleep all night.

I'm only allowed one cup of chai a day at breakfast time so I've sneaked out to the durbar over the main road for an extra

MONKEY ON MY ROOF

cuppa. Then I'll climb in a vikram and go exploring.

The road is full of potholes and bumps, and the vikram is full of people, twelve of us including the driver. On the other side of the bridge a huge statue of Shiva dominates the skyline. I buy a second cup of chai from a chai walla at Har Ki Pauri ghat, when I've drunk it I'll wander to the temple.

*

An Indian couple with a small boy is doing a Puja — a special religious ritual — at a Shiva shrine just inside the temple. The young husband is washing the Shiva lingam, the wife is praying with folded hands while the priest intones. The husband anoints the lingam with oil and the priest brings milk for the husband to pour over it, then curd is tipped over the top. The husband takes saffron and red dye and paints swirls and flowers on the tip.

Sitting against a pillar I smile to myself; *beats a condom every time*; and find myself wondering if Stephan has ever been to Haridwar? I imagine him here with me. Imagine our conversation.

'What's a lingam?' Stephan is asking with a twinkle.

'Don't ask me,' I say, 'you'll have to work it out for yourself!'

We look deeply into one another's eyes.

Stephan's eyes get that smoky look, 'I think Shiva would've been happier for the man to pray with folded hands,' he'll say, 'while the woman anoints his lingam!'

Oh stop it Sally! You must stop this. Must stop these thoughts.

At the Goddess Durga temple on the ghats a man beckons me to enter.

MONKEY ON MY ROOF

'Don't worry Ji,' he says, 'you are safe with me. I'm a Panda.'

'A Panda,' I say, trying not to laugh. 'You don't look Chinese.'

'Chinese?'

'Pandas come from China, don't they?'

Now he looks annoyed, 'Not a Panda!' he growls, 'a Pandit!'

'Forgive my ignorance,' I say. 'But what exactly is a Pandit?'

'I have the ability to invoke the gods through my chanting,' he tells me.

He paints my forehead with red ochre and yellow saffron then takes a few small sweets from a bowl placed in front of the Goddess and gives them to me.

'Eat! This is Prasad,' he says, 'for good health.'

Then he pours water from a brass jug into the palm of my hand, 'Drink,' he says, 'for a long life.'

Has he washed his hands? And where has the water come from? Maybe he walked down the steps to fill his water jug from the Ganges. When he turns his back I secretly empty the water onto nearby plant. So this is the second time I've missed out on a Long Life Blessing.

The Pandit picks up a small flower boat from under the altar and hands it to me. 'Float it on Holy Mother Ganges at sunset,' he says, there's a wicked gleam in his eye, 'to bring you a good man.'

I scarper double quick before he asks me to anoint *his* lingam.

From a nearby stall people are buying small boats made from banana leaves. The boats are filled with flowers with a candle sitting in the centre of each one. In the Shiva temple during the ceremony the candles are lit, and the boats are launched to glide gently on the water. A mystical fleet of flowers and candles drifts along the Ganges.

    The boat the Panda gave me floats among them. Will it float upstream I wonder? As far as Rishikesh? I'll be catching the bus there tomorrow.

MONKEY ON MY ROOF

62

Rishikesh.

I'm staying in the Lakshman Jhula area — jhula means bridge in Hindi. Today is India Independence Day. Three days before Mark's birthday, and nine days before mine. Will he remember?

At eight o'clock this morning, from where I sit in the Ganga View Restaurant by the side of the river, I can see a crowd of schoolchildren in red and grey uniforms carrying banners and chanting 'British out! British Out!' as they march across the bridge.

The suspended bridge over the Ganges is charming; a cobweb construction of steel and concrete too narrow for cars or rickshaws, it looks too fragile to support the odd motorbike winding through the throngs of Indian and western tourists.

This morning red monkeys are swinging from the steel cables and trying to grab the hats, cameras, and bags of the people crossing over. Behind the chanting school kids, a newly married woman in a red and gold sari walks with her young husband. He is wearing a long satin Mughal coat.

Four Adivasi women in rust, green, orange saris, carrying sacks on their heads, walk behind three packhorses piled high with sacks of building materials. A boy in white shorts is geeing the packhorses along with a stick.

A monkey swings down from a stanchion to interrupt the conversation of a sadhu and an old Sikh wearing a bright purple turban. The monkey is snatching at the old Sikh's long grey beard. Behind the sadhu and the Sikh a man pushes a bicycle laden with steel butter churns, while another man's bicycle has been altered to carry a contraption to sharpen knives. Two spiritual-looking people in white robes with long hair piled up on top of their heads are

MONKEY ON MY ROOF

helping a western tourist fend off an inquisitive cow. The cow is sniffing at his back-pack.

Every single one of them, except for the western tourist, the cow, and the seven monkeys are chanting 'British out! British out!'

As I watch this procession, it seems to me that, just for today, it might be healthier to change my nationality. If anyone asks I'll say I'm Australian!

Rishikesh is full of beautiful western souls walking around looking... well, soulful I suppose is the only word for it. Most of these beautiful Western souls are being used as cash cows by even more beautiful Indian souls! These Indian men — it's usually the men — are very good-looking with their dramatic dark eyes, long black hair, and glowing skin. Some of them really do believe what they are teaching.

Maybe it's a good idea to let one of these gorgeous gurus rip me off for some meditation lessons! What have I got to lose, except a lot of my cynicism, and little bit of money? Or should that be a little bit of cynicism and quite a lot of my money. And there's always the Ashram where the Beatles sought enlightenment and got mixed up with the Maharishi Yogi.

What was good enough for the Fab Four should be good enough for me.

A Brazilian woman in the coffee shop tells me where to find the Beatles Ashram, 'It's been closed for a long time,' she says, 'but if you talk nicely to the watchman he could be persuaded to let you in for a small baksheesh.'

The sun is baking hot but I follow her directions along an unmade road full of potholes. At a small portable chai stall by the side of the road four men are sitting on plastic garden chairs gossiping. I stop and ask them for directions.

MONKEY ON MY ROOF

Indian men will never tell you they don't know the answer your question; plus even when they do know the answer, their replies are kind of hard to follow.

'It's straight on around the backside,' one of them says when he's done head nodding and neck swaying.

'First you go left,' says another.

'That's right,' exclaims the third, 'then you go right around the backside.'

I wander around the backside, the front side, my left side and my right side, get myself thoroughly lost and there's still no sign of the bloody Ashram!

So is it so surprising that I've ended up in this forest clearing, sitting on a blue plastic mat under the shade of a tree with two sleazy looking men. One of the men looks as if he's a forestry worker; his only item of apparel seems to be an orange lungi. The other man is wearing the red and saffron robes of a sadhu.

When he saw me staggering through the trees dripping with sweat, the man in the orange lungi had patted the mat. 'Come. Sit,' he'd said. Head spinning, hot, flustered, convinced I had sunstroke, it had seemed a good idea at the time. At the very least I'd be out of the sun, and could give my feet a rest; so I sat down beside him.

They've set up shop on a cardboard box which is piled with a few boxes of cigarettes, a couple of packets of crisps, half a dozen packets of biscuits and one or two bottles of Maaza. Behind the box is a tea caddy, a saucepan, a paraffin stove, a plastic milk bottle and two tiffin mugs.

The sadhu smiles at me, picks up the saucepan and goes to fill it with water from a stand pipe. Coming back he puts a match to the stove and starts the business of brewing up.

While he waits for the water to boil the sadhu pulls a chillum,

MONKEY ON MY ROOF

a conical clay pipe open at both ends used by wandering Hindu monks, and randy hippies to better facilitate the smoking of hashish, from somewhere in his robes, and prepares his charas — his weed, pot, ganja. He gets the chillum lit, takes a drag and passes it to the man in the orange lungi, who offers me a drag.

Alone in the forest with two stoned men? I don't think so!

'No thanks,' I shake my head. 'Don't you have any beedies?'

'Let's get it up,' the man in the orange lungi smirks, 'charas, charas,' he pats my thigh and leers.

I push his hand away, 'What part of "NO" don't you understand!'

He puts his hand back on my thigh again, brown bony fingers probing for my crotch.

I scramble to my feet, 'Gerroff me!'

The sadhu grabs the man by the arm as he moves to follow me, and speaks sharply in Hindi.

And, 'Sorry Momma. Sorry Momma,' orange lungi says, 'stay drink chai.'

I hesitate.

The sadhu looks me in the face, nods, and 'Stay no problem.'

Orange lungi looks ashamed. The sadhu is a holy man; I could do with a mug of chai, so …

Nothing I've experienced can ever beat smoking beedies and drinking chai out of a filthy mug in the forest.

*

In the cool of the evening the three kilometres walk to the Ram Jhula is very pleasant. The temple bells ring all along the river, and the sound of chanting can be heard coming faintly from

MONKEY ON MY ROOF

the ashrams, with, believe it or not, what sounds like Auld Lang Syne being sung somewhere in the distance. Is it something I've carried with me from the Mohyal Ashram, those pesky ants perhaps? Visions of ants wearing kilts, holding drunken parties next to my ear-drum, singing and doing the 'Hokey Kokey' as if it's Hogmanay, make me smile.

Or is this some kind of supernatural message telling me to remember my husband. To prevent me fantasising. That would be unfair, I can't help the fantasies.

Anyway, Mark wouldn't give a damn; odds-on he's too busy rolling around in the hay with the new shop assistant; that blonde who's been mooning around him.

'Oh Sally, your husband has a lovely smile,' she gushed just before I left for India.

'Yeah,' I said, 'it looks good at bedtime soaking in a glass on the bathroom sink.'

It didn't put her off; she was still mooning round him when I left. They're probably getting it on right now. Being manager of a store is so handy for finding fresh totty.

My hotel is next door to an old temple, "Om Shanti, Shanti, Hare Krishna, Hare Krishna, Hari Hari, Kali Kali." The chanting doesn't bother me, it's the chorus of Auld Lang Syne thumping against my eardrums, getting louder and louder, combined with dizziness and nausea, that keeps me awake all night. The altitude is the most likely cause, though Rishikesh is only fifteen hundred metres above sea level. Six nights now without sleep, as if I have a giant hangover.

It's only rained once since I got here. The locals are saying that the monsoon has failed. It's too hot for me in Rishikesh, too hot to risk sunstroke in the baking heat, nothing for me to do except lie

275

MONKEY ON MY ROOF

under the fan in my room and watch TV with the volume turned up loud to drown out Auld Lang Syne.

So I'm away off to Mussoorie tomorrow morning by taxi.

I've booked the taxi from a travel agent at the hotel. Paid him fifteen hundred rupees up front!

Extravagant I know, but I really do feel very ill, in no fit state to go to Mussoorie by bus.

'Don't worry, Momma,' the travel agent told me yesterday, 'your taxi will be there at eight o'clock. I won't let you down.'

Rishikesh is one of the most beautiful places I've been to in India, but something here doesn't like me. I'll be glad to get away.

MONKEY ON MY ROOF

63

So much for that travel agent saying that he wouldn't let me down! Guess what? No taxi! Indian time: we all know what it's like!

There's no answer from the travel agent when I phone the hotel so I ask to speak to the manager.

'Please stop phoning,' the hotel manager says, 'this is nothing to do with me.'

'Nothing to do with you? I'm sure the police would like to know that you keep a desk at your hotel for fake travel agents,' I tell him.

'The police! You go to police?'

'Too right I'll go to the police. Either get me a car or give me back my fifteen hundred rupees.'

It's half an hour later and a dilapidated car has arrived, amazing what can be achieved in India by threatening to call the police! We drive off... for a mile. Less than a mile. All of a sudden, a crowd of men are in front of the car. They fill the road from one side to the other. Each and every one of them yelling, shouting, waving bamboo sticks; spoiling for a fight.

'What's this?' I say in alarm, 'What's happening?'

The driver doesn't answer, he changes gear, throws the car into reverse, backs fast along the road. There's nowhere to go, he has to put the brake on or we'd be swimming in the Ganges.

'Tell them this is your car,' the driver hisses, 'tell them it belongs to you!'

Before I can tell them anything the crowd has caught up with us and dragged him from the car. They all disappear somewhere up the street and I am left there alone, wondering what the Dickens is going on. Consoling myself with, 'At least they haven't dragged me

MONKEY ON MY ROOF

from the car, so they don't intend robbery.'

There's nothing else for me to do but open the car door, grab the keys from the ignition and look around me. The only sign of life is a couple of dogs sleeping at the side of the dusty road. There is no one in sight. Like magic everyone has disappeared. But I can hear shouting, raised voices. The voices are coming from a shop just up the street.

A taxi stops outside the shop, the driver runs inside followed by his fare. The fare is a tall, slim man with thick greying hair who looks like…

No it can't be! Can it?

Inside the shop there's a wooden counter, a bench against the wall, a small table with a pan of chai bubbling on a stove. It's a small shop, too small for the ten or twelve men it contains — the men with the bamboo sticks who all belong to the taxi drivers' union. According to them the car I hired is a private car and the driver doesn't belong to the union.

And Stephan is sitting on the bench.

My heart skips a beat as I watch his eyes crinkle, his lips widen in that familiar smile.

'Hello, Sally. Just as I'm arriving, you're on your way out of Rishikesh.'

I lick my lips, a quiver climbs along my spine, and my smile widens to match his as I recall the feel of his mouth on mine the last time we met. 'Hello, Stephan,' I say, 'ships that pass in the night again?'

'Yes.'

I sit down on the bench beside him.

He takes my hand in his. 'Do you have to leave? Can't you stay a little longer?'

MONKEY ON MY ROOF

I want to say yes! But it's impossible.

I shake my head. 'I have to get away from Rishikesh. The altitude is making me ill.'

He looks at me quizzically. 'The altitude?'

'It's not an excuse, Stephan, I really am ill.'

I stand up and lean across the counter to the man in charge, 'I have to get to Mussoorie. Can't all this be sorted out later?'

He listens to me politely, turns to the other men and says something in Hindi. The others start shouting again.

The man in charge shakes his head.

'I've already paid fifteen hundred rupees to get there,' I say.

At which my driver exclaims: 'You shut up, woman. Keep your mouth shut.'

Stephan jumps up from the bench and faces the driver, 'Don't you speak to my friend that way. Show her respect!'

'Don't worry, Ji,' one of the others says apologetically, 'here, drink chai!'

As if a mug of chai will cure anything!

'I don't want chai,' I thrust the mug back across the counter, 'I want to get to Mussoorie.'

'You'll have to pay for a taxi then,' says the man in charge.

'I've no intention of paying for another taxi,' I tell him. 'I've paid this man,' I point to my driver, 'once already; I'm certainly not going to pay twice.'

'You paid him?'

'Yes!'

Stephan leans across the counter, 'Now get this mess sorted out before I call the police.'

Half an hour later I am on my way in a nice comfortable taxi with an extra four hundred rupees in my purse. The threat of the

MONKEY ON MY ROOF

police worked. The man in charge took my ex-driver's wallet from him, pulled out fifteen hundred rupees, paid the going rate for a taxi and gave me back the extra. According to the taxi drivers' union the travel agent had overcharged me.

At last I am on my way out of Rishikesh! At one point I'd begun to think I'd never get away! Feeling even more drained because of the trouble in the taxi office, I put my head down on the back seat and sleep all the way to Mussoorie. Funnily enough, when I wake up the noises in my ears have stopped. I can't hear Auld Lang Syne any longer, it must have been the altitude after all.

And now Stephan knows which town I'll be in.

When the yoga class he booked into in Rishikesh has finished he'll be coming to Mussoorie he says.

There's no point in pretending any longer. I've agreed to meet him there.

MONKEY ON MY ROOF

<u>64</u>

Camelback Road in Mussoorie is an apt name for the road my hotel is built on, mainly because the room the hotel manager gives me smells predominantly of camel dung. There's no accounting for smells in India, and the room looks clean enough with a double bed, thick blankets and clean linen. There's an upholstered headboard and, wonder of wonders, even a wardrobe... somewhere for me to hang my clothes at last. The bathroom is a joke, dirty clay floor, squat toilet, no shower, but at least there's a tap for hot water and a bucket for a bucket bath. It will have to do. I'm so exhausted that all I want is to lay my head down and sleep. I've almost forgotten what it's like to sleep.

Two o'clock in the morning, my third night here, I've had two nights of blissful sleep, now I'm full of energy. I've tried meditating, chanting mantras, Reiki self-healing, reading a book, but I'm still wide awake. Maybe if I turn out the bedside lamp and snuggle down?

Something hairy is brushing against my bare leg. Thinking of rough blankets I readjust the bedclothes. The something hairy moves, skitters across my leg to the opposite side of the bed.

Throwing back the blankets I turn on the lamp.

Mice are running across the bed! The upholstered headboard is full of them; they've obviously nested in there, and are now playing tag all over the bedclothes.

What is it about Indian mice? Haven't they any fear? Nothing seems to faze them; it's almost as if they are laughing at me! Someone once told me that mice don't stop for a wee or a crap; they empty themselves as they run. The thought of mice weeing and crapping on me as I was sleeping is enough to make me throw up

MONKEY ON MY ROOF

my vegetable curry. I'm going to need a long hot bucket bath to even start to feel clean.

It's beginning to get light; the mice are giving up their games and disappearing back into the headboard. I open the bathroom door, and the biggest, hairiest spider I've ever seen is on the step. It jumps five feet in the air towards my face; and I slam the door. I've never slammed a door so fast in my life. Mice in my bed are bad enough, but spiders... Ugh!

In the passageway I call for the watchman-come-waiter-come-porter. A door closes somewhere along the passage and he walks towards me fastening the brass buttons on the dark blue livery jacket he wears, which looks as if it's a left over from the British Raj days, 'What you want?' he says.

'There's a spider in my bathroom. I want you to get rid of it.'

Twirling the points of his black moustache he stomps his size eleven black army boots into the bathroom, 'Spider, where spider?'

'There! There!'

Stomp, an army boot crashes down, 'No spider now. Spider gone,' he says.

I'd been expecting him to scoop it up and take it out to the garden. 'I didn't mean you to kill it!'

He grins and says what he always says when he can't understand, 'Yes madam, yes.'

When he's gone I turn on the hot water tap, there's no hot water for my bucket bath, no water at all. This is the last straw.

I call the watchman/porter again and tell him to fetch the manager.

'Manager says prayers,' he complains.

After the night I've just had I don't give a damn if the manager is in paradise shagging seventy-seven virgins.

MONKEY ON MY ROOF

'Go fetch him!'

'Yes madam, yes.'

The half-hour delay before the manager arrives does nothing to cool my temper.

'I wouldn't put a dog in this kennel you laughingly call an en-suite room,' I tell him, 'I'm moving to another hotel.'

'You must pay for room,' he says with a smirk.

His smirk infuriates me, 'You can forget the bill, I won't be paying it.'

'You must pay.'

'The editor of 'The Lonely Planet' is a friend of mine,' I lie, and pull my mobile phone from my pocket, 'I'll give him a call, shall I?'

This alarms him, 'I have another room on upper floor,' he says. 'Same price.'

'Show me.'

Wow is the only word for the room I'm in now.

Ankle-deep carpet, separate living room with a TV, a lovely bedroom with a huge tiled bathroom, and a veranda that runs along the side of the house.

*

It's my birthday.

A beep beep beep from my mobile signals a text coming through.

HAPPY BIRTHDAY SALLY SEE YOU SOON. MUCH LOVE FROM STEPHAN.

No other messages. Nothing from Mark. Perhaps he's e-mailed?

MONKEY ON MY ROOF

There's an internet café in the Landour market. Mark hasn't mailed, but there are birthday greetings from each of my daughters. And e-mail and card from Ailsa. Not so long ago I dreaded floating that small arrow over the little white envelope on the computer screen to open e-mails from Ailsa. Now, impatient to hear her news, my finger clicks the mouse eagerly.

A message and an e-card. I open the card first. The card has me and everyone else in the cyber café laughing. Now for the message.

28th August 2006
Hi Aunt Sally,
This is to wish you Happy Birthday and let you know that all is well with me, every day I get stronger. Last week my specialist told me that I could go back to work part time. So it's back to the office on Monday for me. Who'd have thought it?

Just now I came across the folder on my computer with the e-mails I sent you when I was so sick. Reading those e-mails brought back to me how tired and afraid I was then, how black my life had seemed. And how you were always there for me with just the right words to help me make sense of what was going on in my life. Now it feels like I've awakened from a bad dream. It's made me realise how short life is and how a person should always follow their dreams, good or bad.

Perhaps you should think of that the next time you see Stephan?

Yesterday, to celebrate my news, Greg brought me a lovely present, an adorable Basset Hound puppy with long floppy ears. Don't think Greg bargained on our new family member throwing up all over his shoes before dinner though. Poor Greg! Seems like

MONKEY ON MY ROOF

he's always clearing up someone's vomit, first it was me, now it's the dog!

Lots of love and hugs Ailsa xxx

*

My fingers fly over the keys in answer.

30th August 2008

Hi Ailsa, thanks for the long, newsy e-mail. It's good to know what's going on at home and that you are still keeping well. Hurrah! Keep yourself fit, go for plenty of healthy walks with your puppy, eat lots of fruit and veg, and be careful crossing the road. Pity about your puppy throwing up! One way to think of it is that at least he threw up before you ate dinner and not after, otherwise your own Technicolor yawns might have been something to be remembered. How's about next time Greg buys you a puppy for a present he gets a smaller breed? Something along the lines of a Yorkshire terrier; with a commensurate reduction in the size and scope of projectile vomit? Cheaper with the price of disinfectant, kinder on the stomach, and less strain on the nerves!

    That rude card you sent for my birthday gave me the biggest laugh I've had for ages and awed the boys in this cybercafé so much that they keep peeping over my shoulder to look at it. I tell them that all Englishmen are endowed like that, and the size of that particular Englishman's protuberance is rather small!

    You may be right about Stephan, only time will tell; anyway we'll be meeting here in Mussoorie sometime this week. More later.

Love you lots from Aunt Sally.

MONKEY ON MY ROOF

<u>65</u>

This morning a roan horse with bright leather trappings is parked under the NO PARKING sign. The owner is sitting on the bench talking to the vegetable seller. He looks at my walking stick, grins and offers me a free ride!

'Only if you lift me on, Ji, and fetch an ambulance when I'm ready to get off again,' I tell him.

It's a weird feeling to stand by the black, wrought-iron fence opposite the Barista Coffee House with the cloud gently rising towards me. Of course I've often seen clouds from above: the windows of an aircraft for example, the Mall at Shimla, but never before have I felt them tickle my ankles or crawl little by little up my legs until I'm completely enveloped in white mist.

When I was a child I imagined that clouds were shopping bags full of snow and rain, it only needed someone to reach up and poke them with an umbrella for there to be a snowstorm. Not wanting to get caught in a blizzard or downpour on the way to school I spent most of the winter keeping my little sister and me well away from tall men with black spiked umbrellas.

My sister was "delicate" my mother said and had to be kept safe; it was my job to look after her on the way to school. Like all big sisters I resented this, and dragged my little sister along by the hand until she kicked me on the shins and yelled at me to slow down. There were never any tall men with spiked umbrellas around to poke the clouds and make it rain. If there had been my sister might have been compelled to walk faster and my shins might not have been bruised so badly..

In Mussoorie it rains when there isn't a cloud in the sky, and not necessarily when there is. What happens in winter I'll never

MONKEY ON MY ROOF

know since I've no intention of staying to find out. This morning the delicate light at the back of the cloud gives the impression of a silver lamp being turned on and I am there in that room, in that light, with that cloud all around me.

It isn't cold, only damp and rather eerie, reminding me of an old black and white movie I saw many years ago about Jack the Ripper. If the fog in the East End of London was anything like this when Jack was going about his grisly business, it's no wonder he got away so easily.

Here in Mussoorie a woman is being chased by a large, violent-looking man who is pushing passers-by out of the way as he pursues her. The sound of her screaming almost has me imagining that I'm in the East End of London listening to old Jack going about his bloody business.

Assuming the man is an irate shop keeper pursuing a thief I half turn towards the Barista Coffee House. The man snatches at the woman's plait of long black hair and drags her against the wrought iron fence. Her screams turn to gibbers of terror. Gibbers — there are no other words to describe the noise she makes or the expression on her face.

The man raises his fist, draws back his arm.

I can't just stand there and watch him punch her, so I yell loud enough to be heard on the other side of the street, 'Hey you! What d'you think you're doing? Leave her alone.'

He turns around and yells something back at me in the local language.

'Leave her alone! Or I'll get the police,' I shout. 'I'll have you locked up.'

The man lifts his fist again, but this time he is lifting it towards me.

MONKEY ON MY ROOF

I raise my walking stick, 'Try it. Go on. Just try it.'

The owner of the roan horse hollers something in Hindi, and the man hesitates, then he lets go of the woman's hair and slinks away up the street, and she slumps against the fence. She's holding her jaw, her face wet with tears.

'What's wrong?' I ask her, 'What's the matter?'

She takes her hand away from her face; her jaw is swollen to three times its normal size. A huge nasty-looking abscess almost as big as her mouth has formed on the side of her chin.

I say, 'How did that happen?'

The fruit seller is listening and answers for her, 'Her husband beats her. He gets drunk. He's always drunk. He beats her every night. Always he punch her face, punch the same place.'

The woman is whimpering now with pain. In my handbag I have some Disprin; I give her two tablets and tell her to mix them in water. Pointing to her mouth she gives me to understand that she could neither eat nor drink.

'Can you tell her to meet me at the coffee house at ten o'clock tomorrow?' I say to the fruit seller, 'I'll take her to the Community Hospital at Landour and pay to have the abscess treated.'

'She's afraid to leave her children to go to Landour,' the fruit seller translates.

So I tell him that we can take the children with us to the Government Hospital, which is just around the corner from my hotel; then she won't have to leave her children. She nods in agreement and we arrange to meet outside the Barista Coffee House. Poor woman she's got a bad man there.

*

MONKEY ON MY ROOF

5th September 2006
Dear Ailsa,
Since I last wrote I've been wondering if I should go on with these e-mails with my electronic scribbles about India, particularly as you've never been to any of these places. Perhaps you are looking at your computer screen and thinking, 'Oh damn, another e-mail from Sally, I wish she wouldn't bother,' before deleting them. Yet I can't seem to stop, I've come to rely on our messages to chill out.

And I do need to chill about the woman with the abscess on her jaw. The other day I waited around until half past eleven but she didn't turn up. Later in the afternoon, when it was too late to go to the hospital, I saw her with her children and took her to the chemist for Betadine and pain killers. The chemist says she needs proper treatment from a doctor, an antibiotic injection and other treatment.

The woman has two anxious-looking little boys who look as if they have never learned to smile, or if they ever did they have forgotten how. Their younger sister is a beautiful little girl who *has* learned to smile. She hides behind her smile as if it were a protective shield; as if already even at her tender age, about three years old, she knows the usefulness and shelter of a charming smile.

What can I do? I can't force their mother to go to the hospital against her will, but if she doesn't get treatment for that abscess it will give her blood poisoning, and it could be fatal. Then who will take care of the children she loves so much?

I realise that my friendship could be dangerous for her, could anger her husband and cause him to beat her again. How can I to talk to him? Apart from the language difficulty, he's a big man, nearly six feet tall, and looks quite violent. I could be putting myself — as well as his wife and children — in danger.

At the Barista Coffee House, when I sit at the table in the

MONKEY ON MY ROOF

window the woman's children come to me holding their hands out for food. Occasionally I've given them fruit or chapattis. Their mother does not beg. She sits in the shadows and watches. I've never seen her ask any person for anything, it's as if all her vitality has been lost, her get-up-and-go has got up and gone.

I haven't seen her for the last couple of days, though the children are around and come to talk to me. I'm no saint; I don't particularly need to give help, but children and hurt animals always touch my heart. The woman is like a hurt animal, so dumb with fear and pain that I can't pass her by. I realise that this is her Karma. But I can't help thinking that perhaps it's my Karma too. Maybe it's my Karma to help her.

One of the customers in the Coffee House is a doctor at the Landour Community Hospital. I talked to him about her; asked him what I could do.

'I'll make some enquiries,' he said.

Then this morning the waiter told me that the doctor has become involved with the family. She's been taken in for treatment.

Sally X

MONKEY ON MY ROOF

66

The waiter in the Barista smiled when I took my seat at the table by the window this morning, I don't need to order, he knows what I eat for breakfast.

My mobile plays its little tune and a shiver runs from the base of my spine to the top of my head, I know who is phoning even before Stephan's name appears on the tiny screen. I press the green button and listen.

'Hi Sally.'

The soft husky growl as he says my name has my lips stretching in a smile.

'Hello Stephan.'

Can he hear the smile in my voice?

'I'm in Mussoorie, just got here. Where are you?'

'Eating my breakfast at a coffee house. Fruit salad, chocolate croissants and coffee. Do you want to join me?'

'That's why I'm here!'

Through the window I watch a vegetable seller spread his mat on the pavement below as I give Stephan directions to the coffee house.

'I'm just up the road, see you in a couple of minutes,' Stephan says.

The vegetable seller arranges a pyramid of corncobs and empties a sack of green chillies on the mat. The chillies take on a shine like emeralds in the morning sun. A young grey monkey sitting on a water tank on the roof of a nearby house watches the vegetable seller. Pine covered mountains behind the monkey glower greenly in the distance.

I order a pot of coffee and more croissants just as Stephan,

MONKEY ON MY ROOF

backpack slung over one shoulder, walks through the door. He's smiling.

'Is that smile for me,' I say, 'or is it for the coffee and croissants?'

'Come and give me a hug so I can show you!'

It's so good to feel his arms around me, to feel his body push against mine. The bristles on his chin prickle my cheek as he kisses me, a long slow kiss; I breathe in the scent of his shampoo, the mixture of coconut oil and sweat from his skin.

Stephan leans back, holds my hands, 'Let me look at you.'

We stand there, smiling at one another. Like an idiot child I can't stop grinning; neither it seems can he.

The waiter passes us carrying a tray, 'Coffee and croissants here,' he says as he puts the tray down on our table.

I pour the coffee.

On the street outside a young man places a contraption of wooden shelves along the Coffee House window sill. He stocks the shelves with packets of crystallized ginger, dates, and dried figs, then he smiles at me through the window and puts his hands together, 'Namaste Momma.'

'Where are you staying?' Stephan says.

'I'm in cheap hotel on Camelback Road.'

'Are there any vacancies?'

'The Israelis in the next room to me are leaving today,' I say demurely.

Stephan grins, 'The next room! That's handy.'

I can feel my cheeks getting hot, I haven't blushed for years, but I never seem to stop when Stephan's around.

To hide my embarrassment I turn my head towards the window. The monkey jumps from the water tank to the pavement

MONKEY ON MY ROOF

and reaches a long arm to make a grab for the corncobs. The vegetable seller yells and swipes at the monkey who manages to grab a handful of green chillies instead. He jumps back on the fence, puts one in his mouth, chews, spits it out, and throws the rest of the chillies at the vegetable seller.

Stephan tilts his chair back and laughs, and I laugh with him. The vegetable seller is laughing as he shakes his fist at the monkey.

Stephan picks up his backpack from the floor, 'Let's go!'

'What about your breakfast?'

'I couldn't eat it, Sally,' he said softly. That low husky growl in his voice again, 'I just want to be alone with you!'

Our eyes meet, my voice trembles as I say, 'Yes.'

The guest house is deserted. Everyone except the watchman is out.

Stephan says, 'My sister says you have a vacant room for rent?'

'Yes madam, yes,' says the watchman — who addresses every westerner, male or female, as 'Madam' — and shows us both to the empty room next to mine. The room the Israelis vacated this morning.

A good big room with a good big double bed.

'I'll take it,' Stephan says.

He puts down his back pack and looks at me. We both look at the bed.

I nod.

'My sister will stay and help me unpack. If that's alright?' Stephan says for the benefit of the watchman.

The watchman grins, 'Yes madam, yes.'

Sister! I'm hard pressed not to laugh! Is this a game only families can play?

MONKEY ON MY ROOF

As soon as the watchman has gone, Stephan slams the door and pulls me to him.

'So you want your sister to help you unpack, do you, brother?' I pant between kisses.

Stephan doesn't answer. Fingers busy on the buttons of my blouse, hands warm against my back, he pulls the blouse off my shoulders. Now he's fumbling for the hooks of my bra, bristly chin nuzzling my neck, smell of coconut oil, sweat and desire.

We tear at one another's clothes. I hear a rip that sets my breasts burning. Then his mouth is on my breast, hot tongue licking, scorching mouth gulping. And I do what I've wanted to do very nearly from the time we first met; I take hold of the zip on his jeans and pull it down. He isn't wearing underpants, my hand doesn't need permission to curl itself around what I find inside them. I trail my fingertips up and down. My voice shakes as I say, 'Shall I unpack this?'

All at once his hands are gone from my back and are scrabbling at the belt of his jeans, then his jeans hit the floor. There's a fast blur of velvet skin, the delicate curve of bare brown buttocks.

'Ah God! You're so beautiful,' I gasp.

Stephan throws his head back and groans, 'Thank you. You too.'

And we are on the bed naked. I fall on my back, he climbs on me and I pull him down, down, down, inside me; where I want him to be.

*

Afterwards, as we dress, as I button my blouse, a shudder rips

MONKEY ON MY ROOF

through me…Oh, what have I done! I burst into tears.

Stephan drops his tee shirt, draws me to him.

I turn my face away.

He takes my chin in his hand and, with his finger, wipes away the tears trickling down my face, 'Sally! What's wrong?'

I can't bear to look at him.

'Regrets?' he asks.

'I've never cheated before,' I say. 'How can I ever look at myself in the mirror again knowing I've cheated on Mark? How can I ever look my husband in the face again?'

'Don't go back to him. Stay with me.'

'It's not that easy!'

He pulls me to him again, his eyes probe mine. 'So why are you travelling on your own? Don't I deserve an explanation?'

If he puts it like that…

So we sit on the bed and he holds my hand as I tell him how my joke of last year became reality this year.

'Apart from Ailsa, you are the only person I've told… I've always kept it to myself, haven't even told my best friend. Mark cheats on me,' I say. 'It started while I was pregnant with our third daughter. He says it makes no difference, it's only sex and it's me he loves. But it hurts.' I bury my face in my hands, 'Each time it happens it hurts more,' I say through my fingers.

'Go on, get it off your chest.'

So with Stephan's arm around my shoulders I tell him about Mark and me. About our marriage. 'You'd think I'd have got used to it by now,' I say, 'but I never do. Always at the back of my mind there's been the hope that things would get better.

'You've heard of the complaisant wife willing to do anything to please her husband? Anything to keep him happy? That was me.

MONKEY ON MY ROOF

Because, despite everything, I still loved him. I wanted to believe him, to believe his act. Believe the show he put on when we went out with friends. The way he dances attendance, holds my hand. Then last year because of what happened over the tsunami, I realised that's what it is…just an act. A sham. Mark doesn't love me. If he cared he'd have been out there looking for me not lying in bed watching TV. But still I hoped… I thought if I got away on my own…absence might make the heart grow fonder. For both of us. Then when the bombs went off in Delhi…I could hide it no longer; there was no hiding. Everything about our marriage is false. But I can't give up on it. Not yet! Three daughters and thirty years have to be worth something.'

We sit quietly for a while, and then Stephan breaks the silence. 'He's an idiot! How can any man treat his woman that way? Especially you. There is life after divorce, you know. Think about it. You and I could be happy together. We could travel. You like travelling don't you? Money wouldn't be a problem. I have enough for both of us.'

'Money! I've never considered that aspect,' I say, 'the financial stuff; but Mark will be certain to take it into account. He's a lot more money orientated than me. I could be left with nothing.'

Stephan gives my shoulders a little shake, 'That's not important I've enough for the two of us. We could buy or rent a place, somewhere to come back to when we get fed up travelling. A flat, small enough for the two of us. With an extra bedroom for your girls to come and visit if they want to.'

How will my children feel about that? What about my daughters, my daughters?

Oh what shall I do?

MONKEY ON MY ROOF

67

The bus to Palolem — I'm on the bus because I've run away from Mussoorie, run away from Stephan — I have to think; to sort myself out. The bus is decked with garlands, masses of yellow and gold marigolds and creamy white jasmine. Incense is burning in the driver's cabin, and the smell of roses mixes itself up with the scent of the jasmine. There are so many flowers that I wonder how the driver can see through the windscreen to drive the bus. And all that can be seen of the small shrine on the dashboard are the fairy lights twinkling through the petals. I've no idea which God the driver worships. Not that it matters; in India he can take his pick of about three thousand.

Music is playing — Hindi love songs, all those lovely male baritones and the not so lovely tones of the screechy female singers. The sun is shining for the first time in days, and along each side of the road between the palm and banyan trees the paddy fields sparkle pale green.

The bus conductor is standing in the gangway, holding his hand out for my fare. 'What are the flower garlands for?' I say. 'Is there a special festival?'

'No, Momma,' he answers with an enormous smile, 'festival for driver.'

'Festival for driver?'

'Driver's wife gives birth to fine healthy boy night-time,' the conductor says, 'before night he have three daughters only.'

'Tell him well done, but girls are good too.'

'Oh, he loves his little girls but now he thanks God for proving him a man, isn't it?'

An old Sikh sitting at the front of the bus turns around and

MONKEY ON MY ROOF

waggles his white beard in approval, the other men all nudge one another and call out congratulations in the local language to the bus driver. The village ladies pull the ends of their saris over their heads and murmur in agreement.

  Half way to Palolem the driver stops his bus besides a fruit stall at the side of the road, scrambles out of the cabin and buys bananas, then he climbs in the passenger door to walk along the gangway and give each passenger a banana each.

  The old Sikh with the white beard waggles his banana in tandem with his beard at the bus driver, and says some words in the local language. The male passengers laugh and the ladies in saris titter behind their hands. I smile; is the old man reminding the rest of the passengers of the local legend about bananas being an aid to virility? Better than Viagra because of the iron content some people say. Or maybe he's comparing the curvature of the banana to the shape of the bus driver's male organ? I'll never know! But what a lovely bus ride. Only in India!

  It's out of season but my room is waiting for me in Palolem, the same room I shared with Ailsa. Cuthbert strolls nonchalantly across the beam as I unpack. He's early today but the restaurant he usually graces with his presence is still closed, so I suppose he has to look further for his meat and two veg.

  Nervous of reading mails from Stephan, I haven't checked my mail since leaving Mussoorie, and only turn on my mobile to check for texts from Mark and my daughters. At the Sun and Moon internet shop monsoon rain drips from a gap in the wall down the screen of my computer. The rain is warm, but when the sun comes out everything turns to steam. I feel as if I'm living inside a steam iron, except that an iron would dry my clothes and not leave everything damp and smelly.

MONKEY ON MY ROOF

There are six e-mails from Stephan, one from Mark and three from Ailsa. The small white arrow hovers over the little envelopes on the screen. Of its own accord my finger clicks the mouse to open the e-mails from Stephan.
SALLY WHERE ARE YOU? PLEASE GET IN TOUCH. TELL ME WHERE YOU ARE. I LOVE YOU. STEPHAN.X

The next five are the same except for the latest where he's added: ANSWER THE PHONE AT LEAST!

Mark's e-mail asks: when will you be coming home?

What can I write? How can I answer their e-mails when I don't know the answer myself?

*

Ailsa's e-mail reads:

12th September 2006
Sally how are you?

Where are you? What's happening to you? I've tried phoning but your phone always seems to be switched off! I have some more good news, I'm keeping well and I have a new job! It's OK, only for 6 months at this stage. I've been there one week already. I work in the legal/consumer products dept. Good to be earning money again. Me and Greg have started meditation at the local Buddhist Monastery down the road, once a week. I love your e-mails, hearing your tales — I miss you, I miss India, especially the food. I miss everything, even the things I hated — the noise, the spitting, the howling dogs at night. But hey, I don't miss the squitters!

What's happening with Stephan?
Hugs and Kisses Ailsa X.
PS GET IN TOUCH!

MONKEY ON MY ROOF

*

My fingers fly over the keyboard. At least I can answer Ailsa's mail!

21st September 2006
Hi Ailsa,
Sorry about the delay in writing. You must have been wondering why I haven't been in touch. I'm in Palolem at the moment to replenish my tan which has disappeared somewhere in the mountains, most likely licked off by those mice that were in my bedroom YUCK.

Replenish my tan? Who am I kidding! You may as well know; I had to get away from Mussoorie and Stephan. Did I say get away? Run away more like because I can't trust myself around him.

The guy at the Mussoorie internet shop got me a train ticket from Dehradun to Delhi, I had to take a taxi from Mussoorie to Dehradun, and I sneaked out while Stephan was asleep. What a coward eh? I'm still trying to get my head around everything that's happened. Mark and the girls, Stephan and me, bloody hell, what have I got myself into? Oh God. What to do? What to do?

The Shathabdi Express was really good. Chair class is like being in business class in an aircraft — not that I've ever been able to afford business class. High tea of samosas, cakes, crisps, sweets and a pot of tea, then later a dinner that would have rivalled any of the best restaurants. Arrival in Delhi was 10.30pm; the train for Margao was scheduled for 6.00am the next morning, so I took a rickshaw to the station at the other side of the city and spent the night in the ladies waiting room, which brought me down to earth with a bump I can tell you!

MONKEY ON MY ROOF

Then two days and two nights on an AC2 sleeper. I'm getting used to the sleepers, even when the rocking of the train sends me to sleep during the day, then keeps me awake all night!

Spent a few days with Sheila and Doug in Candolim before I got homesick for Palolem. Isn't it funny how a person can get homesick for a place that isn't really their home?

There weren't any shops open when I got back to Palolem, in fact there weren't any shops at all, I was beginning to think the bus had taken me to wrong village! If it hadn't been for Nicky's bar and the internet shop, I wouldn't have recognised the place; it looks so completely unrelated to the Palolem I remember. The beach road is deserted, here and there the skeletons of steel and bamboo that should be full of tee shirts, beach-bags and tourist junk are now filled with rubbish and foraging dogs. And the cows scavenging in the ditches have red and gold tinsel around their necks. They look for all the world as if they've just come from a party.

Maybe they have

Yesterday the guest-house where you and I had our room celebrated the Festival of Mother Mary. Her statue, followed by a candlelit procession, was brought to each house in turn; there was a service in the courtyard and then a feast. I managed to chicken out of the service on the grounds that not being able to speak the language I wouldn't be able to understand what was going on.

But in the evening the beach is flamboyant with coloured lights. There are bonfires and barbecues on the seashore and the smells of roasting fish and chicken. Honeymooners from Bombay walk hand-in-hand, only stopping to make love behind a beached fishing boat.

Don't you wish you were here?

Love and light and 100 hugs from Sally.

MONKEY ON MY ROOF

*

The Festival of Mother Mary calls to my mind memories of my mother, my sister and me kneeling at the bedside each night, hands folded, eyes closed; intoning Our Father Which Art in Heaven. Then it was God Bless Mum and make her strong (Dad was never allowed to get a mention), God Bless Grandma and Granddad and keep them safe. All I got from that was sore knees from kneeling on the cold lino.

Mum would take my sister and me to Sunday school at the local Methodist Hall where we were told to pray to God to make us good so that the Devil couldn't take us. By the time I was seven years of age I'd worked out for myself that God is just a word people use for good, and Devil another word for evil, and both God and the Devil were inside me.

Enough of that!

The beach clothes I brought with me from England have been shed somewhere along my travels. Very few shops are open because of a dispute with the council, and those that are only cater for young beautiful anorexics. My two bathing suits hang so loose over my naughty bits that I feel positively indecent — I've lost some weight along the way and have to keep checking my boobs to make sure one of them hasn't escaped. Anorexic I certainly am not!

But I'm not worried because yesterday there was a break in the monsoon and busloads of Kashmiris, Rajasthanis and Gujaratis, not to mention Keralan masseurs and Kanaka tribal women arrived. Before long the beach road will be full of motor bikes, taxis. The shops will be open, and we'll hear those wheedling voices again, 'You come look in my shop? Only look! Looking is free!'

MONKEY ON MY ROOF

68

'Sally! I've just read your e-mail. What are you playing at?' Ailsa is on my mobile.

'Hi Babe,' I say cautiously.

'What's all this about you running away from Stephan?'

I take a deep breath, 'Things happened! You wouldn't understand.'

'What do you mean I wouldn't understand? I thought we were friends.'

'We are,' I say distractedly, 'we are!'

'Well then, what happened? Did he do something awful?'

'If you call something awful shagging me till my teeth rattled, then yes. But it wasn't awful.'

I can hear her laughing down the phone, 'So you enjoyed it then?'

'Yes,' I smile. 'Yes, I suppose I did.'

'What's the problem then? Stephan's asked you to shack up with him hasn't he?'

'I'm married, Ailsa, there's Mark and the girls to think about.'

'So you ran away?'

'Not everyone is as brave as you, and I have my daughters to consider. They love their dad.'

'You're in an unhappy marriage; you're in love with another man? And your daughters love their dad?'

'If I left Mark the girls would never speak to me again!'

Ailsa has stopped laughing, 'Don't be such a barmpot, of course they will! Okay Sally, they'll be upset at first. They'd be despicable if they weren't upset. But it won't last; they'll come round in the end. They may love their dad but they love you too.'

'Maybe…' I say doubtfully.

'Tell me again, how old are your daughters?'

'The eldest is twenty-five, the youngest is nineteen.'

'Sally, you're in your fifties, your marriage has run its course. Your children are old enough to lead their own lives. Isn't it time you snatched some happiness for yourself?'

'What about Mark?'

'Let me get this right! Mark has affairs. Do you still trust him?'

'No. But maybe I can get the trust back.'

'Trust is like virginity Sally,' Ailsa says, 'you can only lose it once.'

Ailsa has a way of putting things into perspective. Suddenly everything is clear! I can't keep the smile off my face.

*

27th September 2006

Dear Ailsa,

Thanks for the phone call, it's always good to talk to you. I've been mulling over what you said about Mark and our marriage and it got me thinking: perhaps Ailsa is right? Perhaps I should snatch some happiness for myself?

A couple of days ago I had a quiet word with Prakash and asked him to phone Stephan and mention that I was here in Palolem, but not to tell Stephan that I'd asked him to phone. After all a girl has to keep some dignity. What happens now is up to Stephan.

Rain is lashing down, the leaves on the palm trees are heavy

MONKEY ON MY ROOF

with water, the sea is grey instead of blue, and the honeymooners have packed and gone. Now the beach is empty except for the ghosts I keep seeing walking along it; Stephan, Doug, Sheila and you, all our old crowd — but mostly Stephan.

It's so peaceful without all the hassle and bustle of the beach shacks and roaming souvenir sellers. This must be how Palolem was before the hippies discovered the place and the locals stopped netting fish and began to net tourists instead!

Big hug one each for you and Greg xxxxx Sally

MONKEY ON MY ROOF

69

One of my ghosts is walking on the beach today: Nicole, the partner of the man who teaches Transcendental Meditation.

'Hi, Sally,' she says as if I've never been away.

'You've had your hair cut.'

Nicole pats her head, 'Yes.'

'It's very short, but it suits you. Makes you look younger.'

'Can't stop now,' she says, 'how about dinner tonight? Casa Fiesta, 8 o'clock?'

I nod, 'Okay.'

The supermarket across the road sells me some Hit to get rid of the cockroaches falling from the ceiling in my room. I spray everything in sight. Those cockroaches are going to be legs-up-lying-on-their-backs after dinner; makes me wonder what the heck is in that tin of Hit when it massacres insects that are supposed to be able to survive a nuclear blast. Did the Buddhist vows I took in Dharamsala that I'd never kill a living entity include cockroaches, I wonder? Oh well, I might have done them a favour. Now they'll have the chance to be reincarnated into something higher; a worm or a rat for example!

*

The Mystical Meditation Master is nowhere in sight when I arrive at Casa Fiesta. Nicole has ordered a meal for both of us. She's alone and drinking something alcoholic.

Putting my bag on the floor and my mobile on the table I sit down and ask, 'No Singh tonight?'

'We've split up,' she says.

'That's a pity.'

MONKEY ON MY ROOF

'Not really, our affair had run its course.'

She looks down and twists the stem on her glass, 'I'm with someone else now.'

'Who?'

'I'm not telling you his name,' she says, and smiles dreamily. 'All you need to know is that he's a lovely, gentle Indian boy. A beautiful 27-year-old boy who loves me. Makes a change from Singh, doesn't it?'

'Oh Nicole, take care,' I say, 'I might sound like a prude but some of these boys are only here to have sex with the Western girls. Each season a different girl and usually the girl ends up paying the bills!'

Nicole bristles, 'My new man isn't one of those, Sally!'

'Okay, whatever,' I say. 'You know him better than I do and you look ten years younger *and* masses happier, so it can't be bad.'

Prakash has brought our food, 'You want drink, momma?'

'No thanks Prakash,' I say, 'er…did you?'

He smiles at me, 'Yes, momma, I make phone call for you.'

I'd forgotten to turn my mobile off; it has to pick this moment to ring.

Nicole picks it up; she glances at the screen before handing it to me, 'Stephan,' she says nosily, 'who's Stephan?'

'No-one you know,' I take the phone from her and press the red button to end his call.

'Aren't you going to speak to him?'

'Not at the moment.'

When we finish eating I stand up and say, 'Goodnight, I'm off to bed.'

Nicole grabs my arm, 'Don't go yet! Stay and tell me about Stephan.'

MONKEY ON MY ROOF

I look down at her hand holding my arm.

'He's *my* new man,' I say. 'Now I have to go.'

My new man.

It's so good to be able to say those words! I can't stop repeating them to myself on the way back to my room. Which is full of dead cockroaches: they litter the floor, a dozen or so stretch out on the bed, another six or seven on the only chair. My skin crawls as I fetch a broom to sweep them away. As I turn the mattress and unroll my sleeping bag I can hear mice skittering on top of the bathroom partition. Tomorrow I'll look for another room.

Stephan's name flashes up again on my phone.

I press the green button, 'Hello, Stephan.'

'Sally! At last.'

'How are you?'

'Never mind that,' he says impatiently, 'I'm here in Palolem, got off the bus an hour ago, Prakash phoned to tell me you were here. I've found you at last!'

So Prakash wasn't lying when he said he'd made that phone call!

I laugh, making a joke because I still can't bring myself to admit — not even to myself — that this is what I want: 'What took you so long?'

'Come to my room and I'll tell you,' he says, 'I've a hut on the south end of the beach, where one of the beach camps is still open.'

My heart is thumping like a drummer in a rock and roll band and my lips stretch into a smile, 'It's too dark to walk up the beach.'

Stephan must be able to hear the smile in my voice, because his voice is smiling too, 'Get a rickshaw!'

MONKEY ON MY ROOF

'It's too late. The rickshaw drivers have all gone to bed.'
'Where are you? I'll come to you!'
'No, Stephan, no!' Panic-stricken I look around the room. I can hear the mice — or are they rats — squeaking on top of the bathroom partition. Has my broom missed any cockroaches?
'I'll see you tomorrow,' I say.
'Tomorrow then, nine in the morning,' the smile is still in his voice. Then his voice softens, 'And Sally,' he says in this new, tender voice, 'don't disappear on me again, will you?'
'No, Stephan, I won't,' I answer.

MONKEY ON MY ROOF

70

4th October 2006

I'm writing this in the full knowledge that no-one but me will ever read it. I will never press the send button to dispatch this e-mail through the ether to a computer terminal. This mail will never travel for light years through the ether into outer space. It will never wriggle around the stars to be picked up and read by any other person.

But I can't stop myself from sitting here at this scratched scruffy Formica desk in the Sun and Moon cyber café while water from a crack in the ceiling drips down my neck. Because memory can be faulty. It can play tricks. It can exaggerate or understate events. And I want a record of these events. I don't ever want to lose them. That's why I'll keep on pushing down the keys on this keyboard. And when I've finished writing it I'll save this e-mail to draft, then I'll download it to a folder on my computer.

A folder guarded by a password that no one else but me knows.

So here goes! Are you ready world?

It was the first day of the month. The first day of October, and for once I remembered to say White Rabbits when I awoke. There was a misty glow through the clouds with the prospect of sunshine later. Outside, everything glowed: the sand seemed a deeper gold, the sky bluer, the coconut palms greener. I was glowing too. My skin tingled from the touch of the air, I was walking as fast as I could but my feet seemed to float in slow motion across the sand.

In the middle of the coconut grove Stephan's hut, thatched with palm leaves, had its own small-railed veranda. The wooden

MONKEY ON MY ROOF

shutters of the hut were pulled together, the door closed. A wicker gate on the veranda stood open. Flower petals clustered on the wooden decking, pink, white, yellow, blue. The petals were fresh.

The door opened, and he stood in the doorway smiling.

Bare tanned legs below a short white towelling robe tied loosely at the waist. He was obviously naked beneath that robe. There could be no mistaking his nudity. The robe looked wonderful against his tan. Lifting a finger he flicked away some shaving foam stuck on the ridge between his chin and ear. His hair was still damp from the shower.

Then: 'Sally,' he held his arms out to me.

And I went into them.

The hut smelled of jasmine and roses; incense was burning in a holder on a small wooden table in one corner of the room. The bed — headboard placed against the wall — was heaped with the petals from creamy white jasmine flowers, pink and red roses, golden yellow marigolds.

'Do you like it?' he murmured into my neck.

I was speechless; no one has ever done anything like that for me before. Stephan must have got up early that morning to gather those flowers. The petals on the veranda... never would it have crossed my mind that was meant for me... I took his head in my hands and we kissed, his mouth tasted of toothpaste, his skin smelled of shaving cream and coconut oil.

He kissed my neck and face, soft slow sensuous kisses, I pulled off his robe, ran my tongue across the curls on his chest, curls sun-bleached into tiny wiry coils. He groaned and pulled me onto the bed, the palms of his hands clutching flawlessly at my rear end. My breasts cushioning each side of his face as his lips searched, turning blindly from side to side, and I didn't have to do a

MONKEY ON MY ROOF

damn thing because he was hard and hot and smooth inside me. We made love hungrily. Then we made love again, gently, tenderly as if we knew without telling that this was how it would be for us from now on.

For an instant an image of my husband's face appeared behind my eyelids, I could hear his voice, the derisive note in it, 'Getting fat old girl!' and I pulled my mouth away from Stephan's mouth, 'Oh, how can you love me, why are you bothering with me! An old, fat, ugly woman...'

For a long moment Stephan was motionless; then he quietly got up from the bed and took the mirror from the wall, 'Turn over and sit up,' he said authoritatively.

I did as he said, and he held the mirror in front of me, 'Look at yourself!'

The mirror reflected flower petals stuck to my naked body; from my neck to my feet I was covered in jasmine, roses and marigolds.

'You're not old or fat or ugly! Look at yourself, look in the mirror. You're beautiful. Don't you ever think differently, and never let anyone tell you any different.'

Stephan put the mirror back before taking hold of me again. Giving my shoulders a little shake he said, 'Stop putting yourself down! I love you, Sally. I've only ever said those words to one other woman! I meant what I said when I told you I loved you, Sally.'

And suddenly I was laughing. 'Yes,' I said, because now I knew for sure that the emotions I was feeling couldn't just be put down to my hormones. 'And I love you.' I pulled his hands from my shoulders and held them, 'So what happens now?'

'We can travel together for a while, and then settle down here

MONKEY ON MY ROOF

or in England.'

'I'll have to go back and tell Mark and the girls.'

'How will you tell them?'

I shook my head, 'I don't know. I suppose I'll have to make it up as I go along.'

'I'll come with you,' Stephan said, 'to make sure you don't disappear on me again.'

And we made love once more.